THE DRUMMERS

THE DRUMMERS

Tricia Fields

SEVERN
HOUSE

First world edition published in Great Britain and the USA in 2021
by Severn House, an imprint of Canongate Books Ltd,
14 High Street, Edinburgh EH1 1TE.

Trade paperback edition first published in Great Britain and the USA in 2021
by Severn House, an imprint of Canongate Books Ltd.

severnhouse.com

British Library Cataloguing-in-Publication Data
A CIP catalogue record for this title is available from the British Library.

ISBN-13: 978-0-7278-9247-8 (cased)
ISBN-13: 978-1-78029-759-0 (trade paper)
ISBN-13: 978-1-4483-0497-4 (e-book)

All Severn House titles are printed on acid-free paper.

MIX
Paper from
responsible sources
FSC® C013056

Typeset by Palimpsest Book Production Ltd.,
Falkirk, Stirlingshire, Scotland.
Printed and bound in Great Britain by
TJ Books Limited, Padstow, Cornwall.

ACKNOWLEDGMENTS

A special thank you to Jeff Fields, a longtime Arizona Public Service electric lineman, for sharing his expertise on the electric grid. Any mistakes or exaggerations in the story are purely for fiction's sake and mine in the making. Also, a special nod to This American Life, one of my podcast favorites, for allowing me to share a segment from one of their stories. If you've never heard an episode, download the latest, grab a drink and a comfy chair, and enjoy. It is entertainment at its finest. And, finally, a sincere thank you to Carl Smith and Severn House for bringing Josie back. I knew she wasn't done.

ONE

Leon gripped the windowsill in the Sunday school room and looked out into the cold gray morning, wondering if the sun and promised warmth of the West Texas desert would ever materialize. The window pane felt icy against his forehead, but he remained, anxiety skimming along just under his skin.

'The females need to be watched,' Gideon had said. 'Their nerves are stretched tight. It's our job to calm them. To provide a safe haven for their fears.'

Leon thought about his own nerves, stretched as tight as they'd been in Iraq, except at least then he'd known who he was fighting. Here, they were in a new town out in the middle of the desert, living around people who thought they were criminals or devil worshippers or both, and Gideon had decided to change everything up.

'The warmth will do us all good,' he'd said. 'The desert sun will bring us back to good health, breathe life into us.' Leon remembered closing his eyes and imagining that sun baking his skin to a deep brown, soaking all the way down to his marrow. They'd been in Idaho, cold all the time, counting down the days until they reached the desert. Now here they were, living along the Rio Grande with snow forecast later in the week. A record-breaking cold snap is what he'd heard on the radio that morning.

Leon forced himself to leave the room and walk down the center aisle of the sanctuary where the pews were stacked high with boxes and tubs, clothes tossed everywhere, completely unorganized. Two of the men were stretched out on the benches, covered up in rumpled clothing, flat on their backs and sleeping; as if they didn't know the world was crumbling around them.

Most of the women were downstairs in the basement with Gideon, but Leon knew Gloria would be in the church office. She'd taken that room as her own as soon as they'd settled. When Leon first came to know the couple she would tell people,

'Gideon and I have been married through forty years of trials and triumphs. He's the heart and soul, and I'm the bones that keep us upright.' Now, she looked too tired to stand up from her chair. Leon thought Gideon's passion had worn her down.

Leon knocked lightly on the closed door, painted white with a crooked sign hanging in the center that read, 'Enter. Peace Awaits You'.

He smoothed his sweaty hair back on either side to lay flat over his ears. The temperature inside the church couldn't have been any warmer than fifty degrees, but sweat dripped down his temples.

She smiled kindly. 'Leon. Come in. Sit and chat with me a while.'

She wore a red Harvard hooded sweatshirt, a thrift store castoff that Leon thought looked at odds with her fluffy white hair and deeply wrinkled face. A space heater sat beside her with rods burning red hot, warming the room to an almost comfortable level.

'Quick, shut that door. Keep the warm in,' she said, rubbing her hands together.

Leon did as he was told and unbuttoned his old Marine coat. He took it off and placed it on the back of the wooden ladder-back chair that sat across from her. He sat, clearing his throat, not sure what to say. He didn't like feeling nervous with her. She'd grown to be more like a mother to him than his own had ever been. When he'd returned from the Iraq War in 2011 and found his parents had moved from their apartment in Portland and not left any way for him to find them, Gideon and Gloria had taken him in like an orphan and given him a family.

'Why the long face?' she said, smiling.

'Just having a bad day.'

'This cold can't last forever. Once we get some sun we'll all feel better.'

'We've been here two months. It's not what I thought it would be. I thought we'd be in the desert. Out by ourselves, not in some church next to people that hate us again.'

'It's trying times, Leon. You have to stay true to your beliefs. You of all people should know that,' she said. She leaned forward to rest her large chest on the desk, folding her hands on top of each other in front of her. Her soft pale cheeks and silvery white hair were worlds away from the ragged drunk of a mother who'd raised him.

'It's not that I don't believe. It's just that things have changed.'

She frowned. 'We still have the same mission we've always had. You know that.'

'It seems like Gideon's got different priorities. Different things he wants to focus on now. Like talking to the women separate. Why's he have to do that?' Leon hadn't intended to bring it up. He'd gone straight to the heart of it, opened it up like a bloody wound for her to look at. He felt sick with disgust at his weakness.

'You think women and men don't have different priorities? Different ways of looking at the world? You think the women aren't scared right now, in ways you don't even know about?'

'We need to be united. We need to be speaking the same language.'

She dipped her head to one side in a disapproving look. 'Envy doesn't suit you.'

'I'm not envious,' he said, chastised, knowing she'd judged him correctly.

'Gideon grew up poor, with envy like a cold stone in the center of his heart. But he changed. He turned that envy into drive and determination. Now I see it in you, Leon. I see it in your eyes, that unappealing look of envy, wanting something so bad you can taste it in your throat, but not knowing how to reach it.' She lifted one hand in the air and slapped it with the other. 'Getting slapped down every time you try and touch the very thing you want.' Gloria peered through eyes so round and dark they looked like bullets. 'Cia loves you and Gideon in very different ways. Don't you see that?'

He said nothing.

'You have to accept that or you'll make yourself crazy.' She paused but continued to stare at him. 'Do you think it's always easy for me?'

Leon slumped into his chair, stunned at the question. He'd never thought about her in those terms.

'Gideon loves all of us in different ways, including me. It's hard to share one man with so many.' She held a fist in the air. 'Be brave. Trust in Gideon. We'll have a home here eventually. A place where we can be free and live out our lives in peace.'

He nodded and rose from the chair, sensing he was being dismissed. The counseling session was over, but he felt no better. He didn't think Gideon was building a home. He was building enemies.

TWO

Fourteen years ago, when Josie Gray decided to leave Indianapolis and all of its drama, she searched the internet for the most remote areas of the country and discovered Far West Texas. She'd sat on the couch one night with a six pack of beer and a tattered copy of the Rand McNally Atlas and opened to the page on Texas, followed her finger along the highways for a place where the cities gave way to country, where the people gave way to nothingness. She found a highway that ended in two ghost towns and decided that was her new home.

She had written an email to several police departments asking about law enforcement openings and received a response back from Otto Podowski, who, at that time, was the chief of police in Artemis. He later told her that he'd assumed she had the social skills of a mole rat to inquire about becoming a cop in such an isolated town. They'd talked on the phone and he'd offered her the job on the spot. She'd left the city streets, clogged with people on every corner, for the sprawling Chihuahuan Desert and the dusty streets of Artemis. Traded men in suits, sooty buses and concrete for cowboy boots, gun shops and the occasional man on horseback clopping down the two-traffic-light main street. She had never visited another place on earth that felt more like home than her rugged speck on the map.

Pulling her patrol car in front of the PD, Josie noticed how shabby the faded blue awnings looked over the plate-glass windows and front door. The brutal West Texas sun destroyed anything darker than beige. Color wasn't worth the trouble. She hoped for some discretionary money in January to take care of office maintenance issues, but she doubted the budget would allow it.

The PD was located in a two-story brick building directly across the street from the Arroyo County Courthouse. It connected to the Artemis City Office on one side and Tiny's Gun Club on the other.

She saw Otto walk out of the City Office carrying two boxes
and she called out for him to hang on so she could open the
door for him.

'More to carry?' she asked.

'That's the last two. I'm officially moved.'

'That's the best news I've heard in months,' she said, patting
him on the back.

After Mayor Steve Moss was arrested the previous summer,
the City Council had appointed Otto as interim mayor. His wife
Delores had been thrilled, thinking Otto would spend more time
at home and begin to cut his hours with a view toward retirement.
However, Otto had simply traded one set of dramas for another.
His wife had been frustrated, the police department had been
severely impacted by his absence, and Otto had confirmed his
hatred of politics. It had been a long five months.

The three-person police department should have been
sufficient for a town of 2,500 people, but the Arroyo County
sheriff's department was also located in Artemis and was two
men down in a county that bordered Mexico, rife with cartel
and immigration issues. Sheriff Roy Martinez relied on the PD
to take the majority of county calls because his office spent
most of their time manning the overrun jail.

While Otto stopped to chat with the dispatcher, Lou Hagerty,
Josie took the stairs to the room where the three officers shared
desk space. She opened the door to find Marta Cruz, the third
officer, standing on a chair in the back of the office, taping a
Welcome Home banner across the wall.

'Your cake looks lovely!' Marta said.

'You know my cooking skills consist of opening cans and
dumping. So don't get your hopes up,' Josie said. 'You need
some help? Otto's talking to Lou downstairs.'

Marta stepped down and scowled at her handiwork. She
was a stout woman with permanent frown lines that contra-
dicted her generally positive outlook on life. A hard-living
ex-husband in Mexico, coupled with a wild-child daughter
currently burning through money at college at an alarming
rate, kept her perpetually searching for a glimmer of hope in
her family's dysfunctional life.

Marta was wearing off-duty jeans and a sweatshirt, having

come in to the office to surprise Otto. Josie and Otto worked first shift, with Marta working third, and all officers rotating days, nights and weekends with the sheriff's office in order to have at least two marked cars on duty in the county at all times. The impermanent schedules took a heavy toll on their sleeping habits and occasionally their moods.

Josie poured fresh coffee and Marta placed paper plates around the conference table as they listened to Otto's slow, heavy tread on the stairs. 'I missed that sound,' Josie said.

He walked into the office and stopped in the doorway, beaming at them. Bits of gray flyaway hair circled his mostly bald head, and his puffy face glowed red from the trudge up the steps on knees that needed replacing a decade ago.

'What a sight for sore eyes,' he said. 'I'm back where I belong.'

Marta pulled a chair out for him and he sat down with a sigh.

'We're glad to have you home,' Josie said.

'And, look at this! Josie baked you a cake!'

Otto's eyebrows lifted. 'Is that so?'

Josie grinned at his response and cut them each a piece of chocolate cake with chocolate icing.

After one bite, Otto claimed it was the best he'd ever tasted, and asked for the recipe to give it to Delores.

Josie laughed. 'She must have you on a diet again. It came straight from a box.'

'Don't ever admit that!' Marta said. 'You just promise the recipe and never deliver.'

Otto looked down at the buttons straining against his belly. 'I put this uniform back on this morning and was ready to give up cake on my own. Too much time behind a desk.'

'Too many apple dumplings,' Marta said.

The intercom buzzed on Josie's office phone and Lou said, 'Suzanne Pitcher is calling for assistance.'

Marta pointed a finger at Josie. 'I'm off duty. I'd take a bullet for you two, but I'm not going to the Pitchers' again.'

Josie offered to drive, still amazed every time she walked outside the PD to climb into the hot-off-the-line Police Interceptor Utility. White with Artemis PD painted down both sides in blue and black, full lights and a cage in back, and all-wheel drive with a 400-horsepower turbo V-6 that had more power than anything she'd ever driven. After twenty years of driving military surplus police vehicles, Otto had found a Border Enforcement Grants Program that paid for three new vehicles, fully outfitted. With an outside profile like a Ford Explorer, the inside was made for arresting and transporting criminals, a luxury Josie hadn't experienced since her days working for Indianapolis Metro Police.

'Otto, I will never get tired of firing this engine up each day. You are my hero.'

He grinned as he slid into the passenger seat. 'Makes you dream about a high-speed pursuit, doesn't it?'

On the outskirts of Artemis she turned north onto FM-170, also referred to as River Road. The Pitchers lived ten miles from Ruidosa, a town of less than fifty people consisting of little more than a general store and the ruins of an adobe Catholic church.

Otto pointed toward the sign to Ruidosa. 'Did you know that town was established as a penal colony back in the 1800s? They were called the Condemned Regiment. Then the Comanche came through and massacred them all.'

'What's the population now? Twenty or so?'

'If that,' he said. 'Hard to imagine how you make a living this far from anywhere.'

'The Pitchers make it somehow,' she said.

'On Bill's disability check.'

Officers had been called to the Pitchers' house dozens of times over the past ten years. Josie had no doubt about what she would find in the living room of the doublewide, located just a hundred feet from the Rio Grande. Bill Pitcher would be sitting in his recliner, drunk and exhausted from yelling at his wife for the past several hours about the latest load of junk she'd dragged home from garage sales and stacked up in the already packed to busting rooms of the house. Suzanne would be standing in the kitchen sobbing and walking in circles, furious over her husband's inability to see that she was a thrifty shopper, bringing home only the things that they truly needed.

Josie pulled down the gravel lane that led toward four trailers in the trailer park, each separated by a quarter-acre of dust, not a tree or shrub in sight.

Otto said, 'This is the part of the job that I didn't miss. People who say they want help, but who are incapable of change. They wear me out.'

'She just wants someone to listen to her.'

Otto groaned.

'You can't be burnt out on your first day back on the road.'

Josie parked amid a scattering of chickens pecking in the dirt. The trailer sat atop a precarious stack of cinder blocks that provided shade for two Mexican pit bulls sleeping underneath, oblivious to the turmoil above their heads.

Suzanne stood behind the screen door without opening it. They could hear Bill Pitcher inside the house yelling at her to shut the damned door. She burst into tears again.

Josie opened the screen door and said, 'I hear you need some help. Can we come inside and talk with you for a minute?'

Suzanne backed away from the door and Josie entered, followed by Otto, crowding into the tiny entranceway. The woman stopped crying, as if the tears were operated by a switch. Josie had figured out years ago that Suzanne used the sounds of wailing and weeping to drown out the yells and curses of her husband.

Suzanne focused her attention like a laser on Josie. She grabbed her arm and pulled her into the kitchen, behind a wall where Bill couldn't see her.

'He's been drinking all day. Since after breakfast this morning he's had a whiskey bottle in his hand. All I did was go out shopping, and I come home and he's telling me he's going to beat the shit out of me. Says he's gonna take a ball-peen hammer and split my head open like a watermelon.'

'Do you have a safe place you can stay tonight? Some family or a friend's house?' Josie knew the answer. Her daughter lived in Marfa, but she was as tired of the fight as everyone else.

'I'm not leaving my house!'

'Would you like to press charges against him?'

'I just want you to make him stop saying hateful things to me.'

They heard something bang in the living room and then what

sounded like a dog growling. 'You tell 'em all about it, old lady. Tell the truth while you're at it, why don't you?'

Suzanne started wailing and they couldn't hear the rest of Bill's questions.

Otto looked at Josie and raised his eyes heavenward, as if appealing for strength.

'Let's go have a little chat with your husband, Suzanne. See if we can get this straightened out for you. I think it's probably just a misunderstanding.' Josie motioned for Suzanne to walk through the kitchen door and into the living room. As soon as she walked into the room, Bill started in on her about bringing the po-lice – said as two distinct syllables – out to their house again.

'You want to bring them in here? Then fine. Tell them about how I got one chair in this lousy trailer where I can sit. One dag-blasted place to put my feet up that won't be covered in crap by nightfall.'

'He sits in that chair and drinks and yells at me all day long! Says how he's going to beat me to a bloody pulp. How'd you like to live like that?'

Suzanne moaned with her hands over her eyes but her mouth wide open.

Bill pointed at Otto and yelled over her. 'Tell me you wouldn't want to beat the shit out of your wife if she made you live like this!'

'Let's everybody quit yelling,' Josie said. 'Just take a deep breath and we'll talk this through.'

'Show them the mess you dragged into here,' Bill yelled, louder now. 'Show them that pile o' crap on the bed.' He flung his hand toward a hallway with boxes and tubs and clear bags filled with clothes stacked from floor to ceiling along one wall. 'Go on! Show them where you make me sleep every night.'

Suzanne continued to moan and wring her hands together.

'OK, ma'am. Let's go take a look,' Josie said.

'He doesn't know what it's like to make do with no money! He spends it all on that liquor. I do the best I can for us. And he never appreciates anything.'

Josie watched Bill take another swig from the bottle. He had the red bulbous nose of an alcoholic and yellow eyes signaling a liver in bad shape.

'Come on, ma'am. Show me what's happening. Then we'll come back and see what we can do.'

Suzanne led the way back to the bedroom, her moans replaced with nervous chatter. Josie stood in the hallway. She'd already seen the bedroom and heard the story. Bill had taken her on a tour of the house over a year ago, showing her the extent of the hoard. They were a pitiful couple caught in a never-ending cycle of dysfunction.

'How about a compromise with Bill? For every item you bring into the house, you take one out. Right? If you bring in one bag from the store, you take one bag out. That would show Bill that you're trying.'

'Why would I do that? Why would I buy stuff just to turn around the next day and throw it away? You sound like him now. Throwing money out the door!'

The conversation continued in circles to the point that Josie lost patience.

They walked back into the living room where Bill reclined in his easy chair with the half-empty bottle of whiskey propped on his thigh. Otto had walked outside where Josie could see him checking out the welfare of the chickens.

'Bill, I talked to Suzanne. She admits she has a lot of stuff.'

Suzanne started to protest but Josie raised a firm hand to cut her off.

'She wants to make a deal with you. Since she brought in two bags of stuff today, she's going to get rid of two bags of stuff. She's going to do that right now.' Josie turned and stared her down until she offered a slight nod. 'But the deal is, you put the lid on the whiskey and stop yelling at her today. Will you give that a try?'

Fifteen minutes later Josie climbed into the patrol car that Otto had already started.

'I thought you'd want me to warm it up for you,' he said.

'Now I know why I missed you.'

An hour after returning to the PD, Josie received her first summons from the newly elected mayor, Simon O'Kane. Impeccable style, gray shoulder-length lion's mane hair, a wicked intelligence and a net worth in the millions made him as easy to idolize as to despise. Unlike the former mayor, who made decisions based on his own self-interests, Simon had adopted the town of Artemis as his own and seemed to genuinely care about bettering the community. But his agenda for reform didn't always click with the interests of the people living in the town they loved for its unassuming nature. Josie was fairly certain he was the right person for the job, but she was also certain he would make her life hell.

Simon O'Kane had built a vacation home in Artemis after earning his first million during a West Texas oil boom in the nineties. Five years ago, Macon Drench, the man who had literally purchased the town of Artemis in the seventies, had convinced his fellow millionaire pal to make it his primary residence. There were those in Artemis who despised the money and power that O'Kane and Drench had brought to the town, although few would turn away the improvements the two had lavished on the schools and the trauma center. Josie hoped that with the mayor's office adjoining the PD, he might send some money her way for updated radio equipment.

Her first hurdle to talking to the mayor was Helen Stockridge, the former mayor's devoted secretary. She blamed Josie for her boss's demise, even after overwhelming evidence had convicted him of aiding and abetting first-degree murder. When Josie entered the lobby, Helen slipped her eyeglasses down her nose to consider her.

'May I help you?'

Josie was certain that Helen knew the mayor had requested her.

'I'm here to see Mayor O'Kane.'

'Have a seat right over there.' Helen pressed the intercom and motioned for Josie to sit in the small waiting area. As soon as Josie had taken a seat, Helen said, 'He'll see you now.'

Josie found O'Kane leaning over what appeared to be blueprints scattered down the length of a ten-foot table. 'Have a look at this,' he said, without raising his head to greet her.

Josie looked over his shoulder to where he was pointing.

'I found these in the storage room at the courthouse. They're the original drawings Drench commissioned when he bought this little dust bowl fifty years ago. Looks more like a Midwest town center than a Texas millionaire's vision.'

Josie studied the print, which was a bird's eye view of the courthouse and surrounding streets laid out in a grid with the courthouse in the center. 'When he bought the town, the basic layout was already here, even the courthouse. He didn't have a blank slate to work with. And so much of his money was spent on basic utility upgrades and a system of roads that there wasn't much left for design.'

'Are you taking up for the old bastard?' He finally moved away from the prints and grinned at Josie.

'Without his vision, I wouldn't be here.' She smiled and put her hand out. 'Welcome to the mayor's office.'

'Pleased to be at your service, Chief Gray.' He pointed to a smaller table next to his desk that was large enough for two chairs and a carafe of coffee. O'Kane had wasted no time ridding the office of the heavy mahogany furniture and dark paneled walls that had always reminded Josie of a gentleman's club. The office had been painted white and looked like a place for work.

She accepted a cup of coffee.

'After I have a better understanding of the town budget I'll be asking you for department priorities, so be thinking ahead.'

'I can have them on your desk immediately.'

'That's what every department head has said. What's your top need?' he asked.

'A communications system for city and county that's powerful enough to reach remote locations.'

'Expensive?'

'Yes.'

'All right. Get me a prioritized wish list with a budget and a rationale for each purchase. Meanwhile, I have a group of angry citizens on South Street who think the town's headed toward the proverbial pisser.'

'The Drummers.'

'That's it. What can you tell me about them?' he asked.

'They call the leader Gideon. His former name was Wayne Masters. He legally changed his name to Gideon for religious reasons.'

O'Kane smiled and nodded. 'Gideon. A timid man who received a direct call from God to deliver the Israelites. God ordered Gideon to reduce his army from thousands to three hundred to defeat his enemies. The opposing army had over a hundred thousand men.'

'I assume Gideon accomplished his goal?'

'By breaking glass and blaring trumpets. He confused the massive army who turned on their own men in the chaos.'

'A politician and a religious scholar?' she asked.

'I have varied interests,' he said, looking amused at her surprise.

'I can see the story you described fitting Gideon's narrative. It's his small band of followers up against the United States government.'

'A commune?'

'Not according to him. In his words, they're like-minded people who want to live off the grid without government interference.'

'The locals are calling them a cult.'

'They might be right. The guy has textbook charisma. I've only had one conversation with him but he was smooth. He's a dead ringer for Jerry Garcia in his later years.'

'What did you talk about?'

'I stopped in to introduce myself. Gave him my card in case they needed anything.'

'Did you get a feel for how they're using the church?'

'He didn't allow me in. He walked outside and guided me back out to my car as we chatted. Friendly but no welcome sign.'

'What's the deal with the name? Why The Drummers?'

She smirked. 'Because they march to their own.'

'Ah. Should have seen that coming.'

'They had a farm in Idaho where they were into subsistence farming for about five years. Gideon got into it with the locals over property taxes and a zoning ordinance dispute. It sounded like the locals didn't want a commune in their town and found reasons to run them off.'

'So how'd they end up fifteen hundred miles away in an empty church building in Artemis?'

'You remember Davis Belmonte?'

O'Kane nodded. 'Moved to California about a year ago.'

'He owned the deed to the church. He got tired of paying taxes after the church went belly-up—'

He cut her off. 'Didn't the preacher commit suicide over tax evasion?'

'Sort of. He stole money from the church. He was looking at jail time so he slit his wrists and died in the sanctuary. That left Belmonte with a building nobody wanted to touch. He advertised it all over the internet for a dollar to a responsible buyer. The Drummers found out about it on one of the co-op sites and made the deal.'

'Surely they aren't planning on subsistence farming here, are they?'

'I don't know. I'm not sure how they're planning on making money. If they don't stop pissing people off, they won't find jobs,' Josie said. 'I'll stop by and talk to Daggy when I'm done here. He was the realtor on the deal. Gideon is telling people they're just living at the church until they can buy their own land and start building. But I've heard their money is about dried up.'

O'Kane scowled. 'I heard twenty people are living in there. Is that accurate?'

'Gideon told me twenty-one. He said they've converted the old Sunday school rooms into shared bedrooms for families. He wasn't really clear on how many actual families were living together. Sounds like a hodgepodge.'

'Little kids?'

'Yep. The youngest is five. There are also some middle-school-aged kids. Mostly adults, though.'

'Find out everything you can on these people, including their intentions, and report back. I don't like surprises.'

Junior Daggy's office was located two blocks from the PD. The windows were covered in printouts of houses and properties for sale in the West Texas area. Through the gaps in the flyers Josie could see Junior standing next to his desk with his foot propped on his chair, the phone in one hand, bouncing a ball off a socko-paddle with the other.

Daggy wore gray dress pants and a purple Oxford cloth shirt whose buttons barely closed over a well-supplied beer belly.

His gray hair was long and shaggy, curling over the collar of his shirt. Josie thought he looked like the kind of man who could use someone to help him choose his clothes every morning.

He hung up the phone, flung the socko-paddle on the desk and came at her with a hand extended. 'How the hell are you, Josie? Haven't talked to you in ages.'

'I'm good,' she said. Over the next ten minutes, Junior tried unsuccessfully to drag out details about the ex-mayor's trial, but Josie wasn't lying when she said she knew little about the case. The prosecution was out of her hands. She had moved on.

She finally brought him back to her purpose. 'I hear you were the realtor who sold The Drummers the church. Is that true?'

His hands went up like she'd pointed a gun at him. 'Don't shoot the realtor.'

'I just want some background on the group and the leader. What can you tell me?'

'Gideon.' Junior drew the name out and rolled his eyes. 'He thinks pretty highly of himself, I can tell you that.'

'How so?'

'He brought his little harem with him the day we toured the church. He gave them jobs to do. He made one check the church kitchen, another checked the bathrooms out. He had some young girl running around with a radio, plugging it in to make sure the outlets worked. There was one man that came too. The guy poked around the outside of the place and checked the roof.' Junior narrowed his eyes. 'Keep in mind, this was all over a place he was going to purchase for one dollar.'

'Did the other members do what he asked willingly?'

'That was the worst part! It was the way he ordered those folks around, and they all ran around doing what he said. Gave me a sour stomach.'

'You didn't think much of Gideon?' she asked, smiling at his expression.

'Honestly, if Davis hadn't needed out from underneath that place so bad I would have put the kibosh on the sale.'

'Do you have any contact information for them? I've stopped

by the church a couple of times, but they won't answer the door,' she said. 'I've only talked to Gideon once.'

Junior nodded. 'Count yourself lucky. They about drove me crazy while we were trying to finalize the deal. You won't get ahold of them by phone. They don't believe in cell phones. Technology is evil.'

'What's wrong with technology?'

'It'll be the ruin of us all. They don't want any of their personal information online. No phone, no bills, no credit cards, nothing to trace back to them.'

'Are they doomsday preppers?'

'I don't think so. That's not what I understood. They just want to be left alone. Especially by the government. They don't want anyone in their private business.'

'Did Gideon talk to you about long-range plans?'

'He's got me looking for property. He wants cheap land where they can irrigate their crops off the Rio.' Junior rolled his eyes. 'They're clueless. I got the feeling money's a big issue. I'm worried that church will turn into a flophouse for a bunch of people applying for public assistance.' He smiled and lowered his voice. 'That's just between you and me.'

Josie nodded. 'Understood. What do you know about the sale of their land in Idaho?'

'Free and clear. They sold the farm. That's the money twenty or so people are living off every day. They'll burn through that in a few months.'

'Anything else you can tell me? Just between you and me?' Junior was the biggest gossip in Artemis. He'd provided Josie with some decent leads through the years, but just as many tall tales.

Junior rubbed his palm over the razor stubble on his chin. 'Just watch out for the kids. The men and women can fend for themselves, but there's kids living in that place too. Makes me worry.'

Josie patted him on the shoulder. 'Thanks, Junior. I'll do my best. You stay in touch.'

THREE

Leon sat on the sleeping bag pallet in the room he and Cia shared with David and his wife Alaina. Colorful animal posters dotted the walls of the former nursery school room. Four people in their twenties sharing a fifteen-by-fifteen-foot room wasn't ideal, but they were making it work. David and Leon had agreed to leave the scheduling of the room up to Cia and Alaina. From eleven at night to six in the morning it was shared space – no screwing around during those hours. The girls scheduled private time for each couple during the day. Spontaneity was gone, but Leon liked planning for the hour-long quiet that he and Cia shared once a day. Yet here he was, frustrated and alone, with half their hour wasted. Gideon had called all the girls down into the basement for a private meeting. Again.

The church was set up with four distinct areas. The front entry led to a large foyer that opened into the church sanctuary. On one side of the foyer was the church office where Gloria spent most of her time. Gideon's office was located on the other side of the foyer and was off limits to everyone, even Gloria. No one entered Gideon's office unless invited.

Six small Sunday school rooms, now used as bedrooms, were located behind the sanctuary. The hallway that separated the bedrooms led to a large kitchen and dining area with folding tables and chairs where the members ate together. Another set of stairs off the kitchen led to a basement where Gideon preached, in his words, 'away from the prying eyes of the community'. Gideon had also recently started using the basement for private conversations with members. Leon found it increasingly irritating that Gideon needed to talk with the women and girls almost every day, but hadn't once called the men down to the basement for a talk.

Leon couldn't stand it any longer. He walked past the other bedrooms where he heard kids playing, then through the kitchen where one of the teenage boys, Ringo, was doing his chores for the day. He turned and looked at Leon, who opened the door to the steps leading to the basement.

'You can't go down there,' Ringo said. 'Gideon's having a meeting.'

Leon turned and smiled. 'I know. I'm not going in. I just left something in the stairwell.'

The kid looked at him like he wasn't buying it, but turned back to the sink full of pots and pans.

Leon took the wooden steps quietly, wondering what excuse he would stumble over if the door opened. He didn't care. He had to know what was happening in that room.

The stairs led to a concrete landing and a closed wooden door. He stepped up to the door and put his hand on the handle, turning it, just barely, but the knob stopped before turning more than a quarter of an inch. The door was locked. He pressed his ear against the door and shut his eyes, concentrating on the voice he recognized as Gideon's.

The words jumbled at first, a low drone, but he was finally able to pick out phrases: massing weapons, running the machines, preparing for war. Leon felt sweat bead on his forehead. This wasn't what they were about. This wasn't the group he had given his savings from four years' service in the Marines to.

The door opened suddenly and Thea, a forty-something-year-old bit-part actress, appeared in the doorway looking furious.

'What?' She clipped the word, clearly annoyed at his presence.

'I was looking for Cia. Someone said she was down here.'

'You knew we were having a meeting. You shouldn't be down here.'

Thea looked to the top of the stairs where Leon turned and saw Ringo walk away. The kid had ratted him out.

'Yeah, that's fine. Sorry. I'll catch her later.' He glanced into the room and saw five females sitting cross-legged on a carpet in front of Gideon, who sat in a tattered recliner in front of them. Cia leaned around one of the other women to catch Leon's eye and glared at him. He could feel the burn in his cheeks. With her long blonde hair, she'd always reminded him of pretty

Jenny in the *Forrest Gump* movie. As ridiculous as it seemed when he thought about it, when she looked at him with her big brown eyes, she made him feel like he was somebody important, like he didn't need to change in order to amount to something in life. When she turned her smile on him, open and full of hope and love, Leon felt like the world was his. But lately all she could talk about was Gideon.

Leon walked upstairs and found Ringo leaning against the sink with his arms crossed. Leon couldn't believe the arrogance in his stance.

'You get some thrill snitching on people?' Leon said.

'It's not about that. Gideon asked me to do a job, so I did it. Maybe you should do the same.'

Leon forced a long, slow breath. He had to remember the kid was fourteen years old, and the self-righteous attitude was being groomed. Ringo's parents had entered the group about six months ago and Ringo had gone from being an angry kid to a Gideon zealot.

'What are you talking about, Ringo? You think that's a good way to live? All of us running around snitching each other out? You really want to live that way?'

'It wouldn't have to be that way if you'd follow the rules. Nobody snitches on me because I follow the rules. You should have some respect.'

Leon laughed at the kid's tone. 'You need to remember your place. You talk pretty big for a kid barely past twelve.'

'You need to remember your place with Gideon. Without him you'd be nothing.'

Leon wanted to ask him if he'd had to memorize his little speech. Instead he turned and walked back to the bedroom, slamming the door behind him. He had twenty minutes left. He eased down on the hard floor and lay on his back to stretch out his sore muscles. The air mattress had sprung a leak a week ago, so they were making do with blankets as padding. At least when he'd shared quarters in Iraq, they'd all known the allies and the enemies. They'd understood the plan. Now Leon had started to feel like the orders had changed and no one had bothered to tell him.

The door opened and Cia slipped in and shut it behind her.

Leon had imagined a fight, but she knelt down beside him, allowing her hair to fall around his face like a curtain closing out the rest of the world. Her expression was more concerned than angry.

'Why did you do that?' she whispered. 'You knew where I was. Gideon knew exactly what you were doing, standing outside the door, listening in.'

'How'd he know I was listening?'

'Ringo sent him a picture from his cell phone.'

'Since when does Ringo carry a cell phone when no one else does?' Leon asked.

'So he can connect with Gideon. It's for security. A few of us have them now. You'd be one of them if you'd quit causing problems.'

He ran his finger over her eyelid, the soft skin that protected the prettiest eyes he'd ever looked into.

'Leon, I'm serious. You used to be Gideon's second-in-command. He still thinks of you as a son, but you have to stop acting like this.'

He smelled the flowery shampoo from her hair and wanted to kiss her. He was tired of fighting, of always being on the wrong side of things.

'He's worried about you. He doesn't understand why you seem so angry all the time.'

Leon sighed. 'I don't get what it is you're so excited about anymore. I wish I could feel it.'

She sat cross-legged next to where he lay and took one of his hands in hers. 'When I first joined I thought I was the happiest I'd ever been in my life. I finally had a purpose. I was going to live with like-minded people who I could love as my own family. But I look back on that time and it's like looking at a pretty painting. My life those first years was good but flat. Since we moved here to Texas, it's like I stepped into that painting. My happiness is about living now. It's about the struggles and the heartache, it's about figuring out the plan that's going to lead us to a beautiful life.' She gripped his hand hard and her eyes burned with sincerity. She leaned closer and whispered, 'It's about salvation, Leon. It's like Gideon opened up a whole new dimension of feeling inside of me that I didn't even know was there.'

At that moment Leon couldn't have cared less who had a phone or who was in command. Gideon could have been sitting in the basement with a bomb ready to blow. Leon cared only about Cia. About the girl who'd taken his first kiss, the girl whose letters he'd read a hundred times with a flashlight in a tent in the desert with twenty other guys tossing and turning on their cots in the heat while they dreamt about home.

'Lay on top of me.'

She smiled and placed her fingertips on his lips. 'Pay attention. I'm serious.'

'I'm serious too. I need you, Cia. I need to feel your heat. Lay on top of me.'

'We only have like ten minutes and you have to help with the woodstove.'

'That's long enough. I won't try and go any further, I promise. I just need to feel your skin on mine.'

She stood and pulled her jeans and sweatshirt off, then draped a blanket behind her back and outstretched arms. She looked like a goddess with her smooth pale skin and the blanket around her like a cape. Kneeling down, covering them both, she smiled at the look of need on his face. She stretched her legs out on top of his and he wrapped his arms around her back, pulling her tight against him. When she tried to brush her hair out of the way he grabbed her wrist to stop her. 'You're perfect, just like this. Now put your cheek on mine. I want to hear you breathe. I want to feel your heart beat against my own.'

'You know I love you. That's never going to change.' She whispered the words into his ear and his shivers mixed with the heat from her body; a sensation like no other in the world. 'You're my soul mate. Remember?' she said. Her lips touched his ear and his body ached with a desire for her he could hardly stand. 'We're going to have babies together and raise kids who love us and love life and love this crazy world we live in. You just have to be patient. Wait till we get our own land, where people will let us be happy without trying to control everything we do.'

She whispered on and on, and he wanted to believe everything she said. He wanted to suffocate the dread that had seeped so deep into his bones.

'Promise me you won't leave me,' he said.

'I promise you. I will be with you until the day I die.'

Josie finished with Junior and drove to the middle school to talk with the principal. It was four o'clock, well past dismissal, but kids still hung around the school, waiting for practice to start, hanging out with friends, doing who knew what. Debby Williams had insisted when she took the job that the school would be a hub for the kids and for the community, not a block of buildings locked down in fear. With so many school shootings across the country she'd had to fight to maintain her stand, but it came down to the fact that she loved kids, and parents understood that. Teenagers weren't an easy group to love, but she did.

She'd secured a grant and got locks on the doors and issued each kid and staff member a swipe card worn on a lanyard around their neck. There were areas of the building that were open twenty-four hours a day for a student who might need a quiet place or somewhere safe to crash for the night. The kids knew security cameras would catch bad behavior, but mostly they self-policed. They felt respected and it showed.

As Josie reached the door to the building, Debby was just walking outside and smiled to see her. She wore slacks and a gray jacket, trim and stylish, with short blonde hair that framed a well-preserved sixty-year-old complexion.

'You glad to have your old compadre back?' she asked, shaking Josie's hand.

'You can't imagine. Although he had his first run today and he's already worn out with the drama.'

'He got spoiled in the mayor's office,' she said. 'Speaking of, what do you think about the new mayor?'

'I have high hopes. He's a hard worker and I believe he wants what's best for the town.'

'He wants what *he* thinks is best for the town. But I'll give him a chance,' Debby said. 'Let's step inside out of the cold. My bones aren't handling this cold snap. I ache all over.'

Once inside the lobby, Josie asked Debby if she'd talked to anyone from The Drummers about enrolling their kids for classes.

She frowned, obviously frustrated. 'I've sent two certified letters and gotten no response. I did finally talk to one of the dads. He stopped by one afternoon with questions about the school. He said he's got a son who should be in the eighth grade. A smart kid, he said, who needs some structure. I got the feeling he wanted to send him, but there was some pressure from the people he's living with that he needs to home school.'

'Why?'

'I couldn't tell you. I tried everything I knew to convince him this is a good school with caring teachers. I explained that it's a small school with kids who, on the whole, are pretty accepting. And I'd make sure his boy didn't catch any grief about living in a commune.'

Josie winced. 'They're pretty adamant that they aren't a commune. That seems to be a hot button.'

'Maybe I offended him, and that's why he hasn't been back.'

'When was this?'

'About two weeks ago. I stopped by their place on Monday to follow up but no one would answer the door.'

'They won't talk to me either. I had one conversation with Gideon, but I haven't gotten an answer since.'

Debby smiled. 'I've heard about him. Pretty cocky name change. I sent the certified letters to him, asking him to bring all their kids by so we could sit and talk about the school and what we have to offer. I told him I'd get the elementary principal too and we could all talk together. Nothing.'

'Remind me what the laws are on compulsory attendance,' Josie said.

'Texas recognizes home schools as private schools. They don't have to follow the compulsory attendance laws.'

'So there's nothing we can do to get these kids into school?'

Debby smiled and nodded toward three girls standing in a group talking and laughing. 'There's your draw. Riana, the tallest, has already made friends with one of the boys. She told me she's trying to get him to come to school.'

Debby raised a hand and waved it in the air. 'Riana! Come here a minute.'

The girl approached, smiling but wary. A cop in uniform was rarely a friendly visit when you were that age.

'Chief Gray was asking about the kids at the church. Didn't you meet a couple of the boys?'

She grinned and tipped her head back. 'Ringo. He's so cute! And he's smart.'

'How'd you meet him?' Josie asked.

'I live downtown. A couple of blocks from the church. He walked down to the Family Value store and I was in there getting milk for my mom. I'd seen him around the church so I just went up to him and started talking.'

Debby cocked an eyebrow at Josie. 'Riana never learned the rule about not talking to strangers.'

The girl looked dramatically shocked. 'Ms Williams, when a boy is that cute, and his name is Ringo, he is not a stranger.'

'Was he a nice kid?' Josie asked.

Riana shrugged. 'Sort of. He's super shy and smart. Sort of stuck up. But so cute!'

'Have you talked to him since then?'

She nodded. 'I stopped by the church a couple of times after school. He comes out in the back and we talk. I keep trying to get him to school but he blows it off. I said he was just afraid a bunch of desert rats were smarter than him and he got mad.' She shrugged. 'I think he has a temper.' Her expression changed somewhat; her eyes became more guarded.

'What is it, Riana?'

'He told me the other day he has a gun collection. He said he'd show me sometime, but I don't know. He kind of makes me nervous.'

'Always trust your instincts. If he makes you nervous, there's a reason you feel that way,' Josie said. 'Have you been inside?'

'No. I asked why he never invited me inside since it's freezing out, but he just says he likes it better outside.'

Josie's cell phone vibrated and she saw it was a text from Lou Hagerty, local dispatcher, for a public disturbance.

'You do me a favor,' Josie said. 'Until we know more about them, why don't you just hang out at your place. You can ask him to come to your house when your parents are around. Until we find out what kind of people are living there, don't go inside. Deal?'

She shrugged again. 'OK with me.'

'You especially want to stay away from those guns.'

Riana rolled her eyes and ran back to her friends, who had been staring the entire time as if she was about to be carted away in handcuffs.

'The guns are concerning. That's the first I've heard of that,' Debby said.

'You'll let me know if you hear anything about The Drummers? Kids or otherwise?'

'You know I will.'

As Josie walked back to her patrol car she returned Lou's call. 'What's up?'

'Marta's in front of the church talking to an angry mob. There's a couple of kids in the street singing Nazi songs, marching like Hitler.'

'Tell Marta I'm on my way.'

Josie parked in the bank parking lot across from the church and saw Marta standing in front of a group of about fifteen adults, several yelling and shaking fists, but most of them frowning, arms crossed over their Carhartt coats, watching the spectacle across the street.

Two middle-school-aged boys were marching up and down the sidewalk doing some version of the Nazi goose-step while singing what Josie assumed was a German war song. One of the boys had the good looks that Riana had described and Josie figured he was Ringo.

She counted five cowboy hats and recognized four of them as local ranchers who had either been in town when the commotion started and decided to stop and support their neighbors, or had been called into town by the others in the group. One of the women stepped right up into Marta's space and pointed a finger in her face while she gave her hell. Marta took a step back and put a hand up to make the woman move back.

Josie got out of her car. She approached the group of adults and their attention moved from Marta to Josie, obviously hoping she was there to put a stop to it.

Ned Bates, a middle-aged rancher, ran a handyman shop out of the back of his mother's house just a block over. He pushed his way through the group to reach Josie first. His bald head

and face burned with anger. 'This is bullshit, Chief. Don't come
over here spouting the same crap that she said,' he gestured
dismissively toward Marta. 'It's beyond freedom of speech when
they start running people off from our businesses. You lose your
freedoms when you start infringing on other people's rights.'

Josie could have argued the law but there was no point. She
lowered her voice to a level that forced the people in the back
of the group to step closer to hear. 'By standing on the street
corner, you are playing right into their hand. This is no more
than a couple of boys looking for shock value. You're giving
them exactly what they want. I guarantee, when the crowd
leaves, those boys won't last ten minutes. Go back to work, go
home, don't say anything to provoke this further and I'll see
what I can do. The one thing you don't want to do is this.'

Josie and Marta listened to a few more complaints before
the crowd finally dispersed. Josie walked across the street and
called out Ringo's name. The boys stopped marching and the
good-looking kid stared as she approached him.

Josie stretched her hand out. 'I'm Chief of Police, Josie Gray.'

He shook her hand. 'How d'you know my name?'

'It's a small town.' Josie held her hand out to the other boy
who offered a timid, limp handshake. Like Ringo, he was dressed
in jeans and tennis shoes and a ragged sweatshirt. 'What's your
name?'

'Jacob.'

'What's your last name?'

'Smithton.'

'It's good to meet both of you.' They looked at her warily.
'You guys call yourselves skinheads?'

Ringo scowled and looked offended. 'No.'

'I just assumed, since you're marching like Nazi soldiers in
the street.'

'Lots of countries do the high step. It wasn't just Germany,'
Ringo said.

'True enough. You guys going to register for school soon?
Good teachers, and it'll give you a chance to meet other kids.
Play sports if you want.'

Josie noticed Gideon approaching from the side of the church.
Dressed in worn khaki pants and a threadbare Rolling Stones

T-shirt and slippers, he approached with a smile and an outstretched hand, looking winded. He was carrying a paper in his other hand.

'That'll be all, boys. You can head back inside,' he said.

The boys said nothing, just turned and walked away.

'What's the problem, Chief Gray?'

'No problem. There were some community members who were offended by the Nazi demonstration in front of the church. I just stopped by to check on things.'

'It was just boys playing games.'

'I understand the middle school principal has approached you about getting the kids into school.'

'They already are. We have an excellent school program for our kids. We have a licensed teacher to run the classes, too. She works with the students from nine to eleven, and one to three each day. I guarantee our students are as well prepared as any in your little town here.'

'So, here's the deal. You're starting to isolate yourselves from the community. It isn't that we don't want you here. We respect your desire to live life how you want, but when your kids are marching like Nazi soldiers in the street, it keeps people in town from living a peaceful life.'

'I thought you might be headed down that road.' He handed her the paper. 'This was written by a local church group and posted on the front door of the church yesterday.' Josie read for a moment and saw that community members were asking them to leave the church. They were 'blaspheming the name of God'.

'The boys read the letter first and were angry. This was their response.' He smiled, but his expression was dark. 'You see, we were provoked, Chief Gray.'

'I understand some of your members are looking for jobs. The police department is looking for a part-time custodian from four to eight each day. There are jobs to be had if people feel like you aren't out to screw the community. Keep that in mind.'

'You got it backwards. These people are out to screw us over just like everybody else. They want us gone and we did nothing to provoke that.'

'I understand your point. I'm just thinking about the boys

marching in front of the church during school hours. You don't want to isolate yourselves to the point you can't live in peace here. The desert can be a pretty unforgiving place. It's good to have some friends every now and then. And it's good to be able to earn a pay check.' He said nothing in response, so she tipped her head. 'Have a good day.'

After Josie clocked off at a little past six that evening, she drove to her mom's new rental house a few blocks from the PD. Just two months prior, Bev Gray had left Indiana to move to Texas, hoping to build a relationship. After a decade of occasional long-distance phone calls that typically ended in an argument, the move had caused both women considerable worry, and the verdict was still out. With no clear idea about what kind of a relationship her mom wanted, Josie wasn't sure she could deliver.

A text message her mom had sent earlier that day requested help moving a couch into the house. Bev's neighbor had bought new furniture and left their old couch on her front porch. When Josie pulled up to the house she saw Dell Seapus's green pickup truck parked along the curb, and no couch. Dell was Josie's seventy-something-year-old bachelor neighbor, and her closest friend. Her mom had used men throughout her life to take care of any number of tasks, but the thought of her using Dell was another issue. After Josie's dad died in a line of duty accident when she was eight, Josie had grown up watching her mom flirt to get a leaky faucet repaired or cry to get a tire fixed. Josie had sworn she'd never live her life like that, and she had no intention of letting her mom operate that way on her friends.

The little two-bedroom bungalow was on a quiet street populated mostly by young families and retirees. Bev had already scoped out a retired construction worker who lived several houses down. She'd asked him to give her a price on building a picnic table for the patio behind the house.

Josie walked inside and found Dell sitting on the new sofa next to her mom. A photo album was open and lying half on his lap, half on her mother's. He looked up at Josie with an expression that could only be described as relief. Dell had never married, rarely dated, and considered most women to be, in his words, a pain in the ass.

'What's up?' Josie asked.

Bev wore a sweater and jeans with carefully applied makeup, her hair recently dyed a new shade of auburn. Josie smelled her mom's musky perfume from the front door.

'Josie! I forgot to tell you! I got me a strong, capable man to help move the couch in. Come on in and take a load off. Dell and I were just looking at some of your photos when you were a kid. I can't believe you never showed him any pictures from your years in Indiana.'

Dell smiled politely and stood. 'It's been good talking to you, Bev. But I have to get back to the ranch. Cows need tending. You ladies have a good evening.' He tipped his hat to Bev, gave Josie a half-smile, and headed for the door.

'You don't have to run off! Stay and chat a while!' Bev called.

'No, ma'am. I'm not much of a talker. I need to get my chores done.'

'Thank you for your help,' she called.

He waved and the front door shut.

'You sure know how to run a guy off,' Bev said, laughing at her daughter. 'We were having a nice visit.'

'Dell wasn't lying. Talking and visiting aren't high on his list of priorities.' Josie pointed to the brown slip-covered couch. 'That's nice. It fits in here perfectly.'

'I know! And you can't beat free. And he took my old couch to the dump for me. I have enough room for you and your man friend to come over for dinner and drinks now.'

Josie shrugged, hoping to avoid the topic. She had no idea what the status was with Nick.

'I haven't seen him around in a while. You two still seeing each other?' Bev asked.

'He's back in Mexico. A bank president in Arizona was kidnapped. It's a million-dollar ransom. Nick is in Mexico City trying to negotiate a settlement.'

'You two think you'll ever get a normal life? Settle down and have kids?'

Josie shrugged again. She missed Nick. But she'd reached the point where a serious relationship, something more permanent and stable, had started to appeal. She didn't want Nick negotiating with the cartel. He was the best in the business, but he was up against a multi-billion-dollar crime organization with no regard for human life. Basically, she wanted him to give up his own career when she wasn't willing to do the same. It had started to cause problems that both of them were tired of discussing, so they'd quit talking all together.

'I wouldn't count on us settling down,' Josie said. 'And I wouldn't hold your breath for grandkids. We can't even figure out how to spend a weekend together.'

'Well at least sit down and visit a minute,' Bev said.

Josie sat while her mom poured her a glass of sweet tea and brought it over to her. They discussed the new apartment and Bev's job as a cashier at the gas station.

Then out of the blue Bev said, 'I met a different sort of man today.'

Josie raised her eyebrows, not entirely sure she wanted the story. 'Oh yeah?'

'Said his name was Gideon. I was in the hardware store looking at paint. I was thinking about painting the deck behind the house and he said he'd stop by and give me a quote. Said he lives in the old church up the street.'

Josie's skin prickled at the thought of him coming over to her mom's place. 'You haven't heard people talking about the commune? They call themselves The Drummers.'

'I've heard talk. They seem all right to me. I don't care who he is if he can give me a good price.'

Josie winced. 'Be careful thinking that way. You let a criminal in your house to paint it, and end up getting everything you own stolen. Cheap isn't always good.'

'Honey. Cheap is always good. The hangover afterwards isn't always worth it, but cheap is always good while it's going down.'

At midnight, what Leon's grandma used to call the witching hour, he left Cia sleeping on their pallet and went in search of David. Leon couldn't sleep, and he knew that David hadn't come to bed that night having volunteered to pull guard duty at the front door again. David was a night owl, prowling around the church when everyone else was asleep. He'd been the same way in the military. David and Leon had shared the same infantry division in Iraq, shared the same quarters, and now shared a nursery school room as their bedroom. The irony wasn't lost on either of them.

Leon slipped out of the bedroom and, as he quietly shut the door behind him, he saw the red dot flame of a cigarette being inhaled and flicked as David walked back inside the church through the kitchen door.

'Damn it's cold out there,' David said when he saw Leon. He rubbed his hands over his arms and jumped up and down.

'I heard we're supposed to get snow tomorrow.'

David pointed toward the darkened sanctuary. 'You headed that way?'

'Yeah. I can't sleep.'

Past the bedrooms, they took the two pews in the back of the church that they had designated as their own. That time of night, the kids were in bed and the church was quiet. Leon was glad to have a minute with David, to talk to someone who might share his perspective on where they were headed.

'I'm gonna lose my shit if we don't get some heat pretty soon,' David said.

'Why'd we leave Idaho?' Leon said. 'At least we could grow crops there. Have you seen the desert? Nothing but dust and sand and cows. I don't even know how they raise cows out here.'

'It's pretty country. I used the bus a couple of days ago and drove around. I can picture us building our little adobes in the desert. I've been reading about how to make our own bricks.'

They both leaned against the side arms of their pews and covered up with coats to ward off the chill. Light from a streetlamp poured in through the long, narrow windows and illuminated the room just enough that figures and shapes were apparent in the dark.

'Any idea if we're anywhere close to buying land?' Leon asked. David was good with math and helped Gloria take care of the books.

'Hell, no. We got screwed royally when we sold the farm up north. Pennies on the dollar. It was a bad deal and we shouldn't have taken it.'

'What was the rush then? I don't know why we didn't hold out for a better offer,' Leon said.

David shrugged and took a moment. 'Just time to get out of town. And we couldn't turn down a building big enough to hold all of us for a dollar.'

Leon thought about pushing it but didn't. A year ago David would have told him everything. But he'd started guarding information, like Leon couldn't be trusted.

'We can't keep this up. It's no way to live.'

'Gideon wanted me to talk to you about that,' said David. 'You have to get a job. The money from the farm went too quick. We need down payment money for land.'

'Why didn't he tell me himself?'

'I've been searching the internet for job openings around the area, trying to match people up with their skills. He asked me to hook everybody up. There's an evening custodian job at the police department. It's perfect because you can walk to work. I thought you'd be a good one to mend some fences, too. Let the police know we're not a bunch of hippy rejects. The Nazi thing was a bad move. The boys should have never done that.'

'I'll apply then.' Leon had been waiting to get the word from Gideon that they were free to look for jobs. He needed to get out of the church before the place made him crazy.

They heard a noise from behind them, back by the offices, located on either side of the entrance to the church.

'Is somebody in the office?' Leon whispered.

David shrugged. 'Beats me. It was dark when I went outside for a walk. I thought everyone was in bed.'

They heard a whimper, a female voice. 'Sounds like a kid,' Leon said.

They walked cautiously toward the foyer and main entrance. David pointed off to the right where they saw a strip of light coming from under Gideon's office door. They heard Gideon's deep voice but couldn't make out his words, and then a young female talking.

Leon placed his head against the door. She was pleading, 'No, please. I don't want to.'

He turned to face David who was in the shadows. 'What do we do?' he whispered.

'This is none of our business,' David said. He grabbed Leon's sweatshirt sleeve and tried to pull him away.

Leon jerked his arm away. 'We can't leave her in there! You know who that is?'

David said nothing.

'You know that's Mandy. Gideon's been eyeing her for weeks now. She practically hides in the corners from him.' Before David could leave, Leon turned and placed his hand on the door knob. He was surprised when it turned. Gideon had grown secretive since they'd moved to Artemis, but maybe he'd grown bold too. Maybe he'd figured no one would question his actions or dare to enter his office. Leon felt David move closer to his back as he pushed the door open a crack, and then further.

Mandy's long blonde hair came into view and her whimpers grew louder through the open door. Leon pushed the door open another few inches. Repulsed, he felt bile rise up from his stomach and into his throat. The man whom Leon had once considered a father figure stood with his pants undone at the waist and his shirt pulled up to his armpits. Her arms were up, bent at the elbow, her hands and body pressed flat against the wall. Gideon's fat midsection pressed against the thin girl. One hand was concealed under his considerable gut while the other ran up and down the side of her body. Mandy's eyes were clenched shut and Leon was relieved to see her clothes were still on.

Without thinking, Leon backed up and pulled the door shut. Then he banged on it with his fist and called out, 'Everything OK in there? We heard voices and just wanted to be sure you were OK.'

There was silence from the other side of the door and Leon turned to see David walking away, heading through the sanctuary and back to the bedrooms. The betrayal felt like a sucker punch.

Gideon finally hollered, 'Everything's fine. Mind your own business and get on to bed.'

Leon stood for a moment longer, tortured at the thought of leaving Mandy but unable to disrespect Gideon by forcing his way in. He listened to the murmurings of Gideon's deep voice, then returned to his bedroom, leaving the door open.

He climbed into bed next to Cia. He could just make out

David's shape lying beside his wife on the other side of the small room. Lying on his back and staring up at the ceiling, he tried to make out what David was whispering to her but couldn't. Instead, he watched the minutes tick by on the digital clock sitting on the floor. Twelve minutes later he heard someone walk softly down the hallway, her crying louder than her footsteps.

Leon wanted to get out of bed and attack Gideon. Rip the hair out of his head and punch his fat gut until he couldn't breathe. Make him feel some of the pain he had caused that girl.

'She's fifteen years old,' Leon whispered, knowing David had also heard Mandy walk down the hallway to the bedroom she shared with her mom.

'Shut up,' David hissed.

Leon could see Alaina sitting up on their pallet. 'What is wrong with you two? What are you talking about?'

'Leon's being an ass. Just lay back down and go to sleep.'

'Tomorrow we do something.'

FOUR

J osie rose early the next morning to get a hike in before work. With a hot cup of tea in hand, she flipped the light on outside her back door and smiled at the big white flakes swirling down through the porch light. It had been three years since Artemis had seen snow. All the more reason to get outside for a walk.

The snow was coming down too hard for her to see if Dell's light was on. Knowing he was an early riser she took a chance and called. He picked up on the second ring and offered to fix up a mess of eggs and bacon and grits. Aside from ranching, his favorite pastimes were cooking and tending a fire, and Josie benefited from both.

Chester stared down at his empty dog dish, waiting patiently for the scoop of kibble to get his day started. Once he'd been taken care of with fresh water and food, Josie brushed her teeth and pulled her hair into a ponytail. Before turning the bathroom light off, she leaned closer to the mirror, searching for crow's feet around her eyes, pressing the light wrinkles that had begun to trace their way across her forehead. She wondered if they were a visual nudge; her body telling her heart that her opportunity for kids was not infinite. She imagined Nick in Mexico City, taking his shower, getting ready for a day filled with drama and heartache, a day filled with no thought of a family or a settled life with her. She didn't begrudge him his career, but it was time to move on. They both deserved something better than an occasional weekend of arguing over all the reasons their relationship wasn't working. But that was a worry for another day.

Once Chester had finished eating she pulled on a pair of insulated hiking pants and a barn coat with gloves and hiking boots. She put her off-duty revolver in a pocket holster in her coat and opened the door to let Chester bound outside in front of her. She followed after him, smiling at the dots of cold melting instantly on her warm face. Excited at the introduction of something new to his routine, the dog zippered back and forth across the pasture, smelling out jackrabbits and ground squirrels, trying to figure out how the thin blanket of snow was throwing off his ability to track in the desert sand.

She followed the driveway back the half-mile toward Dell's, catching occasional glimpses of the sun just rising between the mountains, lighting up the flakes in a magical dance across the desert. Josie laughed watching Chester lope back toward her, forcing his snout under her hand just to get a pat on the head. She leaned down to kiss his head so he could take off again, scouting the way.

Halfway down the drive the light from Dell's front window appeared through the flakes and she smelled the sweet wood smoke from his fire – her favorite smell on earth. As she grew closer, the silhouette of his cedar-planked cabin appeared, with the mountain ridge looming just behind, and the gratitude that she felt at living in such a place brought a lump to her throat. Life was good. She just occasionally had to remind herself of that fact.

When they reached the front porch, the dog bounded up the steps and forced his way in first, galloping into the kitchen like a horse, skidding into Dell who laughed and handed him a small plate of fresh cooked bacon.

She helped Dell move the kitchen table into the living room where they sat in front of the fire to eat. Dell caught Josie up on the latest with his cattle herd, and she filled him in on the latest with The Drummers.

Dell looked disgusted. 'Somebody needs to run them out of town.'

'You need a diversity class,' Josie said.

'I'm a half-century too old for that.'

'It gets worse. I checked my email before I came down this morning. Marta left me a message from her shift last night. She found several gun sales registered to Gideon over the past several months tracked back to Texas. On top of that, I stopped to talk to Debby yesterday, the principal at the middle school. A student told me she'd been approached by a boy living at the church who claims he has a gun collection.'

Dell looked shocked. 'Did he show it to her?'

'No, he hasn't invited her in, but I got the feeling she'd go inside in a heartbeat.'

'Maybe you need to pay a visit to that jackass. Yank his chain,' said Dell.

'I'm walking a thin line. I just talked to two boys yesterday about marching like Nazi soldiers outside the front of the church. The adults are refusing to answer the door. They don't have a phone number to reach anyone. Their kids won't attend public school. It's starting to get ugly.'

The Artemis PD was managed by the first shift dispatcher, Louise Hagerty, who sat at her computer monitoring everything from the police scanner to what was said by someone's hairdresser. Lou missed very little in terms of the goings on in Artemis and never minded sharing the details or her opinion about the people involved in any situation. Lou did not see gray, only black and white.

When Josie walked into the PD she found Lou reclining in her chair, arms crossed over her skinny chest, talking to Otto, who looked as if he was doing little talking but much listening. The conversation stopped as Josie walked around the counter.

'Ms Gibbs wants an update on her husband's DWI,' Lou said.

'Can you write that down so I don't forget it?'

'You got it,' Lou said.

'Smokey will be here in a few. Are you free to meet with us?' Josie said, looking at Otto.

'I'll be right up.'

Josie made her way up the stairs to the second floor office where she unlocked a wooden door and flipped on several rows of fluorescent lights. Three desk areas occupied most of the classroom-sized room, with a large wooden conference table located in the center. Windows covered the back wall, letting in the desert light and heat that made it impossible to cool in the summer, but created a cozy setting in December.

As she made a pot of coffee, she heard the front door bell ring and the sounds of Smokey, the County Council president and lifelong resident of Artemis, chatting with Lou and Otto.

Smokey Blessings was in his late forties and married to a high-spirited ER nurse named Vie. Where Smokey approached life with the calm of a country preacher, Vie took on the world like a jackhammer. They were the perfect *opposites attract* couple and appeared to genuinely love and respect one another. Josie considered Smokey a good friend and appreciated his calm approach to town problems.

Several minutes later she listened as Smokey and Otto made their way up the stairs, chatting amiably.

With three cups of coffee and a canister of sugar on the table for Otto, they talked about the unseasonably cold winter until Josie finally asked Smokey why he'd asked for the meeting.

'We have a major problem and it's getting worse by the day. Something has to be done about those people in the church.'

He paused and she nodded for him to continue.

'I get living off the grid. I get settling out here because you want to live a life free from prying eyes. But they flaunt their weird beliefs. Have you been by there today?'

Josie and Otto both shook their heads.

'They've painted all the windows of the church black so no one can see in. The kids don't go to school. They claim they're home schooled. Everyone sleeps in the same area. They turned that church into a joke, right in the middle of town. I'd like to know how they got the money to buy it to begin with. I hear they're flat broke.'

'I heard they bought it for a dollar,' Otto said.

'That's true. I talked to Junior Daggy,' Josie said. 'He claims Davis was so desperate to get rid of the building that he was ready to pay someone to take it. After the pastor committed suicide in there several years ago, no one would touch it.'

Smokey made a face like he was disgusted with the turn of the conversation. 'Look. I don't want people in my business either. That's why I choose to live here in Artemis. We take care of our own. We don't need the town government and the police looking over our shoulder every five minutes telling us how to live and breathe and raise our kids. I get why they moved here. But they aren't right. They aren't normal.'

'What's normal, Smokey? Normal doesn't exist anymore.

The black and white of how we grew up is different now. I'm not saying that's good or bad, it's just the way it is.'

'You know what I'm talking about. Something bad is going on in there. Somebody needs to go in there before things get out of control. Damn it, there's kids in there!'

'You want me to go to the judge and ask for a search warrant because there's a group of people who aren't normal?'

Smokey's face grew red. 'You've heard the rumors.'

'Rumors! Come on, Smokey. Give me a break.'

'They're all sleeping together. They're taking orders from some old man that calls himself Gideon. The kids don't go to school. There's no family – people just share kids and wives and husbands. Surely there's a law against that.'

Josie leaned her head back and groaned. 'Rumors. You don't have proof of anything. And even if you did, there's no law against communal living.'

'If they'd just taken all this out in the country, you know? If they'd just settled in some house out in the mud flats, or somewhere away from town. But they're flaunting all of it in our faces. We have to walk by that church every day, with the windows painted black and doors boarded up. It's a church! I get up every morning and walk outside to get my newspaper and have to look across the street at the desecration of a church.'

Josie glanced at Otto who was staying surprisingly quiet.

'You can't react to something like this with emotion,' Otto said. 'That's no good.'

Smokey's face turned a deeper red. 'I served my country. I didn't come home and teach my son right from wrong so he'd have to watch some street punk march around like a German Stormtrooper. We ought to have rights too.'

'What the hell am I supposed to do about this?' Josie said. 'What happens if I go back again and they still won't answer the door? There's no mailbox. They removed the doorknobs on all the exterior doors. You can only gain access from the inside now. There's no phone. So if they refuse to talk to me, what do I do? Force down a door over suspicions of educational neglect? It's not like they're the only people in the county who don't send their kids to school.'

'And if we wait and something terrible happens? What then?' Smokey said.

'That's what law enforcement is all about,' Otto said. 'We wait until something bad happens and we go in and clean up the mess. If you don't like the way something works you have to change the laws first. That's not up to the cops.'

'We want freedom of speech until those freedoms don't match our own ideas. Then we want to shut them down,' Josie said.

'Oh, come on.'

'That's exactly right, Smokey, and you know it. I personally agree with you. I'd like to run them out of town too. I think they're up to no good. But I need a reason to shut them down.' Smokey started to protest again but Josie stopped him. 'Hang on. I'm working on the backstory, digging into their history. And Marta's on the kids. We'll make sure there's no endangerment or neglect issues.' She decided not to mention the possibility of the group having acquired guns. She would talk with Otto later, but the last thing she needed was a rumor spreading about a stockpile of weapons in the church.

'I'll check city ordinances. See about limits for the number of people allowed to live in one structure together,' Otto said. 'I know I don't need to say this. I know you've both thought of this already, probably laid in bed thinking about it like I have. But this could get ugly quick. We can't let this turn into another Waco with the ATF rolling in with tanks and shotguns.'

FIVE

At six o'clock Josie unlocked her patrol car and made a mental note to schedule an oil change. As she opened the door she noticed a man who appeared to be in his late twenties walking quickly down the block toward her. She recognized him as one of The Drummers.

She looked at a paper to gain some time until he reached her. She hoped to engage him in a friendly conversation. She was surprised when he approached her first.

'Chief Gray?'

'What can I do for you?' She reached her hand out and he shook it with his own frigid hand. He'd obviously been outside for quite some time. She wondered if he'd been waiting on her.

'My name's Leon Spinner. I heard you were looking for an evening custodian at the police department. I wondered if that job was still open.'

He looked her square in the eyes as he spoke. His hair was scissor cut, short and neat, but not by a barber. He wore a faded woodland camouflage coat with his nametape intact. Josie thought he had the look of someone who cared about his appearance, who cared what others thought about him, unlike several of the people she'd seen associated with the group.

'Job's still open. Let's get inside out of this cold and I'll tell you about it.'

They sat across from each other at one of the intake desks with mugs of hot tea that Leon seemed genuinely thankful to receive.

'So you were in the military?' she asked, gesturing to his coat.

'Yes, ma'am. I was in Baghdad when we pulled out of Iraq in 2011.'

'Infantry?'

He nodded. 'Were you military?'

'No. I've been law enforcement since I left school. How did you end up joining The Drummers?'

He grinned and she did the same to acknowledge his reticence at her question. 'I'm not asking to cause you grief or pry into your business. Just trying to get to know you,' she said.

'Fair enough. Would you like the interview version or the truth?'

'The truth. It's always more interesting,' she said, smiling at his question.

'When I got out of the service I went home to Portland and my parents were gone. People talk about leaving with no forwarding address? That's literally what happened.'

Josie winced but didn't respond.

'A buddy who was in the same platoon as me also came back to Portland. His home life wasn't much better. We were hanging out at Mickey's Pub trying to figure out how to deal with life after war. The job market sucked, especially for a couple of foul-mouthed Marines. Then Gideon came into the pub one night. He and Gloria, his wife, took us in like sons. They fed us, told us about their big dream to live off the grid. Cut off from technology. Raise our own meat and crops. I was out of the service about six months when Cia and I signed on.'

'Is Cia your wife?'

'My girlfriend. We joined, and my buddy David and his wife Alaina came on at the same time. We were all looking for a place to belong, and Gideon and Gloria provided that. Cia loves Gideon, would follow him anywhere.' He offered a crooked smile that Josie found hard to read.

'I take it that you don't feel the same way as Cia?'

Leon laughed, his face reddening. 'I didn't say that. Gideon's great. It's just rough right now with all of us sharing rooms.' He shrugged again. 'So now I'm hoping to get a job to help support things until we move out of town.'

Josie nodded once. 'Any kind of timeframe on the move?'

Leon's confident expression wavered. He looked like a kid in need of someone to confide in. 'We just need to get some money coming in, and then we'll re-evaluate.'

Josie turned the talk to what experience Leon had with custodial work, and she explained what the job entailed and the pay.

By the time he left, she was ready to hire him, but new hires had to be approved by the mayor. She hoped to get Leon into the office soon to learn some more backstory on the group. With the cold weather, money running short and community anger increasing daily, Josie imagined tensions were running high. She hoped Leon could provide information about possible instability among the members.

Leon went to the front entrance of the church and knocked on the narrow window to the left of the door twice, then twice again. He thought it was absurd they were using codes to get into the building. It felt as if the whole situation had turned into a mockery of their original mission.

Jacob, a thirteen-year-old kid sitting guard inside the church, pushed the front door open and gave Leon a bored salute, then locked the door and went back to the chair he'd been napping in.

'Where is everyone?' Leon asked.

'Beats me.'

Leon felt bad for the kid. Sleeping in the same room as his parents. No phone or television. Leon knew from years in the military that boredom was the fastest way to trouble. If they didn't find something to engage the kids soon, they'd be doing far worse than marching up and down the street. Cia had caught Jacob and Bella making out in the back of the sanctuary the week before. Cia had talked to her about saying no to boys. She said the girl knew almost nothing about birth control, and even less about how to get it. Leon figured that would be the next drama, a pregnant teenager.

The sanctuary was empty. He glanced at his watch and saw that it was almost seven o'clock. He walked to the kitchen to find it empty as well. He'd figured the dinner crew would at least be on cleanup duty, but the dishes were stacked and soaking in the sink.

He opened the door to the basement to find the door at the end of the stairwell closed. He considered whether he should make the same mistake as before by trying to listen in, but didn't want to face Cia if someone caught him.

Leon walked the creaky floors to the Sunday school rooms.

The church was dark inside. They were conserving every penny, so lights were off at all times unless they were needed for work. Leon couldn't imagine what Gideon had been thinking when he'd painted the windows black. As far as Leon knew, no one from the community had tried to look in their windows, and the dreariness inside the old church had been magnified a hundred times. He remembered the day the women had come back from looking at the church with Gideon. They'd been excited about the old building, the long, narrow windows in the sanctuary and all the natural light that filled the church. And they'd lost it for what? To say screw you to the people of Artemis; the same people they needed to buy supplies and gas and food from, the same people Gideon now wanted them to get jobs from?

Leon knocked on his Sunday school room door, knowing they would all be in the basement, then pushed the door open. The two couples' pallets were straightened, the patchwork of colorful sleeping bags neatly covering their pillows, with their books and coffee cups and alarm clocks all lined up around the perimeter of the room. Leon noticed the framed photo of him and Cia in their high school graduation gowns, smiling into the sun, heads touching, arms raised in triumph as if the world was theirs for the taking. He kneeled down onto the bed and held the photo, remembering the pounding in his heart that day as he had stood by the prettiest girl in the school, ready to board a plane to South Carolina the next day to become a Marine. Staring at what felt like a former life, he craved the pride he'd felt that day like a junkie craving a high.

Leon heard voices and footsteps and put the photo back next to Cia's pillow, grabbing his paperback book and laying down as if he'd been reading. Cia opened the door and smiled tentatively when she saw him.

'Hey, baby. We just got done.' Her voice was quiet. She shut the door and sat cross-legged next to him, snuggling up against his side. 'How'd it go with the janitor's job?'

Leon put his book down. 'It went well. I liked the chief. She asked a few questions about us, but nothing over the top. Honestly, I think I got the job.' He grinned when her face lit up.

'Good for you! I knew you were the one to get out in the community. When will you start?'

'She has to go through channels, make it all official before she can offer it to me. But I think she wants someone right away.'

'You'll be the first one hired. Jackson might have a job at the grocery working second shift. He'll know in a day or two.'

'What happened in the meeting?'

She raised her eyebrows and tilted her head. It was the 'Oh, nothing much' deflection that she used whenever he asked a question she didn't want to answer.

'Not much new,' she said.

'He hasn't had a group meeting in a while. Just fill me in.'

She looked down at her fingernails, as if absorbed in picking off the chipped pink polish. 'He's zeroing in on the technology. Assigning people jobs.' She paused, still avoiding his eyes. 'Just because we've hit a snag here doesn't mean we ignore what we're about.'

'And what are we about?'

'Gideon preached from Revelations. Leon, it's scary. The prophecies are practically on top of us. Gideon is connected with other groups across the west and they're all preparing.'

Leon felt the blood pulsing in his ears and he forced a calm response. 'Preparing for what?'

She looked at him then, apparently buoyed by his interest. 'Leon, we have turned our world over to the machines. You know Revelations is about a world order. People used to think the world order was about politics, about one country conquering all others and amassing wealth and power. But how could that ever actually happen? There's only one thing on earth that draws *all* people together.' She paused but he didn't speak. He'd listened to Gideon's rants against technology for years. 'What can connect a person in Iran with someone in Australia and Egypt and Israel and the US in a matter of seconds? Technology.'

'What does that have to do with Revelations?'

'Because it prophesies the prince of darkness who rules over the world. Never before has that been possible. Until now.'

'People have been using the same book of Revelations to prophesy the end of the world for two thousand years.'

'But there's never been a world order before now! That's the part of the prophecies that's finally come true. Scholars could never imagine how the world could have one ruler over all nations, but it's possible now.'

He watched her talking and couldn't help smiling at her sincerity. She slapped his arm. 'This is serious! What are you smiling about?'

'Come lay beside me. I'm glad you're excited. I'll be more excited when we get out of this place.'

'We all will. We all want the same thing,' she said, leaning down to kiss his forehead.

'I just want out of this hellhole. With a real bed to sleep in.'

He reached for her to pull her down beside him but she lay on her side and rested her head on her arm instead. Pin pricks of light dotted her face where the rays from a streetlamp outside the window pushed through the tiny gaps in the paint. Her brow was furrowed and he sighed in submission.

'What have I done to make you mad now?' he said.

'Why would you call this a hellhole? Why do you always have to disrespect him? He's doing everything he can for us right now and you're just being an ass. He brought us here to build our little slice of heaven, but it takes time, Leon.'

'OK, OK, I get it.'

'No, you don't! If you could only watch him. His eyes are on fire when he talks. No one has a passion for life like he does. You can feel this spirit channeled through his body when he talks. You just want to touch him to feel that power.'

'I'd love to see it, but I'm not invited. I've been cast out.'

'He's not going to waste his time on someone who doesn't believe in the mission. None of us were ready for this in the beginning. Everything is happening exactly like he said it would. You just don't listen.'

'Just help me understand how it is that you and I came into this group wanting to have a place to start a family and farm and raise kids someday, and now you've gone off in this different direction? All of a sudden he's preaching and taking away our cell phones. I just don't get it.'

'I finally have a purpose that is true and important. The things

I avoided when I was younger, like pain and fear, now make me happy too because they serve a purpose. They make—'

They startled at a knock on the door and heard Gideon clear his throat in the hallway.

'Cia. Come with me, love. We've got work to do.'

Cia pecked Leon on the cheek and jumped up from the mat to open the door. Gideon smiled like a benevolent father and put his arms out. She went to him and he wrapped her in a long hug. Leon stood awkwardly, looking on behind them. Gideon reached up with a hand to pull the hair away from her ear where he leaned in. He spoke softly into her ear, his eyes locked with Leon's, carrying the wicked mirth of someone enjoying themselves at the private expense of another.

Gideon put his hands gently on Cia's shoulders and pushed her away, telling her to go ahead to his office. As she walked away, he leaned into the room far enough for Leon to smell the spearmint on his breath. 'She's a good girl, that Cia. Compliant and trusting. Even more beautiful than our little Mandy.' He winked and shut the door. Leon dropped to his knees where he'd been standing on their sleeping pallet and wept.

SIX

Josie's cell phone rang, jolting her out of a hard sleep. She searched the nightstand for the time on the alarm clock as she felt around blindly for the ringing phone. She answered it, seeing it was 2:05 a.m.

'This is Gray.'

'Josie, it's Jeff Douglas. You live out on Schenck Road, right?'

She sat up in bed, now fully awake. Jeff worked for Tex-Edison Electric. 'That's right.'

'Get outside and look west toward the substation on Basin Road. I'll stay on the line.'

Josie put on jeans and slipped her feet into the boots she left by the front door. She went outside, struggling to get an arm in her coat, the dog following behind her. As soon as she walked out the door she saw what Jeff was calling about.

'What the hell is that?' she asked. The sky glowed blue green, just as she imagined the northern lights in Alaska might look like.

'I got a call from Dave Abbot who said his wife woke up because she saw a light out their bedroom window. He said it looked like fireworks going off. He called me because it was coming from the substation just down the road from where they live.'

'Transformers blew?'

'They're still burning. All of them at the substation. I've never seen anything like it.'

'Power's out everywhere?'

'Oh yeah. This will take a while.'

'What's a while?'

'I hate to speculate, but let's just say probably a few days.'

'Do you suspect foul play?' she asked.

'I can't imagine what would make all these transformers go at once. So I'm guessing foul play.'

'Is help on the way?'

'I made all the right calls. I'm waiting to hear back on ETAs. I'll keep you posted.'

'I'll head that way,' she said.

Josie called the mayor on her way to the substation and filled him in.

'You don't need to make a trip out here. I'm just letting you know your office will start getting calls. From what Jeff said, we could be without power for a while. Maybe days.'

'I'm on my way,' he said.

Josie sighed. She'd hoped he would keep his distance and allow her to do her job.

On her drive to the substation she received several text messages from community members with photos of the blue pulsating light in the sky, along with messages such as *WTF is this???* and *UFO SIGHTING.*

When she arrived, Jeff was on the phone with someone from Tex-Edison Electric working on an emergency power restoration plan. The fire had burned out, leaving the charred smell of oil and smoke in the air. Mayor O'Kane pulled in shortly after Josie.

Jeff finished his call and thanked them for offering support.

'You ever seen anything like this?' O'Kane asked.

'Not at one substation.'

'I've already received multiple text messages from people asking about aliens. That blue light had people freaked out,' he said.

'It's caused by an electric arc flash. When the electricity passes through the air it creates a charged gas. Then the transformer oil catches fire and burns. We may get lucky here and not have as much damage as I'd feared. The fire remained contained to the transformers.'

'Any idea yet what caused it to blow?' Josie asked.

'Yes, ma'am. Let's take a walk.' He escorted them along the perimeter of the substation, surrounded by a tall chain-link fence. 'The fence is intact. Nobody cut anything to get inside,' he said.

'Will you have footage from security cameras, just to be certain there wasn't foul play?' O'Kane asked.

Jeff made a dismissive sound. 'Our security consists of a padlock on the gate. We don't have the funds for security.'

'For part of the electric grid?' O'Kane said, clearly shocked at the news.

'We have the largest service area of any cooperative in the US. Almost forty thousand square miles. And we're only pulling revenue from about 6,500 Rio Grande customers. So, no. We don't have money for security cameras or alarms.'

'I thought the feds passed laws a few years ago requiring security for the electric grid,' Josie said, finding it hard to believe they didn't at least have cameras.

'The new standards were for critical grid infrastructure. We're not exactly a critical part of the grid in Far West Texas.'

'I get it,' Josie said. 'No different than the police and fire service out here dealing with thousands of miles with a handful of people.'

'What's your best guess?' O'Kane asked. 'Natural causes, or was somebody up to no good?'

'If it was one transformer, I'd say equipment failure. But not this. It was just a week ago that we had the meeting about the thirty-million-dollar grid upgrade. We're several years into a process that has plenty of people riled up. There were about two dozen at the meeting. Most people want it to happen. They're just upset it's taking so long. But there were a few from other communities who've been showing up to protest the amount of money it'll cost all customers versus the small number of people who'll benefit.'

'You think these people were angry enough to jack up the system?' she asked.

'You never know.' Jeff stopped walking and pointed his flashlight at the ground near the fence. 'Check this out. I haven't moved anything. If you're careful you can even see footprints in the sand.'

Josie and Mayor O'Kane stopped and leaned in to see spent shell casings glinting in the light.

'I don't know much about guns, but I know those spent rounds are pretty big,' O'Kane said.

Josie pulled her camera out and took several photos of the ground and the casings. 'It looks to me like a .223.'

'Which is what?' he asked.

'It's a bullet used with a high-power rifle, like an AK-47 or an AR-15. Somebody with a good eye could have taken out those transformers,' she said, 'but we don't know how long these have been laying here. Let's not jump to conclusions.'

'Anything else look suspicious?' O'Kane asked.

'No, but I basically just walked around the fence to see if somebody cut it to gain access. That's when I found these.'

'I appreciate the information,' Josie said. 'Can you take me into the locked area to do a walk through so I can get photos before you start repair work? I'll keep this area with the casings taped off until sunrise so I can have some light for photos.'

Jeff held a hand up to take a phone call. He cursed and covered the speaker. 'Two more substations were hit tonight. The line to Big Bend National Park and Terlingua is gone. It's a radial power line, meaning when it's gone, everything along that line goes down. Most of West Texas is without power.'

Josie and the mayor went home to dress for work in the dark, meeting back at the PD at four in the morning where they received an update from Jeff. The substation in Presidio County sustained what was referred to as a minor explosion accompanied by a fire that required foam for containment. They had crews coming from San Antonio and Houston to help assess the damage.

Mayor O'Kane held a news conference with Marfa Public Radio at 8:00 that morning using backup power sources. Without going into specifics, he promised a news briefing as soon as more information was available. While Josie stood listening to the press conference at the City Office, she received a text from Lou at the PD.

Better get over here.

Josie entered the PD and found Lou on her cell phone. She handed it to Josie. 'It's Smokey. He's fired up.'

'What's going on?'

'Thomas Brandy called me a few minutes ago,' Smokey said. 'He's got the Verizon tower on his ranch. He said about five o'clock this morning he heard automatic gunfire. He put his wife and two little girls in the closet with a shotgun and went outside. He saw two men shooting at the tower until they ran dry, then watched them reload and start up again. He didn't think they knew much about guns. They were just blindly shooting up at the satellites. He crept alongside the fence and unloosed his own shotgun. The two men took off on foot. He tried to follow them but lost sight. He never did hear an engine, but he didn't stay outside too long. He was worried about his wife and kids.'

'What the hell is happening?' Josie said. 'The power grid is shutting down, someone's trying to cut off communications . . .'

'I'm telling you, none of this happened before those Drummer people invaded our town.'

'Now hang on. That's what everyone's going to say. But what purpose would this serve for them? They painted their windows black. They have no natural light and it's too damn cold to go without heat. Why would they eliminate the electric that provides them with both?'

Smokey was quiet.

'I'm not saying you're wrong. Just don't jump to conclusions,' Josie said. 'The last thing we need is a mass rush to judgment followed by protests in the street.'

An emergency generator provided light and power to dispatch and the downstairs area of the PD, but the office upstairs was lit only by the dim light from the gray sky outside. Josie stood at the large window and stared out at the dozens of family homes in the perfectly straight tic-tac-toe grid of streets. With the kids home from school and huddled up inside out of the cold, their bicycles and plastic toys strewn across yards and empty swing sets facing quiet streets, the town had an apocalyptic feel. Josie tried to imagine the mass panic if cell phone communication was compromised as well as the power grid. She would never have imagined that Artemis would be faced with terroristic activity, especially from people living amongst them. Publicly, she would continue to tow the innocent-until-proven-otherwise line, but she had little doubt that The Drummers were behind the destruction.

She moved her laptop to a small table by the window to start looking into electric grid sabotage until Officer Marta Cruz arrived to debrief.

Josie started with a connection she had at the FBI's counter-terrorism division. Mark Davis had worked as an officer with Indianapolis Metro Police during two of the years Josie had been there. When he left for the training academy he'd remained in contact for a few years, and had tried to convince Josie to make the move to the feds as well. Had she not moved to Texas she would have followed Mark, and she occasionally wondered how different her life might have been.

'How the hell are you? You moved to the end of the earth and fell off the map,' he said.

'That's a pretty accurate statement. How's the bureau treating you?'

'I am living the dream. Every cursed day,' he said, laughing. 'But I don't guess you're calling to check up on me.'

'Unfortunately, no. I have a bad feeling about a group that's moved to town, and I'd like to run their information by you.'

'Absolutely. I'll do whatever I can.'

Josie spent the next ten minutes giving him a rundown on The Drummers and what she knew about Gideon, as well as the sabotage of the three substations and the attempt to shoot out the Verizon tower.

'How big is Artemis?' he asked.

'About 2,500 people.'

He laughed. 'Who would go to that kind of trouble to disrupt the lives of two thousand people? This sounds like something you'd see in a large city, not a remote desert area. What's their angle?'

'That's what I can't figure. They hit three small substations and took out power to about 6,500 people. But that's also forty thousand square miles of land with no power right now.'

'With that much area, you figure multiple people were involved?'

'I looked at the times when the stations were hit and figured the mileage. It looks like they made a loop, starting in Artemis. It would have taken someone two hours to reach the second substation, and almost another two to reach the third one.'

'So logistically one person could have hit all three during the night,' he said.

'Yes. But why would you come into a town you want to settle in and harass the people you want to hire you, and destroy the power that heats your home?'

'Maybe they aren't planning to stay. You said they're from Idaho. Is there a pattern of moving from one town to another, leaving disaster in their wake?' he asked.

'I have an officer working on their history. I can't say at this point.'

'I'll look into it, but as small as they are, I wouldn't expect much from our end.'

'Obviously our biggest concern is why they'd want to take out the power and communications systems here,' she said.

'Do you know of any other affiliations they might have?'

'No. Why do you ask?'

'We've been following hackers from Russia and China who target Industrial Control Systems, or ICSs. Attacks aren't publicized because the less information hackers have, the safer we all remain. But it makes it hard to forecast when agencies don't communicate. I'm more familiar with the cyber side of this, but I know there have been ground attacks against energy providers.'

Josie took a moment to consider what he was saying. 'So what happens when the cyber hackers partner with the ground terrorists to take out our grid systems?'

'That's called catastrophic failure.'

Josie spent the next hour trying to understand the motivation behind the grid terrorists. Ninety percent of the time motivation came down to money, but that didn't seem to be the case with the group Mark had told her about. Their sole motivation seemed to be the destruction of the United States. The great paradox was that the freedom of speech and information that was so valued by Americans was the trait that made the country most vulnerable to attackers. The country broadcast every detail, every bit of dirty laundry it could find, to every media outlet in the land.

It didn't take her long to find splinter groups all over the US who were connected to grid attacks. They weren't motivated by money; they were motivated by disruption and chaos. Lloyds of London estimated that with a widespread, well-planned attack, there would be an economic loss in the US of well over a trillion dollars.

Marta and Otto both joined Josie at ten that morning and started by working with the Emergency Response Team to get volunteers checking on shut-ins who might be in trouble with no electricity or heat in the cold temperatures. Once they'd dealt with the immediate aftermath of the power outage, Josie quickly brought them up to speed on the attacks and what she'd learned from her FBI connection.

'My lord, Josie. What is happening in the world? What is wrong with people that they would want to shoot out their own electricity and phone lines? And if they don't want heat, what about all the old people who desperately need power? It's shameful.' Marta had pulled the cross she wore around her neck out of her uniform and was absently rubbing the back of it with her thumb.

'What's the name of this group that's the national threat?' Otto asked.

'They're called the EX-Sovereigns. They appear to be training and equipping smaller groups to go out and attack rural areas in an effort to gather and share information that will help them stage a massive attack. Mark said he thinks they're located in Wyoming.'

'How do you fight something like this?' Marta asked.

'We double what we pay for our utilities so that companies can increase security before something terrible happens. Pay it now, or pay it later,' Otto said.

'Had you heard of this group before today?' Marta asked.

'No. After I talked to Mark I got online and found very little about them. I found most of my information posted in the environmental and electric company publications that required a login to access. They don't want this public.'

'And we have no idea if The Drummers might be connected to this group?' Otto asked.

'We don't. I don't want this leaving this room, but I feel very strongly that our local attacks were caused by The Drummers.

Beyond the timing, we also know from Marta that they're connected to gun sales across the border,' she said. 'I also stopped by the middle school and talked to a girl who claimed that one of the boys who was marching in front of the church told her about his gun collection.'

'Did she go see it?' Otto asked.

'No. Fortunately, the boy hasn't invited her inside. But she's a pretty girl. I gave her a lecture about not entering the church, but hormones aren't ruled by intelligence.' Josie turned to Marta. 'I heard from Leon, the kid who wants the janitor's job, that Gideon and Gloria lived in Portland, Oregon, on top of the other places. Did you find anything about their time in Idaho?'

'None of it is good news. I found a news article about some townspeople in a small Georgia town protesting and carrying picket signs outside The Drummers' farm. This was before their move to Idaho.' Marta turned her laptop around so that Josie and Otto could see. 'Blow up the photo of the picketers.'

Josie zoomed in and read one of the signs. *Keep Your Kids Safe! Child Molester Lives Here!*

Otto groaned and cursed.

'Hang on. I followed up with the local police chief. He said Gideon brought on every bit of grief he received, but they never found any evidence to substantiate the child molestation, or even endangerment.'

'What do you mean he brought on the grief?' Otto said.

'He was doing exactly the same kind of things they're doing here. He provoked his neighbors. Tried to get away with tax fraud and then bragged about it when the case was overturned on some religious technicality.'

'I don't guess they mentioned anything about vandalism or shooting out substations?' Josie asked.

'I didn't get into that since I didn't know about it. But I saved the best for last. One of the men in The Drummers, named Clyde Hamblin, has a felony conviction. He is on parole for robbery.'

Otto lifted a fist. 'If they have firearms in the church then he may have violated conditions of his parole.'

'Does his parole officer know he's left the state?' Josie asked.

'He does. Hamblin received eight years for the robbery, served four, and got four years' parole. He's already served three with no problems so he was granted permission to move out of state.'

'But we have no proof they have firearms in the church,' Josie said.

'Hang on. I stopped at the Hot Tamale for dinner yesterday and Lucy pulled me aside. She's freaked out about The Drummers. She told me, "They're the devil's doing." Then she opened her phone and showed me a photo she'd snapped of Clyde Hamblin when he was eating lunch there a few days ago. She obviously knew nothing about his parole. She just knew he was a Drummer and she didn't like him pulling an open carry inside her restaurant.' Marta held her phone up and showed a photo of a man with a gun sticking out of the back waistband of his jeans. 'Then she showed another photo of the same man from the front, which allows us to positively identify him with the gun.' Marta grinned. 'He absolutely violated conditions of parole.'

'There's our entrance into the church,' Otto said.

'Nice work, Marta. I'll submit the arrest warrant today,' Josie said. 'I'd like you to stay on the substation investigation. Get out tonight and interview Thomas Brandy about the cell phone tower shooting. Make sure to get spent casings logged into evidence. If you have time, contact Presidio County about their substations. Let them know we have a prominent lead and we'd like casings from the scene if they can find them. Leave Otto notes and he can follow up in the morning.'

SEVEN

Otto drove the gravel road home to his small farm on the outskirts of Artemis and wondered how Delores had fared with no electricity. He wasn't proud of it, but he couldn't help wondering what supper might consist of with no stove or oven. They were both a good thirty to fifty pounds overweight – depending on the weight chart they chose to follow – but she could bake like no other. The Polish delights the woman constructed were like heaven on earth: sauerkraut balls and paczki, cabbage rolls and pierogi. He imagined a peanut butter and jelly sandwich for dinner and cursed the bastards who had shot up the substations for no other reason than pure hatred.

He parked his car and walked up the concrete sidewalk to where Delores stood with the screen door open, waiting on him with a smile. The woman was the salt of the earth, he thought.

She held the door open and he entered, dropping his briefcase and slipping his shoes off before stepping onto the rug. Delores pecked him on the lips, asking about his day as she hustled off to the kitchen.

He followed her, offering a brief rundown on the latest with the crazy commune people. He left out the theory that they were most likely behind the destruction of the power grid for all of West Texas, consequently hijacking the dumplings she'd planned for their dinner.

'What kind of life must those people have had growing up to want to live in a church and paint the windows black? Where's the joy in that kind of life?' she asked.

Otto stood at the kitchen counter and surveyed the plates. She had spread braunschweiger on crackers and cut up vegetables with small bowls of ranch dip beside each pile of broccoli, cauliflower and carrots. He knew that he should be glad for the plate of food this good woman worked to put before him, but he couldn't help feeling disappointed. Coming home each night was a treat, wondering what she might have prepared for their dinner, and what dessert would end the meal. And the beauty of it was that she seemed to enjoy preparing it as much as he enjoyed eating it. She'd called him her true love for the past fifty years of marriage and he figured after that many years it must surely be true.

'So what now?' she asked, always interested in the latest big case.

'We need to get into that church. We need to gain entrance to a building where they've removed all of the doorknobs, removed the mailbox, painted the windows black, and where no one has a phone.'

Delores poured them each a glass of water from a pitcher and put the plates on the kitchen table.

'No Dr Pepper?' he asked.

'We're watching our weight.' She turned on the battery-powered lantern that cast an ugly fluorescent glow throughout the kitchen. 'Sounds like Chief Josie has her hands full on this one.'

He took a bite of the braunschweiger and sighed. Delicious. 'Did you order this from the Hot Tamale?'

'I did. Lucy said you've introduced a whole group of Texans to liverwurst. She's putting it on the menu because so many people request it.'

'I've done my civic duty.'

'Do you think these Drummers had something to do with the substations all getting attacked at the same time?' she asked.

Otto put his cracker back on the plate. 'Who told you that?'

'It doesn't take a brain surgeon to make that connection,' she said. 'Plus, Lewis Brier, Mary's husband?'

Otto nodded.

'Well, he's been helping them out. Mary talked him into it. I talked to her at the women's group meeting—'

'What do you mean helping them out?'

She looked exasperated that he'd cut her off. He knew it was a pet peeve of hers, but she'd start a story going down one road and end up three counties over by the end of it.

'Mary met the leader's wife at the grocery store. Her name is Gloria. A very nice lady, by the way. She was telling Mary how cold the church was, and how there was a hole in the office wall that they had clothes stuffed into until they could get it fixed. Well, you know Mary. She went home and told Lewis to get his carpenter's kit and get over to the church and repair the hole for them.'

'And did he?'

'Of course he did!'

'And did he learn anything about how they operate?'

'Indeed he did. He said Gloria sits in one office and her husband has another. Lewis didn't know what Gideon might be up to in his office, but he said Gloria is trying to take care of the business side of things, but they're in a bad way money wise. But on Lewis's last day there,' Delores paused to calculate the days in her head, 'which would have been two days ago because I just talked to Mary yesterday . . .'

Otto sighed. Had she not been his true love of fifty years, he would have told her to get on with it, but he said nothing.

'Anyway, this Gloria told Lewis that she'd gotten great news that day. They'd got some kind of sponsor who'd agreed to help them out with money.'

Otto sat back in his chair. 'A sponsor? What does that mean?'

'I don't know. She didn't go into the details. Her point was just that maybe with some money coming in that they'll buy a place in the country and get out of the church. Gloria is upset by the way the kids are acting and doesn't like the turn of things either. She claims everyone is on edge because things haven't gone as planned, but she thinks the money will help.'

'How much money?'

'I told you she didn't give me details.'

Otto laid his napkin on the table and stood. 'Thank you for a delicious supper.'

'Well, it wasn't delicious, but it was the best I could do with no stove.'

'I'm going to run over to Lewis's for a minute. I won't be long.'

'When you break the case open, make sure to give Mary and I credit,' she called after him.

*   *   *

The Briers lived on a cattle and sheep ranch about five miles from Otto's home as the crow flies, or a ten-mile pickup truck drive along a dried-up arroyo that ran parallel to the Rio Grande, the dividing line between the US and Mexico.

The 10,000-acre ranch was dominated by desert grassland with high rolling grama grasses and tabosa flats. The rear of the property fell into both shallow and deep canyons with juniper and mountain oak where Lewis occasionally allowed elk and mule deer hunting. He had ample wells strategically placed on the property and a well-tended horse barn next to a modest home. Otto had told Delores for years that if he ever won the lottery he'd buy the Brier Ranch, knowing full well he'd never win the lottery and Lewis would never sell.

Otto found Lewis backing his truck out of the barn. He stopped and shut the engine off when he saw Otto.

'You headed out?' Otto asked.

'Just checking fence row. Nothing that can't wait.'

'I won't take long. I was talking to Delores at supper, and I guess she and Mary were swapping tales at a meeting yesterday.'

'Did she get me in a pickle?'

Otto grinned. 'No, nothing like that. I'll ask you to keep this confidential, but I'm here about The Drummers. Mary mentioned that you'd done some work for them. Josie has tried multiple times to talk with them recently and can't get an answer. And as far as I know, you're the only one in the community who's actually been allowed inside the church. We're a little worried about what's going on inside, especially with the kids. I wondered what your impression was.'

Lewis waved his hand. 'I wouldn't want my grandkids living in there, I can tell you that. That old building just isn't fit for living. It sat empty for too many years and isn't built for this cold weather.'

'Did you get the chance to talk to many of the members?'

'No. Only a woman named Gloria. She's the leader's wife. I only worked in her office. She had a hole in the exterior wall that was letting in cold air. I just patched it and added insulation as best I could. Not much more than a band-aid fix.'

'Did you learn anything about the group? What they're after?'

'Not really what they're about. The woman talked mostly about how bad the money situation was. I thought she was just saying that so I wouldn't ask her for any payment for fixing the wall. But then as I was cleaning up on the last day I was there, she got a check in the mail from some group who was helping them out.'

'A big check?'

'She didn't say how much, but the way she talked, it was enough to help keep them going. She claimed they were close to having to disband, but then this other national group agreed to help them in exchange for their support.'

'What kind of support?'

'I didn't ask. And she didn't offer.'

'Did she mention the name of the group?'

He thought for a moment. 'I don't think so. If she did, the name didn't stick with me.'

'If you think of anything else that might help us understand their motives, make sure to call me. This substation business has me pretty worried.'

Lewis looked surprised at the comment. 'You don't think they're responsible for that, do you? I mean, it's not just the station close to Artemis, it was two others as well. It could have been people or groups from surrounding towns, too.'

'True enough. Just give it some thought.'

At a little after six that evening Josie received approval from the judge to serve an arrest warrant for a parole violation. She sent a text to Sheriff Martinez, asking if he had time to meet that night. He said he hadn't eaten since a bowl of cereal that morning so they agreed to meet for dinner at the Hot Tamale.

The restaurant was located down the block from the PD, and was the lunch spot for most of downtown Artemis. A scattering of small tables and chairs were rearranged by the diners to fit whatever configuration they needed, from a quiet place in the corner, to a group of twenty in the middle of the room celebrating a birthday or promotion.

Lucy had put a sign in front of the restaurant that she was serving lunchmeat sandwiches and chips via candlelight, cash only. She'd moved her meat into long coolers packed with ice and had promised her customers that she would remain open as long as people brought her bags of ice to keep the meat cold.

Josie took a table in the corner by the window and ordered a couple of Dr Peppers and sandwiches. Roy came into the restaurant and chatted with a few people before finding Josie by the window. A linebacker of a man with a walrus mustache, he looked as if he'd have been more comfortable sitting on two of the small wooden chairs instead of one.

He patted Josie on the back and sat down across from her. 'You saved me. I was getting lightheaded. And you don't want a big burly bastard like me passing out from hunger.'

'Don't you keep a stash of junk food in your drawer? You need those packets of cheese crackers. They'll get you by in a pinch.'

'What I need is a job that allows me to eat my meals like a regular man.' He leaned back in his seat to allow the waitress to put sandwiches and lukewarm cans of soda on the table. 'Candlelight suits you.'

'Can you believe this? I was told at least another twenty-four to forty-eight hours without power.'

Josie watched him stuff a massive bite into his mouth. He closed his eyes and chewed with a look of satisfaction.

'You getting good checkups from the heart doc?' she asked.

He opened his eyes slowly. 'Can you not see that I'm enjoying this moment? Why would you ask that?'

'Because I care about your big bad ass and would like to see you stick around a while. Are you taking your meds and exercising?'

'I have a wife at home who tracks my calorie intake and exercise on a calendar that hangs on our refrigerator. And I have Maria at the jail feeding me donuts and Fritos on the side to keep me from being so grumpy. It's a complicated life I lead.'

'I'm probably going to make your life a little more complicated,' Josie said. 'What's tomorrow morning look like in terms of deputies on duty?'

'Not bad. Two on the road.'

'How about you?'

'I'm in the office.'

'I need you to help me serve an arrest warrant at The Drummers' church.'

His eyebrows raised. 'Delighted. I'd like to take that smug bastard calling himself Gideon out back and teach him a thing or two. Rule number one – don't paint your windows black with children living behind those windows.'

'Have you heard any rumors about weapons inside the church?'

'I've been so busy the past few weeks that I haven't paid a whole lot of attention. You know we've got three members of the Medrano Cartel incarcerated, and the Mexican authorities are not cooperating. But I can definitely put feelers out about guns at the church.'

'That would be good. One of the members, Clyde Hamblin, has a felony charge. He's on parole for robbery. Received permission to move to Texas, and has about five months left on his parole. Lucy Ramone snapped a photo of him carrying a pistol in the waistband of his jeans.'

He grinned. 'We ought to recruit her.'

'We're good on the arrest warrant, but I'm a little worried about what we might find. Marta's been doing some digging.' Josie explained what she'd learned about recent gun purchases.

He cocked an eyebrow. 'You're thinking this could get ugly.'

'I believe it will, yes.'

'All right. I'll bring Philips with me.'

Josie looked around the diner at the half-dozen people talking in quiet voices at the tables lit by candles brought in from the waitresses' homes. 'They have hijacked our town. We can't let this go on any longer. It's not going to get any better if we don't stand up to them.'

He nodded. 'What's the plan?'

'I'd like everyone to meet in the bank parking lot at five thirty a.m. We'll serve the warrant at six before people are out on the streets. I've already called Paul and told him that no employees are to report to the bank until he gives them further instruction. He said they're already on a skeleton crew with the power outage. He agreed to wait for my text in the morning.'

'That's good. You want Philips and I to park in the lot?'

'Yes. We'll park our cars along the street in front of the church. Then I'll approach the front door with Otto and Philips, and you take the back door. I'll put Marta on the side door.

We'll knock and announce the warrant twice. If they don't respond, we do a forced entry on the front door. You and Marta will enter if necessary.'

'Have you checked out the doors?'

'Solid wood. Swinging inward. Unless they're heavily reinforced we shouldn't have any problems. You have the battering rams at the jail?'

'Philips and I will bring two with us. You need anything else?'

'Some common sense on the part of The Drummers.'

EIGHT

J osie parked her patrol car behind the bank at five the next morning, still three hours before sunrise. A clear night sky and a half-moon would help with coordination of officers, but the thirty-five degrees made her knees ache and her nose run. She wore her Artemis PD navy blue winter coat, with a Velcro reflective POLICE patch affixed to the back.

She pulled on gloves and a stocking cap and walked along the side of the bank building to scout out the neighborhood before the rest of the officers arrived. Three blocks back from the courthouse, the streets primarily housed single dwelling homes with a few churches and beauty salons mixed in. When she reached the corner of the bank building and had the church within her sights, she looked toward her mom's house. Located a block over, it wasn't visible in the pre-dawn light. The town was completely silent at that hour, and with no power, even the early risers were fumbling around in the dark, getting by on flashlights and candles.

She felt a stab of guilt that she hadn't stopped by to check on her mom the night before, or at least called to make sure she was doing OK in the dark, but after a decade of little to no contact, checking up on her now felt disingenuous. Josie still felt ashamed at the harsh way she had judged her mom through the years. But in her own defense, her mom had never understood Josie's approach to the world either. They were simply two very different people. And, for reasons that still puzzled Josie, her mom had suddenly decided that she needed to move two thousand miles so that the two of them could live in the same town together.

Josie glanced at her watch. 5:30 a.m. She walked across the street, having no streetlights to worry about illuminating her position, and around the perimeter of the church, quietly trying each door, pushing gently in hope of an easy entrance. Every door was secure. Finding no lights and hearing no movement,

Josie walked back to the bank at the same time that Sheriff Martinez was arriving, with Philips just behind him. They parked their patrol cars facing the church and exited.

Philips, a thirty-something-year-old deputy with the energy and enthusiasm of a twenty-year-old, hopped up and down when they reached Josie. 'It's colder than a well digger's ass out here. Couldn't we have waited till we had a little sunshine to warm us up?' He blew his breath out and they watched it turn to condensation in the air. He cursed. 'This job is bad enough without this nonsense.'

'Don't be so dramatic,' the sheriff said, punching him lightly on the arm.

They turned to see Otto and Marta roll up in front of the church with their headlights off. Josie watched Otto walk toward them and noticed the limp from the arthritis in his knees and the extra weight he was carrying. She worried about the stress that jumping back into this kind of situation would put on him.

When the five officers had gathered, Josie ran through the plan she had explained to Martinez, and then talked through several worst-case scenarios.

'As you know, I'm concerned about stockpiled weapons. They may be sitting in wait for us. The substation blowups could have been a way to draw us to them. This arrest warrant may be exactly what they're waiting for. I don't know how unstable this group is,' she said.

'You know this will all be caught on video. We do this by the book,' Martinez said, scowling at Philips. He was a good officer, but his enthusiasm caused him to rush into situations that at times needed forethought and planning. Josie had heard him tell Philips multiple times, 'Go slow to go fast.' She always doubted that the saying made any sense to him.

'Marta is familiar with the inside of the church,' Josie continued. 'I asked her to go over the layout so we're all clear. Obviously, with no power and blacked-out windows, we're going in blind.'

Marta held out a legal-sized pad of paper where she'd drawn the basic layout. 'Entering from the front of the church you'll be in a lobby that's about fifteen by fifteen. There's an office on either side. I understand Gideon uses one office and his wife uses the other. The lobby opens into the sanctuary with pews to the left and to the right, and one aisle down the middle. I don't believe there is a door separating the lobby from the sanctuary. Just behind the sanctuary is a hallway with six Sunday school classrooms, three on either side of the hallway. Each of the rooms has one window facing the side street. At the end of the hallway is a door leading out the west side of the building. That's where I'll be stationed. If you continue past that door you enter the kitchen and a door leads directly out back of the church where Sheriff Martinez will be located. On the east side of the kitchen, there is a stairway that leads down into the basement where there is another meeting area.'

'Obviously, if Hamblin comes out, we have no reason to enter the church,' Josie said. 'If he doesn't, we need to secure the building, ensuring our safety and the safety of the members, before we go after him.'

'Which means a search of the building for weapons,' Otto said, nodding approval.

'Correct. If I had to guess, if there are any weapons being stored, they're located in the basement,' Josie said. 'After making entrance into the building, the plan is to gather all members in the sanctuary pews where Otto and Marta will be stationed. The sheriff will take up a post at the front of the building. Philips and I will begin with a canvas through the basement, and then move through the rest of the building.'

She glanced at the time. At five minutes until six, the officers synched their watches.

'Let's head out. At exactly six o'clock I'll announce the arrest warrant. I'll wait one full minute and announce again. I'll wait another full minute. If we haven't heard anything, at 6:03 I announce again and we force entry.'

Josie hoped that one of the members would hear the banging, investigate, and allow reason to rule before Gideon could become involved. In her career, she'd had little experience of forcibly entering a home. Unlike the movies, unless drugs were involved, people understood that the announcement of an arrest warrant left little doubt as to the outcome of the cops banging on your door. She could only think of two other scenarios that might convince a person to ignore a warrant: mental instability or the amassing of firepower intended for fighting back, and Josie was confident that Gideon met both criteria.

The officers took up their posts and made contact via their shoulder mics through a secure channel. At exactly six o'clock, Philips used the end of the battering ram to bang loudly on the door and Josie made her first verbal announcement. When she made her second announcement, she noticed what appeared to be flashlight beams from under the door.

'Again, this is Police Chief Josie Gray. We have a court ordered arrest warrant for Clyde Murphy Hamblin. I know that you can hear me. We do not want to tear up the entrance to the church, but we will do so if you do not open the door within the next sixty seconds.'

Josie waited but heard no movement. The light disappeared. One minute later she announced their entry and pointed to Philips. Using a single-man battering ram, he aimed the first hit at the lock along the door frame. At six feet tall and 250 pounds, Philips had a fair amount of power. Josie saw the frame give slightly with the first ram and he pulled back for a second. During the moment of silence she heard the unmistakable crack of gunfire but couldn't tell where it was coming from. She grabbed Philips by his jacket and pulled him to the right of the door, away from the window. Otto took up position on the other side.

Josie radioed out, 'Shots fired! Everyone OK?'

Josie followed Philips and Otto as they crouched and ran for the street for protection behind the patrol cars.

'I'm headed your way,' Martinez responded. 'Using the alley west of the church.'

'The shot came from one of the Sunday school room windows,' Marta radioed.

'I'm behind my car,' Josie said. 'The middle window is open. Do you see it?'

'Yes. It's directly above me.'

Josie tried to keep the panic from her voice. Marta had no cover. 'I'll fire just above the window. With the first shot, you come down the side of the building. On three. Clear?'

'Yes.'

At three, Josie rose up, steadied her shooting arm against the open door of the patrol car and fired three steady shots aimed five feet above the middle window, leaving Marta time to run.

Marta made it to the car and followed Otto and Philips on to the bank parking lot while Josie covered. She heard four rapid shots then another single out the same window but couldn't tell where they were aiming toward.

Josie saw Martinez running down the alley and heard a scream from inside the church.

Marta grabbed her arm. 'Did you hear that?'

Josie kept her eyes on the building.

'Is there any chance one of your shots entered one of the rooms?' Marta asked.

'I aimed well above the window.'

They heard shrieking and women's voices crying and yelling, growing hysterical. A man's voice hollered out the open window, 'You shot her! You bastards killed her! Our blood is on your hands!'

NINE

Leon had been lying awake and staring at the ceiling, trying to imagine how he would get through another eighteen-hour day wandering from room to room, fabricating things to do in a place where the people he once called family now treated him like an outcast. The banging on the wooden entrance door jolted him up and out of bed, the sound reverberating through the silent church like thunder. David jumped up behind Leon and they both stood motionless, trying to hear what was being yelled outside the front door.

David, who was already dressed, grabbed his flashlight and ran down the hallway toward the entrance. Leon heard doors opening and closing and people running into the hallway asking what was happening.

'Cia, get up. You and Alaina go downstairs. Take the flashlight and get into the basement until we know what's happening,' Leon said.

Cia started to protest but he grabbed her arm hard. 'I am not fighting you on this. Go!'

A second round of banging had started by the time Leon had pulled on jeans and a sweatshirt and begun running toward the sanctuary. He reached the entrance and heard a female voice outside the door announcing an arrest warrant for Clyde, who wasn't visible yet. Several other men appeared in the lobby with flashlights. Markus, a man Gideon referred to as his disciple, ran up to the door panting heavily, as if he'd just run a foot race.

'Back away! Do not open the door under any circumstance,' he said.

'They have an arrest warrant. We have no choice,' Leon said. 'Would you rather they bust the door down?'

Markus put his fist in Leon's face. 'If you don't believe in our cause then you should have left a long time ago. We aren't doing anything unlawful here. They can't enter our home unfounded. Now get out of the way and let the men take care of business.'

Leon started to protest, struggling to think of an explanation that would get people to understand they were fighting a lost battle, when the lobby exploded with the shattering crack of what he assumed was a battering ram smashing the other side of the door. Seconds later, gun shots echoed throughout the building.

Leon ducked and crouched, seeking out David behind him. Without a word David pointed to the sanctuary and the two men ran for the Sunday school rooms, where the shots had come from. With their flashlights off, they moved down the aisle in the center of the sanctuary, tapping the wooden back of each of the twelve pews to stay oriented in the dark.

As the two men entered the hall it was suddenly filled with people looking terrified, their flashlights casting erratic beams around the tight space. A couple of members were waving shotguns in the air, with one yelling something about Revelations. It brought back the flash of a night raid in Baghdad and Leon had to stop and take several deep breaths to calm himself. Feeling cold air on his face he looked to his left into the middle Sunday school room to find Gideon standing to the side of the open window, rifle at the ready.

Leon saw Mandy sitting in the corner of the room with her legs drawn up and knees tucked under her chin. He called her name and she looked out at him with tears running down her cheeks. He put his arm out and motioned for her but she didn't move. David caught him by the arm and propelled him toward their own room, handing him a rifle.

David yelled, 'Get to your rooms! You know your positions. Get your arms ready and the women and kids downstairs.'

'What the hell are we doing?' Leon said, trying to make out David's face in the dark and wondering where the hell his own rifle had suddenly come from.

David turned on his flashlight and placed his hand over the harsh light so that they could see one another. 'We've been assigned this room.'

'For what?' Leon felt the blood draining from his head and worried he might pass out.

'This is what we've been preparing for. The men post in the bedrooms and take up arms at each window. The women and kids will be in the basement. Cia and Alaina both have guns. They're rounding up kids now and ensuring no outsiders get to the guns.'

Leon stared at David in disbelief. 'He put two women, who have no experience with guns, in charge of guarding weapons?'

'They volunteered. It's an important job. He said the cops wouldn't storm the room if they knew women and kids were in there.'

Leon put his hands to his head, feeling once again that he was about to lose control. 'This is insane. You're a Marine! When we were in the service, if you'd heard that load of shit, you'd have called Gideon a coward and then beat the hell out of him. And now you're willing to throw your wife to the wolves?'

David's jaw tightened and he stared intently at Leon. The glow from the flashlight in the dark room gave him a demonic look, but Leon could tell that he was at least considering his words. 'I can't deal with you right now. Just man your window.'

David left the room and Leon kicked blankets out of the way as he walked to the window, furious that he felt so incapable of taking a stand. As he reached the window, he heard gun shots from outside, and then return fire from the room next to him. He fell to the floor and crawled toward the hallway. With no flashlight, he crawled in the dark, unsure where the shots were coming from. As he reached the doorway, he heard one additional shot and someone running.

Leon moved down the hallway toward the sound of the gunfire. Others were now crouching in their doorways, some crying, asking what was happening. As Leon reached Gideon's room a woman screamed in anguish. Inside, Leon found Gideon holding a flashlight limply in his hand, leaning against the wall looking pale and weak. To Gideon's right, Alaina was leaning over Mandy, who was slumped on her side with blood gushing from her chest.

David stepped behind Leon, scanned his light around the room and yelled Alaina's name.

'Are you shot?' he yelled.

'No, it's Mandy,' she cried.

'What the hell happened?' David said, kneeling next to Alaina but looking back at Gideon.

'They shot her.' His voice was breathless, his eyes out of focus. 'They shot her. I couldn't protect her.'

Leon dropped to his knees next to Mandy's head but saw the light had already left her eyes. He watched in horror as the girl's blood seeped into David's jeans. He heard Gideon mumble something about the cops shooting her, then his voice became louder and louder in the room. Leon turned to watch Gideon grab onto the windowsill and yell outside, 'You shot her! You bastards killed her! Our blood is on your hands!'

His voice boomed, as if he'd suddenly recharged. He turned back toward Mandy's body and pulled a phone out of his back pants pocket. He turned it on and Leon realized he was going to take photos. He was so overwhelmed with it all he couldn't speak. Then Gideon held the phone up and began talking.

'This is how the police in Artemis, Texas take care of their citizens. They didn't like us. They didn't like that we stood for freedom, for an end to the tyranny. They tried to storm our church this morning before daybreak. When they couldn't get in they began shooting. Now one of our own, an innocent young woman, is dead from their guns.'

Leon turned away from the camera and stumbled out of the way of the video. Alaina turned to face the camera with tears streaming down her face. She screamed, 'Murderers!' before Gideon switched the video off.

'Alaina. Go and get Cia and some of the other women. Take Mandy and clean her up. Prepare her for a burial,' Gideon said. He left the room without another word.

Leon sat on the floor with his back against the wall, watching people flood into the room, crying and screaming obscenities out the window and down to the police officers. It felt as if he were watching from above and he wondered for a moment if he had died in the shootout. He watched Cia enter the room, a look of hatred in her eyes like nothing he'd ever seen before. He realized he was shivering from the cold and noticed the open window and wondered how it could possibly still be dark outside. It felt as if the past few minutes had been days. The sun hadn't even had time to rise and Mandy was dead and his only group of family and friends on earth were all losing their minds in anger and sorrow and he had no idea where he fit inside any of it.

'Leon!'

He felt his shoe being kicked and looked up to find Cia yelling his name. Her face was still distorted in anger. 'Are you hurt?' Her voice contained no trace of compassion or worry.

He shook his head.

'Then get off the floor! There's work to be done.'

He pulled himself up and watched Cia turn away from him in disgust. He looked around the room at the men and women in distress and tried to understand how any of it could be happening, and then he saw that Billy, the youngest boy, had wandered upstairs into the middle of it and was crying.

Gloria entered the room with a bucket of water and towels. She seemed to have aged another ten years overnight. David walked in behind her with an air of self-importance that made Leon turn away.

'Listen up everyone. I've talked to Gideon about next steps. Markus and John will be carrying Mandy to the bathroom at the front of the church where the women will take care of her. Everyone else, except for Leon and I, will report to the basement to talk with Gideon about a plan. Leon will remain up here to guard the windows. I'll do the same at the front entrance. When Markus is done he'll take the back entrance and side door.' David handed Leon and Markus a two-way radio. 'Use this to communicate if you hear anything.'

Even amidst the turmoil, Leon was confused at what he was looking at. 'Where did we get this? I thought we were against technology.' It was a brand new radio and David had several more in a bucket.

'We have people helping us. Gideon will explain downstairs. I'll fill you in later.'

Leon looked at the rest of the adults in the room who had quietened and appeared docile, ready to take orders. The only sound in the room was the little boy crying and beating his fist on his mother's leg.

*   *   *

Once Mandy's body had been carried out and the walls washed down, David handed Leon a roll of duct tape. 'Tape cardboard up to keep people from seeing in, but leave a space where you can see out. Watch what's going on across the street with the cops. Report anything out of the ordinary.'

David turned and left and Leon had to stifle an urge to laugh. What the hell was out of the ordinary anymore? There was nothing ordinary left in their world.

He faced the place where Mandy had lain and dragged Gideon's mattress over the top of the blood stain. The image of her face, looking out at him with terrified eyes, hit him like a punch to the gut. If he had intervened between Gideon and her, then she would have most likely not been in his room that morning. He couldn't imagine why he'd found her in Gideon's bedroom at such an early hour, and not Gloria.

It wasn't until the room was empty and quiet that he allowed the terrible doubts he had about the shooting to pierce his thoughts.

Gideon had ordered Gloria to wash down the wall where Mandy had been shot. But the image of the blood was forever imprinted on his mind, and he could still see faint traces of red on the paneling.

Leon positioned himself about five feet back from the window. The blood marks were on the wall to his right, but less than a foot away from the window wall, and about four feet up from the floor. It appeared to Leon that Mandy had stood from the corner where he had seen her sitting, and been shot in the chest.

The windows in the Sunday school rooms were approximately eighteen inches square, and were positioned high enough so that kids could get no benefit other than the natural light they allowed into the rooms. He and Cia had joked about the poor kid desperate to daydream about playing outside, who got nothing more than a glimpse of the top of the house next door.

The room was now dimly lit from the sun making its way between the two buildings and through the small open window, so Leon took his flashlight and shone it along each of the four walls, being especially careful as he considered the area where Mandy had been shot. He found no bullet holes.

Leon carried a small child's chair from down the hallway

back to Gideon's room. He placed it to the side of the window and stepped up to get a good look out toward where the police were parked. He followed the path a bullet would have taken from the road to Mandy's chest. It didn't take tape measures or tools or the need to understand the trajectory of bullets to figure out there was no possible way that a bullet from outside could have hit Mandy. Leon figured Mandy was just over five feet tall, the top of her head reaching just above the sill. The only way a bullet could have traveled from the window to where Mandy was standing was if the officer had been outside on a stepladder. Leon considered the house next to the church, but there was no opening located on the side of the house that would have allowed for the shot.

After taping cardboard over the window, as he'd been instructed to do, he scratched black paint off a small area of each window in the Sunday school rooms to better see outside. It was now ten o'clock in the morning and flashing lights surrounded the building. As far as he knew, the police had not made any additional attempts to enter the building, and there was no way for Leon to call out. He knew other members had phones, such as David and Cia, but Leon had surrendered his as he'd been ordered to do. He imagined Cia in the basement, most likely holding a gun, preparing for what? For battle with the police? A battle they stood no chance of winning.

Leon forced himself to re-enter Gideon's bedroom. His thoughts were a jumbled mess and more than anything he needed a plan. He sat on the floor in the corner opposite where Mandy was shot and tried to come up with a situation that could explain how she had died.

What he wanted was to find Gloria and ask why she'd not been in her bedroom at six o'clock in the morning. He tried to remember passing their bedroom when he had run for the banging on the front door. Leon had used his flashlight to guide his way down the hall, but he couldn't remember any details about the rooms that he'd passed. He wondered if Gideon had asked Gloria to go get Mandy when the banging had started. But Gideon had ordered the women and children down to the basement. The only reason Mandy would have stayed in that room was if he had ordered her to. She had been crying and looked terrified when Leon had called her name. He felt confident that she'd wanted nothing more at that moment than to have run as far away from that room as possible.

The more terrifying concern was that Leon was certain that a stray bullet from the police had not killed Mandy. Someone had shot her, in the room with Gideon. So why had Gideon told the world that the police were murderers when he had to have known what happened?

When they were living in Idaho, people had begun calling The Drummers a cult. At first it had been a joke, but then Gideon had begun to spin the insults as offensive to their beliefs. That's when the 'us against them' philosophy had first started. A neighbor who had befriended Leon had warned him against drinking the Kool-Aid. At the time Leon had laughed it off, but now the thought of Cia sitting in the basement with the other members all listening to their beloved Gideon made him sick with fear.

He'd read up on Jim Jones when they were back in Idaho, back when he still had a phone and internet access. Jones had convinced his followers to drink cyanide-laced fruit punch. Over 900 people had died within minutes.

Leon had watched Gideon's tactics change over the past few months. He wondered now if Gideon could have convinced Mandy to sacrifice herself for the good of mankind or some such bullshit. She was a quiet, sweet-natured girl. If Jim Jones could convince 900 people to give up their lives, it was no stretch to imagine a young mixed-up kid could be convinced of the same.

Leon considered running, just walking out the door, or sneaking out the side door while Markus was patrolling the back. But he couldn't leave Cia. He loved her, the old Cia, before she had become a blind follower. If he left her and something happened, he would never forgive himself for giving up on her.

TEN

Within an hour of the first shots, every police car, fire truck and ambulance within thirty miles of Artemis was parked in the bank parking lot or the surrounding block. The area had been cordoned off and three sheriffs' deputies were in the process of ensuring all families and businesses were evacuated within a one-block radius. The bank manager, Paul Navarro, had provided the police department access to the bank lobby for a staging area. He had given Josie the keys and helped move desks back and set up tables for law enforcement to use. Using the back entrance, Paul had gone home to bring back two more long plastic conference tables, and stopped by the bakery to buy out every pastry and donut in the shop, as well as four decanters of coffee. He had promised to keep the coffee coming through the back door, and Josie had readily agreed. She hoped his prediction that they were in it for the long haul wasn't founded, but it was hard to imagine anything less.

The SWAT team from the Texas DPS ranger division was located in Austin, a six-hour drive from Artemis. Josie had been told they would send an advance group via helicopter with another following by land. The Texas Highway Patrol had two officers from their special response team already on site, as well as two other patrol officers in unmarked cars.

By eight o'clock, Josie had set the perimeter around the church and moved the fire and EMS vehicles two blocks over to free up space.

She requested Sheriff Martinez and the SRT officers meet with her in the bank at 9:15 to debrief and come up with a next phase response. Control of the scene would revert to SWAT once they were on scene, but because the shooting took place within the bounds of the city, the chief of police was the lead until that happened. One of the biggest issues with large-scale events like a standoff or hostage situation was not a lack of help, but a lack of communication and clear chain of command. She was determined not to let that happen.

As Josie walked toward the bank at a little before nine, she heard someone bark her name.

'Gray!'

She turned and watched Mayor O'Kane walk around Otto, who attempted to stop him from entering the secured area, but gave up when he saw Josie motion him forward. O'Kane wore a moleskin military-style jacket that most likely cost more than a soldier's monthly paycheck, along with a plaid scarf and tailored trousers.

'Yes, Mayor?'

'Why is it nine o'clock in the morning and I'm just finding out about this?'

Josie gestured toward the bank.

He followed her into the building with a rant about his next-door neighbor, whose wife worked at the bank, calling him and asking why she'd been told not to go to work that morning. 'I had to play detective in my own town. I believe I'm owed a bit more courtesy than that, wouldn't you agree?'

'Absolutely. I've been so consumed with getting people evacuated and the block secured that I hadn't gotten that far.'

He crossed his arms and considered her. 'Next time, if you don't have the thirty seconds it would take to fill me in, ask one of your officers to do me the courtesy. Can we agree to that?'

'Absolutely.'

'What's the status?' he said.

'The command team is meeting here at 9:15 to go over next steps. You're welcome to attend.'

They turned to see Martinez walk into the building. The men nodded at each other but didn't speak.

'What's the status on the evacuation?' Josie asked.

'We had two houses with no response. The neighbor of one of the families said they're on vacation in Florida. We've left notes inside the doors for the other one. Beyond that, every designated home and business is empty.'

'Can we back up a minute and explain how we got to this point? All I've heard is community gossip,' O'Kane said.

The sheriff raised his eyebrows at Josie, obviously surprised she'd not contacted him.

She went through a brief summary, ending with the officers retreating before serving the warrant, and Gideon yelling out the window that one of their female members had been shot.

'By one of our officers?' O'Kane asked.

'I was the only officer to fire,' Josie said, 'and I shot above the windows. Three shots were fired and they were good shots.'

'So, what you're telling me is, you can't be certain that you didn't kill that young girl?'

'I can tell you that I'm ninety-nine percent certain, but until we have the results from the autopsy, and the ballistics test comes back, we can't be completely certain.'

O'Kane nodded and asked, 'Have you seen social media?'

Josie and Martinez glanced at each other. She shook her head.

The mayor opened his phone and passed it to Josie. She looked down at the dead body of a girl who looked to be about sixteen years old wearing a white nightgown saturated in blood. Vacant eyes stared out from a pale face. She was clearly dead. Josie felt the blood drain from her face. Following the original shouts from the person inside the church claiming that someone had been shot and killed, they'd not heard anything. Knowing that she had not fired on anyone, Josie had assumed it was theatrics, that Gideon had made up the story.

She scrolled up to see that the photo had been posted on Facebook by Gideon. Underneath it was a rant about the police in Artemis shooting innocent citizens after trying to use a battering ram to tear down their door at six o'clock in the morning.

'I have Helen working to get the photo and accompanying video removed, but that will take time. This photo and the video will be all over the internet. Probably already is,' he said.

She handed the phone to Martinez who shook his head and swore at the sight of the young girl.

'Why would they shoot one of their own, let alone a young girl like this? It doesn't make sense.' O'Kane's tone was not accusatory, but Josie felt the sting from his words.

'I spoke with Marta about the location of the windows. She's been in the church many times and is familiar with the Sunday school rooms. She said they're located high up on the wall. From where I was standing in the parking lot, with my gun pointing well above the windows, I don't believe a bullet could have entered the room.' She motioned toward the phone. 'It looks as if the bullet hit her in the center of her chest. I would have needed to have been standing above the window, shooting down into the room for her to have been hit like that.'

'Even without the location of the windows, what are the odds that a stray bullet would enter a window from across the street and hit a person dead center in the chest? It looks like a direct hit from a person in the same room,' Martinez said, handing the phone back to the mayor.

'Then what does this say about the leader of those people locked in that church? He has guns, has convinced this group of people to lock themselves away, and he's willing to kill his own. This has too many similarities to Waco for me. What kind of help do we have coming in?'

Two special response team officers from Texas Department of Public Safety entered the bank.

'Good timing. Mayor O'Kane, this is Officer Eric Downey and Officer Mitch Townsend.' She explained their involvement and asked for an ETA on the SWAT team.

'Two members are in the air now. Probably an hour out, then drive time from the landing strip. Because of the gunfire and the possibility of stockpiled weapons, I've been told they're sending the BearCat. It's slow, making fifty-five miles an hour at most on the highway, but it should be here by nightfall,' Downey said. He was a middle-aged officer who lived with his family in Marfa. Josie was glad he was on site. He was a straight shooter who didn't get into politics or bravado.

'Let's hope we're done long before nightfall,' Martinez said.

'And what's the BearCat?' O'Kane asked.

'It's an armored personnel carrier, sir,' said Downey. 'It will allow officers the armored protection they need to get closer to the building. It can also be used to force entry into a building.'

'It looks like a smaller version of an army tank,' Josie said.

Downey pointed to the dim overhead lights being run by the bank's standby generator. 'How much longer before power is restored?'

Josie looked to the mayor who said, 'I was promised within twenty-four hours. They're still waiting on equipment to arrive from Houston. I was told best guess is tomorrow morning.'

'Do we know if they have a generator, or even candles in the church?' Downey asked.

'No generator. I saw what appeared to be flashlights under the entrance door this morning when we announced the warrant. They may have solar chargers,' Josie said.

The fire chief and trauma center emergency room director came into the building along with Otto, and Josie convened the group. They took seats and each person introduced themselves and explained their role.

Josie asked a representative from each group to provide an update on their status in terms of the operation. The SRT officers gave a rundown on the SWAT team and their role, and said the hostage negotiator would be arriving shortly via helicopter. The fire chief and ER doc both stated their teams were prepared with staff on call for the next forty-eight hours. The sheriff had three deputies stationed around the church, with the rest of his staff at the jail.

Josie explained that Otto would be stationed in the command center to serve as the liaison for all of the various agencies. She took a deep breath. 'At this stage, I think we have the right people in place, and we're as prepared as we can be. One of my biggest concerns is that we have no contact with any of the members. They shun technology, so I doubt most of the members even have cell phones.'

'Let's get some throw phones in there,' Downey said.

O'Kane, who was sitting directly across the table from Josie, raised his eyebrows in question.

'They're protected cell phones that connect directly with one of our team, usually the hostage negotiator. Part of our problem is we have no access to the building. The windows are painted black. The one window that was open has been taped up,' Josie said.

'Shoot those windows out, throw the phones first, followed by gas bombs,' Martinez said.

'They're already claiming we shot one of their own. We don't want to escalate with gunfire,' Josie said.

Downey put his finger up. 'I've got Lieutenant Hernández on the phone. Should I ask him to join the conversation?'

'Absolutely,' Josie said.

They waited while Downey caught Hernández up to speed, and then he introduced himself to the group.

'Any contact with any of the members since the shots were fired?' he asked.

'Nothing. We were just discussing ways to get a couple of throw phones into the building,' Josie said.

'I do know one person who has made contact,' Otto said.

Josie looked at him in surprise.

'I just found out last evening and hadn't had the chance to tell you,' he said, looking at Josie. 'A neighbor of mine told me that his wife ran into Gideon's wife Gloria at the grocery store and she mentioned how cold the building was, and that there was a hole in the wall in her office. My neighbor's wife convinced her husband to take his toolkit and offer to fix the hole. Gloria invited him into the church. They texted details about the repairs, so he has her phone number.'

'That's great. Let's get him in here. Ask him to make contact with her.'

'I agree that you need to bring him to the command center with his phone,' Hernández said, his voice coming from Downey's cell phone on the table. 'But I'd like our hostage negotiator to talk with him first, before he makes the call. Agreed?'

'We'll do it,' Josie said.

Otto stood from the table to call Lewis.

'Let's talk about the location and security of the building. Can someone send me pics of the church, all four sides, as well as close-ups of the windows and doors, and then the alleyways and streets that parallel it?'

'I'll have one of our officers take care of that now,' Downey said.

'And what about a search warrant? We'd like that to be taken care of before we arrive.'

'I'll submit when we're finished here. We were trying to serve an arrest warrant for a parole violation when the shooting began,' Josie said. 'Given the shots fired at law enforcement,

I'm sure the judge will grant a search warrant for weapons at this point.'

'Good. It'll make things easier for us if that's out of the way.'

'Sure thing,' she said.

'We're about ready to land, so we should be on site within the hour. Let's get your neighbor with the phone ready to go. We need to know more before we start throwing teargas. Remind me how many kids?'

'We believe four kids, ranging in age from five to fourteen. Plus the teenage girl who was shot.'

'Confirmed dead?'

'No, but the photos would indicate so,' Josie said.

'Do you know the location of the members? Where they're stationed inside the building?'

'No.'

'What about a floor plan?' Hernández asked.

'We have a drawing I'll send you a picture of,' Josie said. 'One of our officers is familiar with the interior and should be able to answer any questions you have.'

'Excellent. Obviously you have a perimeter set and the building surrounded with officers?'

'We do. And a command post across the street. The bank parking lot, the church parking lot and city street are between the bank and the church. I'd prefer we were further removed, but shots fired at the bank would have to come directly from the front door of the church, and I don't see that happening. The area around the church has been evacuated,' Josie said.

'We've got two snipers with us in the air, and four more on the road. We'll get them positioned immediately.'

Over the next hour, the early response SWAT team arrived and Josie gave them a detailed history of The Drummers and their motivation, at least as far as the police were able to understand it. She explained her belief that they were responsible for knocking out the substations and power to most of West Texas, that they had stockpiled weapons but that the police had no idea on numbers. The team walked the area at a distance, becoming familiar with the building and the block surrounding it. One of the team members entered the house next door and had a bead on the back door of the church. When Lewis arrived, the hostage negotiator worked with him inside the bank to discuss everything he knew about the inside of the building, and what he had gathered about the mental state of Gideon's wife. Lewis made two attempts to call her on the number he'd used before, but she didn't answer the phone. He was stationed in the bank with Otto, ready to talk in case she returned his call.

Lunch and dinner came and went with little outward change. They discussed breaching the building with drones and small robotics, but with the suspected firepower inside they would be shot down immediately. The BearCat had arrived and was sitting at the ready pointing directly toward The Drummers. They hoped its presence would act as a deterrent, but trying to predict the mental state of any of the members at that point would have been impossible.

Over the course of the day, media outlets from across the country had posted throughout Artemis. The location in Texas, along with the religious connection to the church, was too similar to Waco for the media not to be consumed with it. The police had barricaded the area so that reporters weren't able to get footage of the church, but helicopters had flown overhead and live video was streaming over all the major news channels. One reporter had described the 'powerless town', in reference to the lack of electric power, and then went on to describe in detail the young child who had been killed, 'presumably' by a stray bullet from one of the city officers on scene in an early morning shootout. Josie's name was all over the news and her mother had sent multiple texts asking what the hell was going on.

By nightfall, a battle over which agencies should be present was raging. ATF had not been called in because it had been established that no federal crime had been committed. The debate was that the man from Idaho had been given written permission to leave the state by his parole officer, thus negating the federal crime. However, the ATF said the search warrant that had been issued for a weapons violation had turned it into a federal crime.

Josie assumed part of the debate was whether bringing the ATF into the equation would enflame what was already a very tense situation. While they had been exonerated for their role in the fifty-one-day standoff with the Branch Davidians, there were still conspiracy theorists who believed the federal government had started the fire that led to seventy-six people dying. Hundreds of law enforcement officers had eventually surrounded the compound, and Josie could not fathom how such a situation would play out in the downtown streets of Artemis.

At nine o'clock that night, Dr Jennifer Bell, a psychiatrist from San Antonio, arrived to debrief with the team. She had worked with law enforcement on numerous occasions, and her specialty was mass psychology as it related to cults. Mayor O'Kane had picked her up from the local airstrip and delivered her to the staging area.

Bell was an attractive middle-aged brunette wearing a slim-fitting gray skirt, cream-colored blouse and four-inch heels. She walked into the bank with a laser focus, as if she had several additional meetings to get to and time was of the essence.

Josie introduced her to the group and skipped the briefing. Lieutenant Hernández had already provided her a detailed account of their situation.

Bell spent the first few minutes presenting her academic background, before talking about her experience with trauma.

'I was born in Guatemala. My father moved my family to Juarez when I was a teenager after my mother was killed by the Sinaloa Cartel. My father raised my brothers and I in what was then considered to be the most violent non-warzone city in the world. I grew up amidst the ravages of trauma. I was fortunate enough to receive a coveted scholarship to a school in Brazil where I received a degree in psychology and criminal behavior. My dissertation focused on cult leaders, and the positive and negative outcomes to be gained from police intervention. I say all this only to assure you that I have sufficient background and experience to be standing here before you. Any doubts?'

She took a moment to scan the group of officers who sat in complete silence.

'Excellent. Then let's jump in. We have several things in our favor,' she said. 'Chief Gray's conversation with Leon about hiring on as the evening janitor. The information you received about the member wanting to hire on at the grocery. And Mr Brier's contact with Gloria. These interactions all make me believe that the group hasn't escalated. The fact that they invited an outsider into the church to make repairs just this past week is a very positive sign. But, as I said at the outset, the death of one of their own members by a police officer changes everything.' Several officers started to speak up and she raised her hand. '*Allegedly* shot by an officer.'

Josie's face reddened in anger.

Dr Bell apparently read the look. 'You need to understand that my goal is to help you get inside the thinking of the members inside that church. I guarantee that everyone in that church believes that you killed that young girl. Whether you did or didn't doesn't matter to us at this point.'

Josie clenched her jaw to keep from saying something she would regret.

'When the young girl was killed inside their home, it fundamentally changed the way they think about the police, and the way they think about their leader. There's nothing quite so powerful as "you and me against the world". That's how these charismatic leaders get people to follow them.'

'By killing one of their own?' Otto asked.

'By sacrificing one of their own. But in this instance, it isn't even a sacrifice. The members believe you, the police, killed the girl. If he indeed killed the girl, it was an incredibly strategic move on his part.'

Otto looked tortured by the conversation. 'I just can't understand how intelligent people can be so gullible.'

'Cult leaders often start by comparing themselves to other biblical prophets, such as Isaiah and Jeremiah. Jeremiah was scorned by society, considered a failure by some, and revered by others. It gives them instant credibility. They site stories from the bible that illustrate a prophet's misunderstood genius. They cast themselves into the light of a martyr. It's what David Koresh did with the Branch Davidians. He changed his name from Vernon Howell to David Koresh and called himself a direct descendent of King David, from whom the new messiah would descend. I know that Chief Gray has shared with you the story behind Gideon's name, and his attempt to connect himself with a biblical figure.'

'But who follows a man calling himself a prophet into the desert to live in an abandoned church?' Otto said.

'People who are longing for a family, longing to fit in. People who feel abandoned by society or by their own family and friends,' Bell said.

'When Leon interviewed for the custodian's position,' Josie said, 'he talked about coming home from Iraq to find his family had moved with no forwarding address. He fits that description perfectly.'

'What about other members? Do you have anything on why they joined or their experience in Idaho?' Bell asked.

'We have news accounts and we've talked to law enforcement and former neighbors about why they left Georgia and Idaho. We've not talked closely to any members other than Leon.'

'It's helpful to know the mindset of the group in order to target a response. For example, members typically die for either altruistic or fatalistic reasons, depending on their personality and their experience in the group.'

'What's the difference?' Hernández asked.

'An altruistic follower is one who is selfless and willing to die for the cause. A fatalistic follower is one who dies because they've given up all hope. Knowing the mindset of the people inside can help you target a response. My advice is, don't rush a response before you know more about who you're dealing with. You don't need me to remind you that the children inside that building deserve none of this.'

'Given what you've heard today, who do you think we're dealing with?' Hernández said.

'The term traumatic narcissism is used to talk about certain cult leaders, and I think it fits this instance well. Gideon forms relationships in which he coercively pressures people to support and validate his grandiose ideas. His followers are allowed to develop their own identities, but only as an extension of his own ideas. The problem for law enforcement is that these situations are often years in the making. It's not like a hostage situation where a person has a psychotic break and can be talked off the ledge. This is a group of almost twenty adults and children who are operating with a complicated sense of right and wrong that they've developed together.'

'So you're saying, even if we make contact with someone inside, maybe even manage to get a throw phone to one of the members, we can't convince them this is crazy? That they need to stop this before someone else gets killed?' Townsend asked.

'How many cult standoffs have you seen where members leave of their own free will?' She waited a moment and scanned the room as the officers thought about the most notable cases. 'Davidians, Jonestown, Heaven's Gate. They didn't end well, did they?'

'So why even talk about this if negotiation won't work?' Townsend said, clearly frustrated with her response.

'Because you need to understand it going in. I'm not saying it isn't worth your effort to try and make contact, but keep it in perspective. Trying to change someone's mind at this point would be extremely difficult. Trying to understand their thinking, trying to predict their next move based on past behavior, that's where your focus should be.'

ELEVEN

The nine o'clock meeting that night in the Shelter was the first group meeting that Leon had been invited to attend in days. The only members not included were Ringo, who'd been posted to watch the side and back doors, and David, who had clearly been briefed on Gideon's plans and instructed to guard the front. They had both been provided with two-way radios to communicate directly with Gloria while Gideon spoke.

The Shelter was the new name given to the basement where all group meetings took place. Gideon was convinced that the police had bugged the sanctuary and that it wasn't safe to speak openly.

As Leon filed down the candlelit stairwell he had the terrible feeling that he was walking into his own grave. Inside the basement room, a half-dozen kerosene lanterns gave the low-ceilinged room an orange glow, casting long shadows that swayed erratically in the flickering light. The pungent smell of kerosene felt like a hot poker in Leon's gut. He'd not eaten anything since the day before and was beginning to feel weak and nauseous.

Long tables had been set up on either side of the lectern where Gideon preached. Rifles and ammunition were laid out in an orderly fashion. Markus stood behind the tables with a clipboard and pen, appearing to take an inventory. Leon could see several large crates underneath the table that seemed to hold additional weapons. He knew they'd only had a few rifles when they left Idaho, and he couldn't imagine how they'd been able to afford that many guns given their current situation.

Rows of folding chairs faced the tables and people filed in and took a seat without speaking. Leon watched Mandy's mother, Charlene, sit in the front row. Her face was splotchy and swollen from hours of crying, but her expression was resolute and her eyes filled with an angry fire. Cia sat down next to her and wrapped an arm around her shoulder. All of the women had spent the day together, supporting Charlene as best they could. The building was miserably cold, but Leon had no idea how long Mandy's body could remain inside before they would have to contact someone about a burial or cremation.

He noticed the people around him rustling and sitting up taller in their seats before he realized Gideon had stepped out from behind a screen in a dark corner of the room. Leon thought back to the early days when they all walked in and sat together as a group in meetings, with no one more important than anyone else, and everyone sharing their opinions in an honest manner without fear of scorn. Now Gideon wore a kind of robe that appeared to have been made with a white sheet, tied at the waist with a rope. He stood at the lectern and grasped it with both hands. His thick white hair had been carefully combed back and his beard trimmed to give him the look of a biblical sage.

'Over the past three months, I have witnessed the demise of my country in ways I never imagined possible. I have watched law enforcement turn our government into a police state where citizens have no rights. The police break into homes and murder innocent people. My friends, this is the day of the resurrection of the righteous!' He raised his hands into the air and people clapped and hollered, *Amen*. Gideon looked into the rows of people with a feverish intensity that Leon had never seen before. 'This is the day when the world is split between the believers and the unbelievers. Today we are united with our brethren across the world as the unrighteous attempt to destroy us.' He picked up a rifle from the table and held it high. 'But we will not give in.'

Several members began to clap again as others stood and cheered. Cia kept her arm around Charlene but raised her fist in the air to show her support. Leon felt the energy in the room and considered stepping up to the podium to tell everyone that they were listening to a fraud and a murderer, but he knew he wouldn't survive ten minutes if he did. As he looked around the room at the believers, he knew that he stood only one chance of saving them all, and it had to be that night.

After the meeting, before David and Alaina had made it back to the bedroom, Leon pulled Cia away from Charlene's room, convincing her that she needed to rest to be strong for the days ahead. He had lit a candle in the corner of the room and straightened their bedding, hoping he'd have a few minutes alone with her. He knew it would be his only chance.

He closed the door behind her and put his arms out. Tears clouded her eyes instantly and she went to him, lying her head on his chest and crying. He stroked her hair, wondering for the hundredth time how they had fallen so far so fast.

'I'm so tired, Leon. I know we need to fight, but I'm so tired of it all.'

Leon felt his pulse quicken. He felt as if he were handling an animal in a trap, desperate for freedom, but ready to fight to the death if provoked. He knew that the wrong words would destroy their chance of making it out of the church alive.

He put his hands on her arms and gently pushed her back to look into her face. 'Cia. We have to talk before David and Alaina get back.' To his surprise she nodded agreement.

'I have to sit.' She sank down onto the mat and he sat next to her, their legs and arms touching.

'I know that you love Gideon. I know he's like a father to you and that you would do anything for him. But just this once, remember what you and I used to have, and take just a minute to hear me out. Will you do that?'

She sat hunched over, staring at her legs, and said nothing.

Leon began telling Cia about his run to the front of the church when the police arrived with the arrest warrant, and about how he had come back to find Mandy in Gideon's bedroom, cowering in a corner. Leon watched as tears dropped onto her jeans leaving dark circles. He explained that there was no way the police could have shot Mandy, that it had to have been someone from The Drummers, and that Gideon was in the room when Mandy was shot.

Leon laid his hand on her shoulder. 'I know you don't want to hear this, but I believe Gideon shot Mandy.'

Cia jerked back and slapped him across the face. 'You won't stop! Why are you still here?' she cried out. Tears streamed down her face and she crawled away from him as if touching him repulsed her. 'I knew you'd say just about anything to discredit him, but murdering Mandy? My God, Leon, that's horrible. So you know what? That's fine. In the morning, go outside and throw yourself at their guns. Let them shoot you down like they want to kill all of us. At least in here we all die together.'

'I'm not trying to—'

She pointed to the door, her expression changing suddenly from sorrow to fury. 'Get out. I don't want to talk to you. I can't even stand to look at you.'

Leon heard the floor creak outside the bedroom as he stood. He figured David had been out there listening to the whole conversation.

He grabbed his coat and opened the door into the dark hallway. He pulled his flashlight from his pocket and turned it on, noting how dim the light had become. He'd be lucky if the batteries made it through to the next day, and he knew no one would issue him additional supplies.

The sanctuary was completely dark but he walked along each pew to see if anyone else was sleeping there. The only person he found was James, sleeping sitting up with his head against the wall next to the front entrance; the men were taking turns pulling front door guard duty. Markus slept on a cot in the kitchen to keep watch at the back entrance. Leon had thought guarding the doors was absurd when Gideon first set it up; now he had to wonder if the conflict had been part of the plan all along.

Leon put his coat on and lay down on a pile of clothes in one of the back pews, layering sweaters and random pieces of clothing across his legs for warmth. He had not been issued a gun when they'd left the so-called Shelter. Gideon had said he would receive his in the morning after it had been sufficiently inspected. Leon had noticed that Jackson was the only other male who'd not received a gun that night either. He wondered if Jackson had expressed doubts as well and been shunned by Gideon. Leon planned to seek him out in the morning and find some way to talk.

Staring at the ceiling, he listened to the creaks and moans of the old building and wondered what the police were planning across the street. He felt as if a bulldozer might plow through the front of the building at any moment and he wondered what the response would be. Gideon had made it clear that they would not give in to the police. Leon wondered if faced with their own demise, or the chance of life outside, how many of the members would fight to the death.

TWELVE

A t a little after five in the morning, Lewis opened the door of the old cast-iron woodstove in the kitchen, slipped in a handful of bark and pieces of kindling and watched the leftover coals quickly ignite the dried wood. He listened to Mary pouring water from a pitcher into the metal coffee pot they'd been using since the power went out. She brought it over and set it on top of the stove so the water could boil, while chatting about how she planned to try baking biscuits on the stove for breakfast.

Between the kerosene lanterns and the two woodstoves in the house, they'd not had it too bad. Some winters were mild enough that they didn't even need the furnace to heat the house, so Lewis had plenty of wood stacked outside to get them through. Mary had told him she liked the lantern light; she even thought it was romantic. He wasn't so sure about that, but he was glad she was making the best of it. After sixty years of marriage, they had at least figured out that much.

The ringing of the cell phone startled him in the quiet house, and he had to remember where he'd put it – somewhere he wouldn't forget. The police had charged his phone the night before, just in case he received a call.

Mary handed it to him, her eyes wide with worry. 'It's the number!'

He glanced down and saw that, indeed, Gloria was calling. 'Hello?'

'Is this Lewis?'

'Yes it is.'

'This is Gloria. You did some work in my office?'

'Yes, of course. I remember.'

'I'm sorry to call you so early,' she said.

Lewis noted the worry in her voice and tried to remember the words the negotiator had told him to use, and the words he'd told him *not* to use. 'It's no problem. I'm up lighting a fire in the woodstove. Are you staying warm in this cold weather?' Lewis motioned for Mary to pick her cell phone up.

'I'm calling you with a problem,' Gloria said. 'I don't know anyone else in town so I'm hoping I can count on you.'

As Gloria talked, Lewis covered the phone with his hand and whispered to Mary, 'Call the negotiator and tell him what's happening. The number's in my wallet.' He motioned toward the kitchen counter.

'I'll do what I can for you. I still have my toolkit in the car even. As cold as it is, I bet you could use some work on those walls. Some insulation even.' He talked slowly, trying to draw the conversation out as he watched Mary connect with the hostage negotiator from her phone.

'No, we've had something terrible happen. One of our members, a young woman, has been killed.'

'What? Someone was killed in the church?' Lewis feigned ignorance as the negotiator had asked him to do, trying to engage Gloria, to pull out details.

Mary stood next to Lewis with the phone close to him so the negotiator could hear but still talk with Mary.

'That's terrible. What happened?' Lewis asked.

Gloria began crying and Lewis covered the phone and looked at Mary who was whispering, 'Ask if she can bring the body out. Tell her you know the police won't hurt her. They just want everyone out and safe.'

Lewis repeated Mary's words and waited for Gloria to continue. She finally said, 'Just call the police and tell them we're sending someone out. Tell them not to shoot.' And the call ended.

Mary handed her phone to Lewis.

'This is Terry, the negotiator you spoke with yesterday?'

'Yes, I know. What should I do?' Lewis asked.

'Can you get to the bank with your phone? Or we can send someone out to pick you up. I know it's early to be dealing with this.'

'I'm fine to drive. We're on our way.'

Josie was asleep on a cot in the waiting room of the bank when Lieutenant Hernández woke her.

'They're sending someone out of the church. Sounds like they're claiming responsibility for the female who died yesterday from the gun shot.'

Josie sat up and rubbed her eyes, trying to make sense of what he was saying. 'Sending who out?'

'She didn't say. Gideon's wife called Lewis and had him relay a message to the police that they're sending someone out. She wanted the police to know so they wouldn't fire.'

'That doesn't sound right. That destroys their whole narrative about the cops killing innocent people,' she said, standing and trying to smooth out the wrinkles in a uniform she'd been wearing for twenty-four hours. 'You think they could be drawing us into gunfire?' she asked.

'We have SWAT team members stationed around the front of the building and snipers at the ready,' Hernández said. 'My guess is this is their form of negotiation. They've got a dead body they can't leave inside for much longer, and they know an investigation is going to point to one of their members. Either way, it's a touchy situation. I want to be sure we know where every law enforcement officer is located so we don't get crossways if they do start to fire.'

Josie spent the next few minutes ensuring every city officer and sheriffs' deputy was accounted for and knew the plan, while Hernández took care of the state personnel. Josie positioned herself outside the bank, shielded behind a patrol car next to Hernández. 'We're watching all three doors,' he said. 'We storm the place if we get a clear entrance but not without knowing the location of the kids. We'll take whoever exits the building and immediately interrogate. If we get the right information we may push in through the back. One of the snipers got a clear site into the kitchen when someone opened the door to throw a trash bag outside about an hour ago. He got a couple of photos with a night-vision camera that showed the room was empty.'

Josie watched the front door of the church open and a man step out slowly. Two SWAT members located behind the BearCat stepped to the corner of the machine with weapons drawn.

'Put your hands on top of your head and walk straight ahead, slowly, and into the street. We will not shoot.' The officer inside the BearCat repeated the message over a loudspeaker several times as the person moved forward.

Spotlights appeared and lit up a man as he walked down the sidewalk toward the street. 'That's Leon. The kid that applied for the custodian's position,' Josie said. 'I thought they were sending a body out.'

'The woman Lewis talked to wasn't clear. She said that a female had been killed and they were sending someone out. We had thought they would send a person out with the body. Maybe the body comes next.'

They watched as the two SWAT personnel ran into the street, pulled Leon down and dragged him behind the BearCat then back behind a police car in the parking lot.

As the officers surrounded him and moved him toward the bank, Josie pointed to the church entrance where another person had exited and was standing with arms crossed. Hernández motioned toward the BearCat and he and Josie took off at a low crouch, running for the cover of the machine. Once there, the officer inside gave the same instructions and a female wearing jeans and a long parka walked toward the BearCat. When she reached the street, Josie and Hernández ran and grabbed her, using her coat to pull her back behind the safety of the machine.

Inside the bank, Leon was placed in a manager's office with a police guard outside the door. The female, named Alaina Jonas, was located in another office on the opposite side of the building where the two members wouldn't be able to overhear one another.

Josie asked to talk with Leon first since she'd had contact with him and had already established a decent rapport. Hernández agreed and she entered the room with a phone to record their conversation.

The lobby and main entrance of the bank were powered by a generator, but the offices were not. Two battery-powered Coleman lanterns cast a harsh glare in the small room.

Josie quickly talked through the formalities and received permission from Leon to record the conversation. When they started to talk in earnest, she changed her demeanor to that of a sympathetic friend, an approach the hostage negotiator had suggested.

'Leon, before we get started, I need you to tell me where people are located in the building right now. Where are the kids?'

'When they found Cia this morning they took all the kids to one of the Sunday school rooms. I don't know which one.'

'Where are the adults?'

He shook his head. 'I don't know. It's a mess. People are coming apart. Maybe they're in the basement while Gideon tells them what to do.'

'What about weapons? Is everyone carrying a weapon?'

'I don't know. The men are supposed to carry, but things were crazy this morning so I don't know.'

'Are there additional weapons stored anywhere?'

'In the basement.' Leon shook his head and looked away from Josie.

She turned toward the door where one of the SRT officers was standing. He gave a thumbs up that he'd heard the information and left to work with SWAT on next steps.

'What happened to make you leave the church this morning?' Josie asked.

He looked terrible, as if he'd not slept or eaten in days, as if he were ready to break down into sobs.

'Tell me what's happening, Leon. I'm here to help you.'

Leon pressed his finger and thumb into his eyes to stem the tears that had started to flow. 'I'm so screwed. I don't even know how to explain what's happened.'

'Gloria called and told the police that someone had been killed. We thought someone would be coming out along with the body.'

'I didn't kill her. I swear I didn't. I would never have done anything to hurt her. Someone killed her and is blaming me.' He looked at Josie with eyes that were crazy with grief and fear. 'I loved Cia with every bone in my body. I would have never hurt her.'

Josie thought she'd misunderstood. 'I thought the girl who was killed was named Mandy?'

He nodded. 'That's right. Both of them are gone.'

'You mean that Cia was killed too?'

'I found her body this morning and they're blaming me.' He broke down and sobbed.

Josie stood. 'I'll be right back, Leon. I'm going to find you a box of tissues.'

She stepped into the hallway and found Downey, who had been standing next to the door to listen in.

'Did I catch that right?' he asked. 'Did he say two females are dead?'

'That's correct. Mandy and a young woman named Cia Mulroney. She was Leon's girlfriend. I need you to pass that on to the team while I continue.'

Josie re-entered the room with a box of Kleenex and waited until Leon had gained control before continuing.

'Why would someone want to kill your girlfriend?' she asked finally. Her voice was quiet, her expression compassionate, hoping he saw her as a friendly figure.

'Last night, I tried to tell Cia that Gideon killed Mandy.'

'Hang on,' Josie said. 'Mandy is the young girl who was shot. She was the girl that Gideon says was shot by the police. You're saying that Gideon shot her?'

Leon nodded. 'I tried to tell Cia last night what happened. I tried to explain how there was no way that the police could have shot her from outside of the building. She was furious with me and threw me out of the room. But someone heard me telling her.' He stopped talking and leaned his head down between his legs as if trying to keep from passing out.

'OK, let's slow down. How long has it been since you've eaten?'

He sat up slowly, looking pale and sick. 'It's been a while. A day or two.'

'Let's get you some food before you go any further.'

Josie had one of the officers give up his breakfast sandwich that he'd brought in from the gas station. She asked Otto to deliver the sandwich and a cup of coffee, letting Leon know that people cared about him and believed his story.

While Otto chatted to Leon, Josie found Hernández and filled him in on what she'd learned so far. 'What about the female who left the building just after Leon?' she asked.

'Her name is Alaina. Her entire purpose for leaving the group seems to be nailing Leon for the murder of Cia, who was apparently Leon's girlfriend and a dedicated follower of Gideon.

Alaina claims that Leon was trying to sabotage the group and frame Gideon for murder,' Hernández said.

'And Leon claims he tried to fill Cia in on the truth about Gideon, and he woke up this morning framed for her murder.' She nodded toward the SRT officers and several SWAT team members who were huddled around a table. 'Are they moving in?'

'We're getting people in place. We're moving in through the back door. Once we're inside, we'll use the drone to advance. This is the time to make a move.'

After Leon finished eating and looked as if he were regaining some strength, Josie started back in on the questioning. With coffee and food in his stomach, he finally broke loose with his story.

'We fought last night. I tried to give her facts, to show her what Gideon had done, but she wouldn't listen. She said she couldn't stand to see me anymore. I took my coat and left our room.'

'What time did you leave?' Josie asked, her voice gentle, not accusatory. She had no idea yet what Leon's role might be in The Drummers, but she hoped he would serve as a lifeline to their group.

'It was around ten thirty. After the big meeting, Cia and I went back to the room to talk before David and Alaina came back.'

'What do you mean by big meeting?'

'Gideon was getting people ready for a fight.'

'With who?'

'With everyone. With the police. With anyone who might be against us.'

'You mentioned David and Alaina. Who are they?' Josie asked.

Leon explained the basic structure, including which members were staying in which of the six Sunday school rooms, and how he and Cia shared a room with David and Alaina.

'And what is your relationship with Alaina?' she asked.

He took a moment to answer. 'David and I were best friends in the military. David is married to her. When we joined The Drummers we were in complete agreement about living off the grid. Then Gideon started to change his focus once we got here and David and I grew apart. And Cia too. They all believed everything Gideon had to say, but I didn't.'

'What made you feel different than they did?' she asked.

'Everything turned into this mission. Everyone was out to get us, but we were doing things to piss people off at the same time. A few days ago, Gideon got two of the boys to march around like Nazis in front of the church. What was the point in that? I felt like he was setting us up for conflict.'

'Were there other people who felt like you?'

'I don't know. They started giving me door duty and keeping me out of the meetings for the group. I don't even know the big plans. There was one other guy, Jackson, who wasn't issued a gun last night. I don't know what his story is. We weren't really close. He's quiet, sticks to himself.'

Josie spent the next hour questioning Leon about the members of the group and getting as much detail as she could about their beliefs and loyalties. Next, she focused on the details of Mandy's shooting and Cia's death. Leon said he'd found Cia's body in the basement.

'When I found her, I just lost my mind. I was screaming and crying for help. Gideon was the first person to come downstairs and he accused me of killing her. He told everyone that he found me over the top of her, after I strangled her to death.'

'Had she been strangled?'

Josie watched his face contort with anguish and he struggled to keep from breaking down again. While grief presented itself in endless ways, she had found suspects basically fell into three groups: not enough grief, over the top grief, or trying to hold it together. Leon fell into the more believable barely holding it together.

'I don't know. Honestly, my first thought was that someone had drugged her. She was just lying there, lifeless. It didn't make any sense.'

'Did she have any medical conditions that could have caused her to die from natural causes?'

'There was nothing wrong with Cia. She was perfectly healthy until we joined The Drummers.'

THIRTEEN

When the power kicked back on, Manny Colombo stood in his tiny kitchen, looking in awe at the brightly illuminated countertops and shiny kitchen sink. It felt like it had been days since he'd seen bright light. He had been facing the prospect of cold soup and potato chips for lunch that day, and had been considering a drive to a town with power just to get a hot meal. A two-hour drive for a grilled hamburger and crispy French fries was not out of the question.

His first order of business was brewing a hot pot of coffee and toasting a bagel to golden brown, allowing the butter to melt over the edges. Next, he would get caught up on the news. He watched the news each morning with his breakfast to stay abreast of the issues, then turned the idiot box off. He had not realized how much he enjoyed that hour in the morning until he lost the ritual.

With his plate fixed, Manny turned the lamp on beside his recliner and settled in with his breakfast and TV remote and smelled the furnace as it started up, ready to blow out warm air. His fat old body couldn't deal with the cold like it used to. It needed modern comforts like heat and toasters.

As he enjoyed his breakfast he flipped through the local channels, shaking his head. He had sold a lucrative Holiday Inn franchise more than twenty years ago in order to move to Artemis for a new beginning: a quiet life, free from drama. He watched the overhead footage of the church with police cars and ambulances and fire trucks on all sides, SWAT officers dressed in black hiding behind armored vehicles, and all just a few blocks from his motel. All those people crammed into a sacred place, and for what? Because they thought the government was out to get them, that technology was destroying the world? What did they imagine they were doing to their own children, he wondered?

The wall phone rang and startled him up and out of his seat.

'Manny's Motel. How can I help you?'

'It's Josie. Are you all lit up again?'

'Fresh brewed coffee and electric light. Two of life's greatest pleasures restored this morning. And how is your day?'

'It depends. I have a big favor to ask.'

'You know I'll do anything for you, Chief.'

'Have you seen the news this morning?'

'It's like a train wreck. You can't take your eyes off it.'

'Then you know they've evacuated the remaining members. They've been transported to the Arroyo County Jail for questioning. With two deaths under investigation, and the number of people involved, this could take days. But the majority of the members haven't committed any crimes. Technically, they're free to go, but we need them to stay until we have answers.'

'Do you figure they even have family to go home to?' Manny asked. 'I'd guess most of them severed ties when they joined up with this animal.'

'I would guess you're right. Our biggest problem is that we can't hold them at the jail because there's no evidence that they committed a crime. However, we don't want them leaving town,' Josie said.

'Ah.'

'You see where I'm headed with this.'

'I do. And, as luck would have it, with the power off, it's not as if I have a motel filled with guests.'

'How many rooms do you have open?'

'Five vacancies.'

'The sheriff said he has some probationers' fees that he can use to pay you for rooms. I imagine we'll need all five. We have thirteen adults and four kids.'

'I'm glad to help.'

'Send me a text of how many beds you have in each room, and I'll have Maria work with someone from the group to assign people to rooms before they arrive this afternoon. Is that OK?'

'That would be helpful. I'll call Maria so I can coordinate and have the keys ready.'

Manny hung up the phone and looked down at the neon Rooms for Rent sign that hung crooked in the front window. He unplugged the sign, pleased to have all his rooms filled but unsure what kind of drama that might bring. From family reunions to wedding parties, rarely were all rooms filled without chaos to accompany the full load.

Seventeen members of The Drummers were evacuated from the church and taken to the Arroyo County Jail for questioning. Four of the seventeen were children who remained with members of the group in the waiting area while their parents were questioned in one of two interrogation rooms. Clyde Hamblin was arrested on gun charges and lodged in the jail. The two females were both taken to the morgue, also located at the jail complex, for an autopsy. Leon and Alaina were still at the jail for questioning. Sheriff Martinez had called in every staff member on payroll for support.

The jail was located on the outskirts of town on a lonely stretch of desert that reached all the way to the Rio Grande. The state-of-the-art jail and trauma center were paid for by a Homeland Security grant that the town received after 9/11. The facilities were first-rate for such a remote town, but increased border violence had provided the need.

It was a brown cinder-block and brick building with a brown awning over the entrance door. Josie entered a vestibule and pressed a buzzer, stated her name, and a second set of doors opened into a central hub where Maria Santiago, intake officer, sat in front of several computers. The octagonal-shaped room led to several other areas of the jail, such as the booking room, the interrogation room and the prisoner pods.

Josie chatted with Maria for a few minutes about the logistics of settling in almost twenty people for questioning, feeding them lunch, and then planning for transportation to Manny's for lodging. Maria finally received a phone call and buzzed Josie through another set of doors, with the words County Coroner painted in black on them. Josie pressed an intercom button and announced her name. A moment later the door clicked and she entered to find Mitchell Cowan wearing a white lab coat, a mask and a blue surgical cap, leaning over a body on a stainless-steel gurney.

Mitchell, known for his gloomy disposition and lack of social skills, had always been one of Josie's favorites. Never one to put on airs, he dealt with every person, regardless of their status, in a completely honest and forthcoming manner; a manner which tended to offend, especially those who thought their status in life owed them something a bit more refined.

'Good morning,' Josie said.

'Let's just stick with morning. Not too much good in this office today,' he said, talking into the cavity of a severely bloated body.

'Fair enough. If you have a minute, I wanted to fill you in on the two females who were delivered this morning.'

He murmured something unintelligible and spent a few minutes packing up the body and washing.up at the sink across the room. The chemical smell of the soap, mixed with the stench of the decomposing body, made it hard to breathe. Josie couldn't imagine working in that environment all day long.

Cowan approached her as he dried his hands. 'Let's have a chat in my office. The odor isn't near so bad.'

Behind the closed door, the smell was certainly better, or at least masked by a plugin deodorizer that smelled like fabric softener. He motioned for Josie to sit in the chair across from his desk.

'On top of the mess we have in our own county, I received a drowning victim yesterday from Presidio. Thus the bloated body on my table. They're full up and begging for help.'

'What kind of timeframe are you looking at for the two females?'

'I'll finish up Presidio's today. I've got another one back-logged, then I'll get to your two women. However, when they came in this morning, I did take a preliminary look.' He turned from Josie to face his computer screen. 'The sheriff sent me crime scene photos from when they moved the bodies.'

'Can I have a look? I've been in interviews this morning and haven't been inside the church.'

Cowan turned the screen so she could view with him. They leaned in to look at a photo he had enlarged. 'This is where victim one was shot, located in one of the Sunday school rooms.' He turned to Josie. 'This is the one that every conspiracy theory nut on the planet is saying you murdered, correct?'

Josie nodded.

'This first photo shows her location in the room in relation to the door and window. You can see the outline of where the police believe she lay before people in the church moved her. I believe the police found the body in the church bathroom. From my initial examination I would estimate she was shot at point blank range. That bullet did not enter her chest from thirty yards away.'

Josie nodded, more relieved than she would have thought.

Cowan took a moment to look at her. 'Your bullet did not kill this young girl, and forensics will certainly bear my speculation out.' He pulled up the next photo. 'This is the wall, directly behind where I believe she was shot.' He clicked to the next photo. 'This is a close-up of the wall. Notice the pinkish hue? It's apparent someone tried to wash the blood off, but it's obvious that the blood splatter was centered at around four feet off the ground. With the bottom of the windowsill measuring five feet off the ground, the only way for a bullet to have hit this young girl would have been from the room she was standing in. Obviously, this is more your crime scene tech's bailiwick than mine, but I'd say this is a fairly straightforward finding.'

Josie nodded. 'Good to hear.'

He clicked through another two dozen photos of Mandy and the room she was murdered in before reaching another grizzly photograph.

'This victim, however, not so straightforward. I believe this woman died of asphyxiation. However, after doing a quick examination this morning, it appears she was knocked out with a blunt object before the asphyxiation. Her head burst open from the blow.'

'Is there blood apparent in the photos?'

'Yes, but not significant. She obtained a large hematoma on the back of her skull. Let's look here first.'

Josie pulled her head back from the screen to get a better angle on what she was looking at.

'It's not a well-composed photo. This is the basement of the church. It took me some time to figure out the layout of the room. The long white area is a table and next to it is a wooden stand that appears to be a lectern. Speculating, I'd say she was standing in front of this table and someone clubbed her from behind with a heavy object.' Cowan used his mouse to enlarge the photo and pointed to a long gray object. 'Most likely this iron pipe. Whoever killed her didn't care to conceal the evidence.'

'What would be the point? It had to be someone in the church that killed her, and there was nowhere to dispose of anything. May as well do it quick and leave the items where they lie. Even if we find good prints, every member in the building had the potential to leave their prints on that pipe.'

'True enough.'

'You don't think the blow to the head is what killed her?'

'As I mentioned,' Cowan said, pushing the computer screen back around to his side of the desk, 'when I examined the body I found a large hematoma on the back of her head. Given the amount of swelling and insignificant bleeding, I doubt that the blow was enough to cause her death. But I also found bruising just above the laryngeal prominence.' He pointed to the area just below the chin on the neck.

'So just above her Adam's apple?'

'Correct. There was a line of bruising that extended several inches from both sides of the' – he paused and looked at Josie – 'Adam's apple.'

Josie began nodding. 'You think someone tied something around her head to asphyxiate her, to ensure she was dead?'

'Obviously this is preliminary, but, yes.'

'Did it look as if she struggled?'

'Not that I could see.'

'This is helpful, Cowan. I appreciate the early information.'

'I won't know for certain until I get in for the autopsy. And the sooner I get the smell out of my examination room, the sooner I can move along to your females.'

Josie started to leave, then turned back. 'I know you're swamped, but until we get the bullet and can run ballistics and prove otherwise, I'm being labeled a child murderer.'

'I understand.' He considered her for a moment and said, 'I have to get the Presidio victim complete, but I should be able to get the bullet processed today.'

Josie thanked him and left, but she knew the photos incriminating her would remain on the internet: innocent or not, there would always be people who chose to view her as guilty.

FOURTEEN

L ieutenant Hernández requested a debriefing at the command post at four o'clock that afternoon with the command group and Mayor O'Kane. He intended to assign two officers to continue working the murder investigations of Mandy Seneck and Cia Mulroney, and to determine expectations for the rest of the group as they disbanded the post.

He provided a summary of the questioning that had taken place at the jail earlier in the day, starting with Alaina, the female who left the church at the same time Leon was forced out. Alaina stated that she and David shared a room with Leon and Cia, and that all four were in the room together the morning that Mandy was shot. Alaina said that David had run to the front of the church when the banging on the door started. She said that Leon stayed behind and told Cia and Alaina to go to the basement with the kids and wait for more instruction. She said that he got dressed and took off to 'supposedly' go help David at the front door.

Alaina claimed that she went to the basement as instructed. She stated that Cia left to get Mandy. She claimed there were people walking and running and crying, and that it was a chaotic environment.

Then, when she came up from the basement, she walked into Gideon's room and found Cia standing in the doorway. Mandy's body was slumped on the floor, with Gideon standing at the window in shock.

'We spent a lot of time questioning her on this part of her story,' Hernández said. 'We've heard three very different narratives about who killed Mandy Seneck. We first heard from Gideon that a bullet from a police officer stationed across the street killed her. Now he's changed his story and is saying that Leon killed the girl. Next, there's Leon's theory that Gideon killed her. Leon claimed that he tried to explain to his girlfriend

Cia that the only person who could have killed Mandy was
Gideon. Cia got so angry that she threw him out of the bedroom
to sleep on one of the pews that night. Leon says someone then
killed Cia in order to frame him for her murder, and also for
Mandy's murder. And now we have Alaina's story, which may
put Cia in the room at the time of the murder.'

'Do we know what the relationship between Alaina and Cia
was like? Did she actually say that Cia could have killed
Mandy?' Josie asked.

Downey said, 'I interviewed Alaina. Early in the interview
she said that Cia was Gideon's favorite. When I followed up
on that statement she laughed and tried to brush it off as mean-
ingless, but I got a sense there was some jealousy between the
females in the group. Then when I asked her to elaborate on
seeing Cia in the room with Mandy, who had just been shot,
her exact words were' – Downey flipped through his notes, then
read – '"I just don't know. I know Gideon would have never
killed Mandy."'

Hernández said, 'But Alaina wouldn't go so far as to say she
thought Cia shot the girl?'

'Correct.'

'What was your take on Alaina?' Josie asked.

'It was odd. She started the interview stating that Leon was
responsible for both murders. But by the end, I got the sense
that she was trying to point the finger at Cia, but didn't want
to be the person who came out and said it. I didn't find her
very credible,' Downey said.

'Could she have been trying to draw attention away from
herself? Maybe she was jealous of both Cia and Mandy, and she's
behind the move to frame Leon and discredit Cia,' Josie said.

Otto cut in. 'Hang on. I keep hearing how everyone is trying
to frame Leon for both murders. Every person in The Drummers
agreed to frame the man for two murders? You can't get five
people to agree on the weather, and he says all those people
agreed to frame him?'

'Leon claims he was in the Sunday school room with David
when Mandy's shooting occurred,' Hernández said. 'He claims
he and David were arguing about Cia and Alaina being stationed
in the basement to guard the guns.'

Otto put a finger up. 'But I interviewed David. He claims he left the room to make sure everyone was in place. David says Leon went to check on Mandy next door to their room, and shortly after, shots were fired.'

'Did Alaina see Leon in the room, or leaving the room, after Mandy was shot?' Josie asked.

'No. She only saw Cia, but she's still sticking to the group story that Leon shot Mandy. She believes the police were shooting and he went into the room and made a split-second decision to kill Mandy in order to make it look like the police did it.'

'Which is the same thing Leon is saying about Gideon,' Downey said.

'Correct,' Hernández said.

'If that's the case,' Josie said, 'if Leon killed Mandy, why would Gideon have told everyone that the police shot the girl?'

'Both Alaina and Gideon have the same story on that. They claim they were so shocked that Leon would have done such a thing that Gideon just made up the police story to try and save Leon. Then when they found Cia had been murdered too, they knew Leon had to pay for what he'd done,' Hernández said. 'That's why they forced him out in the morning.'

'I notice they haven't cleared anything up online. My mother is sending me crap she's finding on social media calling for me to get the death penalty for shooting children,' Josie said.

Hernández was quiet. Everyone in the room knew that in today's world, an attack by the media could destroy a cop's career.

The hostage negotiator said, 'We shared with several members that the timing didn't support Leon killing Mandy. We explained that Gideon was the only confirmed person in the room with her before she was shot. Several stated that Leon was also in the room, although no one was willing to say they actually saw him there. We were trying to gauge the support of their leader. Gideon appears untouchable.'

'Regarding Cia's death,' Hernández said, 'every single member of The Drummers pointed to Leon as the person responsible for killing her. Not one person believed his story of walking down to the basement and finding her dead on the floor. Alaina claims that David stood outside their door and heard Cia and Leon fighting. Cia supposedly told Leon that she knew he'd killed Mandy. Both Alaina and Gideon say that Leon killed Cia before she could tell everyone else that he was a murderer.'

'They're saying all of this with absolutely no evidence to point to Leon as the murderer,' Josie said.

'Agreed. It's a "he said she said" until we get ballistics and the autopsy results. But this isn't a typical murder investigation. We have a very finite group of people who could have killed both of those women. If not Leon, then who?'

'You honestly believe Leon killed Cia?' Josie asked, looking at Hernández.

'Someone in that church killed her. Again, if not Leon, then who was it?'

'Gideon. We already know he tried to blame Mandy's death on the police, until he found out the shot wasn't possible. Then he blamed it on Leon. He clearly isn't trustworthy. I think he killed both girls and blamed it on Leon, the person he knew the other members would rally around as the murderer.'

'I still don't see that as motive for Gideon killing her,' Otto said. 'From the interviews, it was obvious that Cia was one of his favorites, as was Mandy.'

Josie nodded slowly, thinking it through. 'But if they thought Leon was a killer, why wait until morning to throw him out? If what they're saying is true, they basically gave him the time and opportunity to kill Cia.'

Hernández said, 'Gideon claims they waited because it was a terrible tragedy and it took them time to process what happened.'

Josie smirked. 'Come on. You can't possibly buy that.'

'Here's another piece,' Otto said. 'Cia's body was found in the basement. Someone convinced her to go down to the basement in the middle of the night. Leon makes the most sense.'

'Why would Cia throw him out of the bedroom and then go meet him in the basement a short time later?' Josie asked.

'Because they shared a bedroom with another couple,' Otto said. 'Leon and Cia had a terrible fight. I'd say, one of them got up and convinced the other one to go down into the basement so they could finish their argument without having everyone else listen in. While they were down there, Cia told Leon something that either implicated him or infuriated him.'

'For now, we can hold him twenty-four hours without filing charges,' Hernández said. 'Meanwhile, we wait on ballistics. I believe we found the gun that was used to shoot Mandy. An officer found it shoved underneath a pile of clothes in Gideon's bedroom, the same room where she was shot.' Hernández paused and looked around the table at the group of officers. 'We have a lot of moving parts here, from multiple law enforcement agencies to the number of suspects and victims. Procedures and details are critical. Don't rush. We don't want a killer walking free over a technicality.'

Otto nodded agreement and looked at Downey. 'Where are we with logging the weapons?'

'We've catalogued over forty guns, mostly rifles and shotguns.' Downey gestured for Josie to continue.

'When I interviewed Leon, he drew me a sketch of where each of the members slept, and how the group utilized the different areas of the church. I worked with Downey to map the guns they found in each room to get an initial feel for who the radicals might be. At first look, I'd say David and Markus seem to be the two members who were most into the guns.'

'Otto tracked two of the serial numbers to a dealer from El Paso with connections to certain groups on the FBI terrorist watch list,' Downey said. 'We're several days away from knowing much more though. And we're waiting on the autopsy findings to hopefully connect the bullet to the rifle left under the clothes. We got a good print on the gun but haven't had time to match it.'

'And what about Gideon?' Josie asked.

'What about him?' Hernández said.

'We can't hold him on anything?'

'What would we hold him on? We have nothing on him, other than conjecture by this group. Everyone who was in that building when the two women were killed claim he's innocent of everything.'

'You're holding Leon, so why can't you hold Gideon for questioning until we get ballistics?' Josie said.

Hernández shook his head. 'I spoke with the prosecutor at

length, and given what we have on Leon and Gideon, he won't file charges against either one at this point. Leon gets cut loose tomorrow with nothing further.'

'So we know we have at least one murderer, maybe two, among that group. And we're going to let them all go?' O'Kane said, his tone incredulous.

'Mayor O'Kane, I'm not trying to be a smart ass here, but if the prosecutor filed against those two, he'd have to file on Josie too. We have the same amount of evidence pointing to her as a murderer as we do Gideon and Leon.'

'That's out of line,' Otto said.

Hernández scowled. 'I'm not saying Josie murdered anyone. I'm making the point that the prosecutor can't arrest someone based on someone saying it's so. That's irresponsible and everyone in this room knows it. Not to mention, who would it be? We have too many stories to even write a summary that makes sense.'

'I hate to bring this up,' Josie said, 'but even if Gideon's prints are on the gun found in his bedroom, he'll claim he picked it up to move it. Say he hid it under clothes to keep it away from the kids or some such bullshit. With so many people in and out of that room, how do we tie it to him?'

O'Kane choked out a laugh. 'I am stunned. We know for a fact that at least one of these people murdered two young women. And you're telling me there's a chance they may all walk free?'

'That's always a possibility in any investigation,' Hernández said.

'And what can be done about the misinformation that's being spread in the media about the shooting?' O'Kane added. 'These people murder their own and then tell the world that one of our officers is guilty of shooting children? How can they get away with this?'

'My dad called me this morning to ask how a police officer could get away with shooting someone and still be allowed to stay on the job,' Townsend said. 'He said the national news is painting it that a local officer's stray bullet killed the girl.' His face had grown red with anger. 'At some point, someone needs to be held accountable for blatant lies in the media.'

Josie listened, quietly grateful for the support, especially from the mayor. Throughout the day, none of the officers had mentioned the media frenzy, but she had received a dozen or more texts from community members wanting to know what was happening. Manny had sent a screenshot of a conversation that had taken place on Facebook or some other media outlet that accused her of getting away with murder. Clearly upset, he had wanted to know what he could do to help put a stop to it.

The anger she felt at seeing her name in print next to the slander was no shock, but the shame and embarrassment surprised her. She felt bad for her mom, having to read such hate and lies about her own daughter, and she worried what the bad press would do to her office. And dark thoughts continued to make their way into the front of her mind before she had time to still them, wondering, was it possible that she *was* responsible for the girl's death? If something is said enough times, it begins to ring true. She had willingly submitted her gun as a precaution. She didn't want to give the media any chance to spin a police cover-up. But however irrational, she couldn't stop asking herself the question: what if ballistics came back as a match for her gun?

After each of the groups had presented, Hernández provided instructions on dismantling the command post and logging evidence and filing paperwork with the proper agencies. It was agreed that the two DPS officers would move to the upstairs office at the police department. As the rest of the group began packing up the gear, Josie and Otto left to help those who were being transported from the jail to Manny's Motel.

Otto had moved his patrol car to the PD earlier in the day so Josie offered him a ride back to the department.

'How about a quick stop at the gas station?' he said, sliding into the passenger seat. 'It's after my dinner time and my belly is still hollering for lunch.'

Josie drove toward the convenience store. 'I'm going to order pizzas for The Drummers' supper tonight. Their minibus is impounded and I don't think any of the rest of them have cars. They can't get back into the church yet.'

'That's why you shouldn't piss off your neighbors. If they hadn't been so hateful, there'd be a passel of people cooking dinners and delivering to the motel tonight.'

'Well that doesn't help me right now.'

'Who says you're responsible for feeding those people?' he asked, clearly irritated.

'Otto, if nothing else, there are four kids who need to eat tonight. Why are you so grumpy?'

'Because I'm tired of people. Two young girls are dead because some crazy bastard convinced a bunch of sheep that he was the new messiah. What kind of parent would take their kid and follow a man like that to their death?'

'We don't know what they were thinking yet.'

'You heard the DPS guys. In the interviews, those people swore up and down Gideon would never have hurt that girl. And he was in the room when she was shot!'

'Think about this from The Drummers' perspectives. If they concede that Gideon was even remotely responsible, it means they've devoted their lives to a monster. It's a lot easier to put your head in the sand than it is to accept you've made a horrible mistake.'

'I can accept that until you involve kids. These people dragged their kids into a fantasy land that turned into a nightmare. They ought to be held accountable.'

'Maybe what they need is a conversation with someone who isn't going to judge them,' Josie said.

'Well, good luck with that,' he said.

'I'll have pizzas delivered. Manny said we can use the reception room behind the motel to set up for dinner.' She glanced over to find Otto staring out the front window. 'I'd like to go myself, but you know some of them still buy the narrative that I shot the young girl,' she said. 'I'm not the right person to try and make peace.'

'I know what you want.'

Josie smiled.

'For pity's sake.'

She pulled the car in front of the convenience store. 'We need to have a conversation with them. My guess is we'd learn more about their group dynamic by sharing a pizza than anyone did questioning them today at the jail.'

'And by we, you mean me?'

'I'll be back at the office, with you in spirit.'

He took a moment and sighed heavily. 'Let me get a snack, then I'll run home and change clothes. I'll be back at Manny's in an hour.'

After finding the front office empty, Otto found Manny inside one of the motel rooms with its door open toward the street. He was running a dust cloth around the bedside table.

'Manny, I'm sure no one will judge you over a bit of dust,' Otto said.

'You sound like my daughter. I explained to her a thousand times growing up that worrying about what others think is not the reason for cleaning. You clean because it needs doing.'

'True enough. Are you ready for this?'

He raised his arms in an exaggerated shrug. 'I've had plenty of groups through the years. Plenty of families staying in town for a funeral or memorial service. But never one quite like this. The media portrays them as a bunch of quacks.'

Otto decided to let that judgment pass. 'You have room assignments for everyone?'

'I do. The families with kids are all together. A few of the single members have to share rooms, but Maria said they didn't seem to mind. She said they all seemed grateful for a place to stay. Although I do admit, it's a bit unsettling to have a potential murderer sleeping in my motel for the foreseeable future.'

'I'm not happy about that either. Although, as the innkeeper, you should have nothing to fear.'

Manny raised his eyebrows in surprise. 'I imagine those young girls thought they had nothing to fear as well.'

Otto winced and Manny waved it off.

'I suppose Josie worked it out with you to have pizzas in the reception room out back?' Otto asked.

'She did. The bus is on the way, and Josie already placed the order.'

'I brought a platter of sweets from Delores for dessert. You're welcome to join us,' Otto said.

'Tell Delores thank you. I'm hoping to get everyone off the bus and into the back room. I assume you'll want to say a few words,' he said, his expression hopeful. 'I'm not sure what to tell them about what happens next.'

'I'll be glad to,' Otto said, clapping Manny on the back as they left the motel room. 'We all appreciate you taking this on.'

As they walked back to the office to get the keys, they watched a yellow school bus pull up along the front of the motel. Otto noticed the faces of the adults staring out at them, wary and exhausted. The driver opened the doors and people filed out as if walking to their death sentence. Even the kids looked somber. Manny walked up to each person with his hand outstretched, introducing himself and smiling warmly. Otto led them through Manny's office and into a detached pole barn that was rented as a reception hall for gatherings.

The barn was a simple thirty-by-thirty-foot space with folding tables and chairs, restrooms and a galley kitchen. Manny had arranged half a dozen tables with plastic tablecloths in the center of the room. Once the group had settled, Otto introduced himself.

'First, please know that we're very sorry for your loss. Manny and I want to make your stay here as comfortable as we can until we find out the details about what happened. I assure you that you won't find a better host than Manny.'

A woman who looked to be in her seventies spoke up. 'And we appreciate your kindness, taking us all in like this. It's been a terrible couple of days so we appreciate a place to lay our heads down tonight.'

Otto recognized her as Gloria, Gideon's wife, then noticed Gideon sitting next to her with his Albert Einstein hair and smug look.

Manny stood up from his chair on the side of the room. 'You just let me know if you need anything. There's plenty of good people in this town who are happy to help.'

As Manny talked on, Otto's thoughts remained with Gideon, wondering how a man in his position could possibly seem so smug. The lack of contrition from Gideon, from all the members, from all of society for that matter, appalled Otto. He wondered if it came from his Catholic upbringing, where guilt and absolution were the fabric of life. In Poland, where he had lived until an adult, eighty-five percent of the population was Catholic. They understood sin, but they also understood penance and they had a conscience, something he worried had been bred out of the vast majority of the population over the past decade.

He noticed Manny waving to him and realized he'd been daydreaming, a habit that had recently become worse.

'As far as next steps,' Otto said, hoping he was picking up where he'd left off, 'we'd like to get everyone settled in tonight with dinner and a safe, comfortable place to sleep.'

'Excuse me,' a man said. He sat at a table furthest away from Otto, dressed in a flannel shirt and jeans, with a scruffy beard and unkempt brown hair in need of a good wash. 'And how do we sleep safe in a town where two of our members were killed? One of them by one of your officers?'

'That's enough, Markus,' Gloria said.

'I think it's a fair question,' the man responded. 'They have us right where they want us, stuck in their little rooms to spy on us until we break.'

'Markus, I said that's enough. I'm quite sure the police aren't happy about any of this either. And making people angry with us surely hasn't gotten us anywhere good so far.' Gloria turned in her seat to glare at Markus and he looked away, saying nothing more.

Otto noted the smile that now accompanied the smug look on the bastard Gideon's face. Otto turned to face the other side of the room and tried to keep his own expression neutral. 'We'll be conducting follow-up interviews starting tomorrow morning at nine. Hopefully your rooms here at Manny's will give you a few days to figure out next steps.'

'When can we get back into the church?' a young woman asked. 'The kids need clean clothes.'

'We all need clothes and medications,' a man sitting next to her said.

'I understand. I'm sure by tomorrow we'll be able to provide at least limited access, and if you need medication tonight we can send an officer in to retrieve that for you.'

Otto watched as the side door opened and a wide-eyed pizza delivery boy walked in carrying an armful of boxes. Manny rolled in a cooler with iced down cans of pop and set everything up on a table outside the kitchen area.

*   *   *

Otto waited until the members were served and eating, finally starting to quietly chat amongst themselves, before he filled his own plate. As he moved toward an empty table in the back of the room, Gloria motioned toward him. 'Please, join us.'

He sat down across from Gloria and she gestured toward her husband who was sitting next to her. 'I'm sure you've met Gideon.'

Otto nodded and Gideon did the same. Otto decided Josie owed him a hefty favor after this one.

'And this is Lydia and James. They're original members from back in our Georgia days.' The couple appeared to be in their sixties, with long hair and the laid-back demeanor of what Otto still thought of as hippies, although he had no idea if the term was still used.

James reached across the table to shake Otto's hand. 'Don't mind Markus. He's taken this the hardest. We're all in a bad way.'

Otto struggled with how to proceed with the conversation. These same people had accused his chief of police of murdering a young girl and posted it for all the world to see, and now he had to play nice. His stomach churned and gurgled and he wasn't certain he could get through dinner without having to excuse himself.

'You mentioned Georgia,' Otto said, grasping at something to start a conversation. 'How long were you there?'

'Over ten years,' Gloria said. 'We had over thirty people living together at one point. Farming and sharing meals and chores. Those were great days.'

'What made you leave?' Otto asked.

'We were sharing land with another group. It was a good situation, but we wanted our own place. We went to Idaho because we'd heard there was cheap farm ground.' Gloria put her fork down. 'Please tell your wife that she is an amazing baker. These sweets are heavenly.'

'I certainly will,' Otto said, wondering if Gloria was trying to avoid a conversation with any depth. He looked at Gideon and said, 'Do you mind my asking what made you start the group, back in your Georgia days?'

Gloria wiped her mouth on a napkin and settled back into

her chair. She appeared to be pulling back to allow her husband to take center stage. Otto thought Gloria had the kind, matronly bearing of a mother whose kids had given her endless sorrow through the years when all she wanted to do was love them.

Gideon cleared his throat. 'I suspect that you just might understand our beginnings, and even support our beliefs. We were early critics of technology. I've been warning people for many years that we're giving away our privacy to anyone who wants it, from the government to companies making money off our information. We have cameras on every corner filming our actions, people wearing cameras attached to their eyewear and clothing. People want to catch every word on tape, both private and otherwise. People recording what you say and then posting it for the world to hear.'

'Some people say, if you're not doing anything wrong, why does it matter if someone takes a video?'

Gideon pointed a finger at Otto. 'You don't believe that for a minute. How many people in the past few years have lost their job, their families, their government positions, because of some remark they made without thinking? There was a judge who faced scrutiny over something he wrote in his college yearbook decades ago. Do you really want every conversation you have reportable to the world? And the same with your medical records, your voting records, your financial statements? All this information is available for anyone who wants it.'

Otto nodded, agreeing with most of what he was saying.

'And here's the other problem,' James said. 'You can say something today that's not offensive. But twenty years from now, when society's norms change, that something you said that was posted on social media might be extremely offensive. Might keep you out of a job or get you fired. It's happening all over the country.'

'So what do The Drummers intend to do about it?' Otto said.

'We refuse to participate,' Gideon said. 'We've removed ourselves from the media as much as possible. Do you know the monumental task it is to get false information removed from the internet? If it's not porn or a copyright violation you're basically screwed. We're talking court orders. And even if you get the courts involved it can take years and thousands of dollars in attorney fees. And then the misinformation just comes up again elsewhere. People make up lies and slander your name for no reason.'

It was all Otto could do to keep from bringing up the fact that Gideon had posted horrific things about Josie on the internet and had done nothing to set the facts straight now that he was blaming the girl's death on one of his own members.

'Everything changed for us in Idaho. Gideon was a civil rights leader back in our early days. He was always one to stick up for the underdog. Then, in Idaho, we came up against a group of people who made up terrible lies against us,' Lydia said.

'Mostly against Gideon,' James said, 'but they said terrible things about us all. They claimed Gideon was abusing kids. Taking on child brides. That we were all sharing wives and kids and that kind of nonsense.'

Otto watched Gloria's demeanor change from warm and friendly to quiet and withdrawn. She stared down at her plate and said nothing as James talked on about one of the members leaving with her kids and stirring up trouble. 'She filed a complaint with Child Protective Services and it turned into a two-month investigation that was devastating to everyone.'

'And nothing ever came of it,' Gideon said. 'It was sour grapes by a woman with an axe to grind.'

Lydia laid her hand on top of James's arm and said, 'We had good times there too. It wasn't all bad.'

James glared at his wife and stuffed pizza in his mouth in an apparent effort to stop talking.

'What is your role in the group?' Otto asked Gloria.

Gloria smiled at his question, apparently glad to change the conversation.

Lydia interrupted before Gloria could speak. 'I'll tell you what her role is. She's the glue that holds everything together. Gideon is the leader, but Gloria makes sure bills get paid, people's medical issues are taken care of. You know how hard it is taking care of a family of four, imagine taking care of a family of twenty or thirty.'

'I never had kids of my own, so when Gideon started his crusade, I was happy to take in anyone who needed a place to stay and a family to call their own. The more the better.' Gloria stood from her chair. 'I'm sorry to cut our meeting short, but I need to check on Charlene. It's been a terrible stress today for us all.'

Otto thanked her and got up to throw his trash away and scan the room. He watched three teenage kids sitting at a table together. The two boys appeared to be teasing a younger girl who was trying to ignore them. Another small child was throwing a temper tantrum while a tired woman watched, saying nothing. It resembled a hundred other family gatherings, and made Otto reflect upon the secrets that people held deep inside while carrying on outwardly as if all was normal.

It still mystified him why parents would join such a group. He found it easier to imagine a single parent, like Charlene, wanting to join because of the help the group might provide. But there were also two families with a mother and father and their two kids in the group. He just hoped wherever the families landed, that they would find counseling for the kids. Two young women dying under the same roof within a day of each other would be emotionally traumatizing for anyone, and he hoped the parents were aware enough to understand that fact.

FIFTEEN

After a mostly sleepless night, Josie was up before five the next morning and at the office with a packet of stale donuts by six. She found an envelope with her name on it lying on top of the stacks of file folders on her desk. She opened it and found a handwritten note that said:

> Josie,
> It's been a tough week. Let's discuss the case over a homemade dinner tonight at 6:00. My place. Just let Helen know if you can't make it.
>
> Hang in there,
> Simon O'Kane

She sat down at her desk and reread the note several times, trying to figure out his angle. It didn't sound as if he was asking her on a date because he had involved his secretary, Helen. Maybe he had specifically used Helen's name to make it clear that it *wasn't* a date. And then she wondered what she thought about a date with Simon. Aside from the fact that he was her supervisor and the newly elected mayor, he was attractive, intelligent, and she was certain he came with quite a backstory.

Josie folded the note and slipped it into her pocket, forcing herself to put her personal thoughts aside for the pile of work in front of her.

As she made her way through a dozen phone messages, she came across two from Mark Davis, her FBI contact from the counterterrorism division. The first had come in at 9:00 a.m. the day before, and asked her to return his call when she got a minute. The second message, received later in the day, had asked her to call his cell immediately.

At six-thirty she called and he immediately picked up.

'Did I catch you eating your breakfast cereal?' she asked.

'I'm already on the subway, two cups of coffee down. Hang on.'

Josie listened to the jostling of people in the background, doors opening and closing, and next exits being announced. He finally came back on the phone and said, 'You sent me down the rabbit hole on this electric grid situation.'

She put him on speakerphone so she could type notes while he talked. 'I figured you were calling about The Drummers and the two shootings,' she said.

'I've been following the news on that too. Suspects?'

'Several, but we're waiting on the autopsy and ballistics.'

'That's actually not why I called. We've got bigger issues.'

'Bigger than two murders in a town of 2,500 people?'

'Hear me out and then you decide. I used some connections to get me in contact with an agency lead at the Department of Energy in DC. I explained to him what happened in West Texas, and my own concerns about the EX-Sovereigns. He wasted no time. He put me in contact with a guy named Jason Castro who works at DOE's Integrated Joint Cybersecurity Coordination Center. He was well aware of the EX-Sovereigns. He says they've made it their mission to map the electric, oil and natural gas networks across the US. He believes they have a plan to take down the system, but we only know bits and pieces about the when and how.'

'I assume this is somehow connected to The Drummers?'

'Yes. The EX-Sovereigns group has taken a page out of the cartel handbook. They're organized like a paramilitary group, with small factions all over the US.'

'What the hell? Why haven't we heard about this?' she asked.

'Because most of the groups are small and they're infiltrating remote areas to set up compounds where they can organize with the least amount of outside intervention. From what Jason says, the EX-Sovereigns target these small groups and lure them in with money and the promise of power. They make them legitimate and give them enough money to keep their mission alive. The EX-Sovereigns couldn't care less about the mission of the splinter groups; they're paying to get their own priorities pushed forward. That's how the cartels have taken over Mexico. They go into the small communities and act like Santa Claus.

They build schools and hospitals and provide food and clothing to these desperate people. The communities then become dependent on the cartels who are supporting them. This national group is doing the same thing with these splinter groups across the US.'

'You're saying the EX-Sovereigns are funding The Drummers?'

'Yes. Jason confirmed it.'

'One of our community members did some carpentry work for The Drummers last week. He said the leader's wife told him that they received money from a sponsor who was helping them keep things going. We had heard rumors that they were out of money.'

'Did she say anything else about who the sponsor was?' he asked.

'No, just a sponsor. One of the suspects in the murder of the girls said that the group came to West Texas with a few firearms. After the raid yesterday, we've catalogued over forty that I'm aware of. I'm sure it's more than that. My guess is those guns came from this group you're talking about.'

'What's happened to the group members since the two women were found murdered?' Mark asked.

'One member was arrested on parole violation.'

'And the rest?'

'We're paying for them to stay in a local hotel so we don't lose them for questioning.'

'You got a mess on your hands.'

'Agreed. I'm convinced Gideon Masters, their leader, is behind at least one of the murders, probably both. But with a church full of people worshipping him, it'll be tough to prove. I'll keep you posted.'

'Not so fast. I haven't even gotten to the big news yet,' he said.

She laughed and waved Otto over to her desk when he walked into the office. Josie told Mark that he was on speaker, and that she'd invited her partner to listen in to the conversation.

'No problem.'

Otto introduced himself and Josie briefly explained the connection between The Drummers and the EX-Sovereigns.

'When I talked with Jason,' Mark said, 'I explained that you'd had three substations attacked on the same day, and that it had taken out power over a large land mass but affected few people. He took the information you gave me and called back yesterday evening with an update. He said there were substation explosions reported in eleven different states on the same night as yours, spanning from Maine to Oregon. Each of the outages took place in remote locations that barely made news in the local papers. They took place with small energy providers.'

'What the hell?'

'He said he found out about it by sending a mass email to his connections in the energy field across the country. He received eleven responses. He suspects there could have been far more that weren't reported. From the eleven that were hit, about a hundred thousand people lost power because of the vandals.'

'It doesn't seem worth the effort,' Otto said.

'We believe their plan is to start small, train the troops, then go for a massive attack and catch everyone unawares. Bottom line, Jason said that if they take out our power grid, we're not even a third world country. We are effectively shut down.'

'How the hell do we combat this?' she asked.

'I'm sending a team to Artemis today. And I'm working with the Department of Energy to pull together cybersecurity experts to accompany us. But this is new. And it's going to take us time to get the paper in order and the right manpower. At this point, I have no idea what kind of charges could be drawn, but I know we want to talk to the leader and to the person who said the group has a sponsor.'

'That would be Gideon and his wife, Gloria,' she said.

'How much longer will they be housed at the motel?' Mark asked.

'We didn't give them a deadline because we're still questioning people. We can't keep them here with no arrest warrant. I've got seventeen people at the motel. And at this point, I don't have any evidence indicating that any of them were responsible for the murders. We can't hold them if they want to leave. And who knows where they'll end up.'

'We need to get charges filed.'

Josie laughed and gave Otto a look like she couldn't believe the conversation. 'It doesn't work that way,' she said. 'There's no way our prosecutor is going to detain these people just because we don't want them to leave before the feds get here. That's just not going to happen.'

He was quiet for a moment before speaking. 'Have you heard the term "cascading failures"?'

'No, but it doesn't sound good,' she said.

'In this instance, it's referring to what happens after a catastrophic power outage. It's when the backup resources start to fail. Supply chains are exhausted. It's not just that we won't have lights and heat and cell phones. Those backup generators everyone counts on are powered by gas, which is temporary without a supply chain. We lose water, wastewater treatment, banks would go down, no fuel for transportation, hospitals and nursing homes at a standstill.'

'OK, Mark. I understand what you're getting at, but it doesn't change the way the legal system works. You know I can't just detain someone because the feds want to talk to them.'

'Give me your timeline,' he said.

'I'm meeting with the two detectives from DPS at nine this morning. We'll be splitting up the members for a second round of interviews. It will take most of the day. I'm guessing most of the members will be here through tomorrow, but I have no way of knowing for certain.'

Otto said, 'My feeling is we'll have the opposite problem. They're staying free of charge in our local motel. We'll end up evicting people before it's over with. I doubt many of these people have anywhere else to go at this point.'

'Unless they're guilty of murder,' Josie said.

'Or they think the feds are chasing them,' Mark said.

'Am I free to share this information with our two DPS officers? I think we could try and work the electric grid into the questioning.'

Mark said nothing.

'We'll be subtle with questioning, and only bring it up if it makes sense in the context. Otherwise, if it takes you longer to put your team together than you'd hoped, we could lose them altogether.'

Mark emailed Josie several links that helped explain the electrical grid and the vulnerabilities that he had been describing.

When Troopers Downey and Townsend arrived at nine, Josie explained the details she had learned from Mark, leaving both officers shaking their heads in disbelief.

'Why haven't we been planning for something like this?' Downey said. 'We plan for hurricanes and floods and fire. But the biggest threat to our entire nation's safety, and we put our heads in the sand?'

'From what I gather, it's mostly a lack of communication among the various organizations. We want autonomy in our states and small towns, but then we lose the federal oversight.'

'I'm still trying to wrap my head around this,' Townsend said. 'I don't get how a handful of explosions could take out our electric grid across the entire country.'

'It's because there are just a few major backbone power lines that cross the country, and powerful transmission lines that run through large regions that connect us all. Then there are the small substations and branch lines that fill in all the gaps. Those lines connect to a lot of different electric companies. These producers then buy and sell the electricity from each other to balance out the needs of the country. And because we don't have places to store excess power, we have to basically create the exact amount of electricity that's needed across the country at any given time.'

Townsend looked at Downey, his expression incredulous. 'How can we know nothing about how something we use every day is produced?'

'It gets better,' Josie said. 'There are people whose job it is to balance out the electricity being produced with our hourly needs. So when there's a failure from one provider, they try to draw from others. Transmission lines overload and shut down, and it causes a cascading effect. I read that back in 2003, forty-five million people in the US, and ten million people in Canada, lost their power in a large-scale blackout. It wasn't malicious, but it isn't a stretch to imagine how a massive outage could happen if smaller outages occurred simultaneously across the US. And we didn't even get into the use of EMPs that could completely destroy the power grid.'

'What's an EMP?' Otto asked.

'Electromagnetic pulse,' Downey said. 'It's a pulse of energy emitted from a nuclear blast that fries electronics from miles away. The feds have been worried about that kind of attack for years. China, Russia and North Korea are developing the technology.'

'Let's keep this grounded to right now,' Otto said. 'So this group, the EX-Sovereigns, have already carried out one small-scale round of outages. Does anyone have any indication what's next?'

'No. This new information just came together in the past two days. The problem is that we have this giant grid that's connected for brokering the power, but there are hundreds of companies involved. So when we got hit in West Texas, our priority was getting the substation repaired, not trying to figure out if anyone else got hit. This may not even be the first time this has happened. This could have been in the works for months.'

Townsend leaned back in his chair and rubbed at the stubble on his cheeks. 'I feel like I got dropped into the middle of a sci-fi movie set. With technology as sophisticated as it is, I can't imagine how we've let this happen.'

'This is why Mark wants a team here immediately. He's hoping one of The Drummers can provide some clue to their connection with the EX-Sovereigns. It could be a huge break-through.' Josie held up a plastic bag to show Downey and Townsend. 'These are bullets we retrieved from the substation when the transformers were shot out. Mark asked if you could rush ballistics.'

Otto interrupted, 'I got a message from the sheriff in Presidio County this morning. They did find spent casings at both of their substations that were hit. I'll ask Roy to send a deputy over to pick them up first thing. We need them processed too.'

Josie looked at Townsend. 'If we get a match to one of the guns you seized from the church, it'll make the federal charges a lot more enticing to a prosecutor.'

'Especially if the gun sale is traced back to Mexico,' Otto said.

Townsend nodded. 'I'll get them submitted first thing. If we get domestic terrorism to stick, you could end up with the whole lot of them facing charges.'

'I'm guessing we'll have the bullet from Mandy Seneck's body this morning as well. The coroner said he hoped to finish the girl's autopsy last night. Can you get that bullet to ballistics as well?' she asked.

'Sure thing.'

Downey was flipping through his notes. 'Gideon Masters has a record so his prints are on file. Didn't somebody say Leon was in the military?'

Josie nodded. 'The Marines. He was in Iraq.'

Downey shut his notebook. 'Then his fingerprints are in IAFIS. I'll track them down.'

'How do we handle talk of the electric grid and the EX-Sovereigns during interviews today?' Otto asked.

'Let's start with an interview schedule, and then come up with a set of questions. Mark stressed that we don't want to scare people into running before he gets his team down here.'

By ten o'clock they had made a list of the information they hoped to gain from each witness, and split up the interviews amongst the officers. They agreed to leave notes on Josie's desk by the day's end, which she planned to review for a summary meeting the following morning at 9:00. After determining the list of focus questions and the location each officer would be using, Josie told Otto she would be at the motel within the hour to start her interviews.

She had spent the majority of her time at the bank over the past couple of days and needed to start her interviews with a better feel for the crime scene.

SIXTEEN

Josie stepped outside the police station and stood on the sidewalk smiling up into the sunshine. The cold spell had finally broken, and a balmy seventy-degree bright-blue-sky day had moved across West Texas. She slipped her keys in her pocket and opted to walk.

Between the beautiful weather, the restored hot water and lights, and the drama at the church coming to an end, people were stepping outside without coats, and running errands with smiles and waves. Just past the courthouse Josie ran into Rubin Ortega, affectionately called Happy by everyone who knew him, wearing shorts as he delivered the mail on foot. He was the only person Josie knew who could whistle and smile at the same time.

Pleased to see him away from the postmaster, she waved him down and chatted a moment about the beautiful weather.

'Have you delivered to The Drummers at the church yet?' she asked.

'Not yet. Next block up.'

'They're all staying at Manny's right now. How about I deliver their mail to them? I'm headed that way.'

He grinned and wagged a finger at her. 'You know I can't do that. Even for my favorite police chief.'

She grinned too and considered him for a moment. 'Would you show me how you organize the mail in your bag?'

He narrowed his eyes at the odd question.

Josie pointed to his bag. 'First, you put the mail in order at the post office. Correct?'

He opened the bag and looked down in confusion.

'And the mail is organized by address, so this must be a batch for 112 Carlos Street. The next batch would be 115 Carlos Street.'

He nodded his head, and absently pointed to the batches of mail for Carlos Street that she was referring to.

'Then, after Carlos Street, you cross over to Tenth Street.' Josie pointed down the block to Tenth Street, where the church was located.

Finally understanding what she was getting at, he smiled and nodded in exaggerated understanding. 'Yes, you have the hang of it. See, here is the section for Tenth Street. For example, here is the mail for 210 E. Tenth St.' Josie knew 210 was the street number for The Drummers. He flipped through each piece of mail one at a time, allowing Josie to glance at the addressees. One piece caught her eye. There was no return address, and the delivery address was handwritten to Gideon Masters. Most encouraging, the letter was postmarked from Wyoming, where Mark believed the EX-Sovereigns were located.

'Can you hold the mail at the post office since there's no one staying at the church right now?' she asked.

'That makes good sense,' he said. 'I've carried this pile of mail for them for the past week, hoping to catch one of them outside, since they don't use their mailbox. I'll be glad to get it out of my bag.' He winked and walked off, his whistled song trailing behind him.

On her way to the church, Josie called Mark and left a voice message for him explaining what she'd discovered. She suggested the feds file for the search warrant, hoping the federal request might speed up the process.

The chill in the dark foyer felt especially grim given the beautiful weather outside. With no heat or sunlight penetrating the windows, Josie guessed it was at least twenty degrees colder inside than out.

She kept her flashlight off, allowing her eyes to adjust to the gloom. Standing in the middle of the foyer, she faced the front door, thinking back to the morning of the arrest warrant and the men from The Drummers who had stood in that same place, listening to the police bang on their door with a battering ram, shining their flashlights from one to another in the dark, looking into each other's eerily lit faces, trying to determine what next.

To the right and left of the foyer were the two offices that Marta had mentioned. The door on the left had a hand-painted plaque that read, 'Enter. Peace Awaits You.' Josie gloved up and pushed the office door open to reveal a large wooden desk piled high with stacks of folders and scattered papers and receipts. A coat rack perched in the corner of the room with an old sweater and a bright pink jacket hanging from its hooks. She stepped behind the desk and saw where someone had nailed a piece of wood and a two-by-four frame around it. She could still smell the new wood from the freshly cut pine, and was certain it was Lewis's handiwork in Gloria's office.

Josie sat in the chair behind the desk and tried to imagine making sense of the disordered piles of paper. A checkbook was lying open on the desk along with a ledger detailing items such as cans of peanut butter and crates of paper towels. She flipped through the papers on top looking for anything that might tie the group to the EX-Sovereigns. Mark had asked to have access to all paperwork in the offices so she decided to conserve her time and leave the offices to his team.

Back in the foyer she stood looking out into the sanctuary of the church and felt the hair rise on her arms. Josie had only gone to church as a child when staying with her aunt. Her mother had sent her to vacation bible school each summer, and told her the basic bible stories around Christmas and Easter, but that had been the extent of it. Her aunt, on the other hand, had been a devout Methodist and had instilled a sense of holiness around religion that Josie had never lost. She had spent much of her life wishing she could cultivate that sense, but stepping into a church as an adult had always made her feel like a kid playing dress-up. She relied on inner prayer, and she knew God's presence when she felt it. But now, looking toward the cross hanging behind the pulpit, cast in thick unnatural shadows from the black paint covering the windows, she felt no sense of holiness. She had the urge to flee the building before walking any further into the darkness.

By the time a crime scene was vacated, it typically felt more like a three-dimensional puzzle begging to be solved than a place to avoid. Standing in a room where a crime had been committed usually left her senses alert, her mind soaking up every detail. But this felt like sensory overload, like she wanted to shut it down and walk away. A group of people who claimed to have some special vision for humanity had taken a holy place and dragged in filth and guns and hate and death. Josie didn't have the words to describe it, but she knew that her spirit wanted to avoid it.

She stepped into the room and looked up into the rafters, concealed by the lack of light. In the pews to her left and right she saw dozens of boxes and tubs with clothes strewn over the backs of the benches and in piles that looked as if they were being used as pillows and blankets. The building had the musty smell of old wood and dirty carpet, of people not taking care of the building or themselves.

Leaving her flashlight off, she stepped up past the pulpit and opened the door behind the altar that led to the Sunday school rooms. She imagined Leon and David crouched down in this spot as they listened to gunfire from the room just ahead. She knew that Gideon and Gloria's room was in the middle on the left. Using her gloved hand, she opened the door and was surprised to see sunlight. The cardboard that had been used to cover the window had fallen and was lying on the floor.

Her eyes were immediately drawn to the light pink stain on the wall to the right of the window. She stepped back into the hallway to see the corner of the room where Leon said he had seen Mandy sitting. Josie thought back to Alaina's description: walking into the room after hearing several shots fired, and finding Cia standing in the doorway, with Gideon leaning against the wall, pale and in shock.

Seeing the window, she better understood Leon's description of the room, and his assurance that there was no way for the police to have shot Mandy from the road. The window was simply positioned too high off the ground for a shot to have entered the room and traveled downward to where Mandy would have been standing. The relief Josie felt at seeing it with her own eyes was palpable. She took a long, slow breath in and exhaled, letting some of the tension from the past forty-eight hours exit her body.

Leon claimed to have been in the room to the right of Gideon's, arguing with David. David claimed Leon had left the room to check on Mandy. Josie turned her flashlight on and walked next door. The mats where the two couples had shared the room were still on the floor with their meager possessions stacked around the perimeter of the room. Josie picked up a picture frame with a photo of Leon and a smiling young woman whom Josie assumed was Cia. Her wide open smile lit up her face. Josie imagined the young woman trusting Gideon, thinking her life would have meaning and purpose with The Drummers. The terrible waste of a young life, and Josie's part in it – however necessary it might have been – left her feeling nauseous.

She used her phone to take photos of each of the six Sunday school rooms before she continued on to the kitchen. A large table made from twelve-foot planks of wood screwed into a base of industrial pipe looked long enough to feed all of the members at once. She snapped photos of the contents of the cabinets and drawers, and a schedule that hung on the wall designating the cooking and cleanup crews for the month.

On the right side of the room she found the door that led to the basement where the members described Gideon's meetings taking place. She opened the door and winced at the over-powering smell of kerosene oil mixed with the stench of a musty damp basement. The wooden steps creaked as she made her way down, ending abruptly in front of another closed door. She noticed splintered wood around the hinges where the door had recently been hung. The door didn't lock from the outside, but when she stepped into the room she found two massive dead-bolts, one near the top of the door, the other near the bottom.

She slowly panned the room with her flashlight, imagining the space filled with adults eager to learn from their leader. From the way members had talked about Gideon's sermons and speeches, and the self-proclaimed importance of the work they were preparing for, she had imagined a more dignified space. It was nothing more than a concrete floor with metal folding chairs facing a homemade lectern constructed from pallet wood. Plastic folding tables flanked the lectern, formerly stacked with guns that were issued to members. She tried to imagine the mentality of a person who would be locked in a filthy basement by a man who had enough money to purchase guns for his members, but not enough money for beds; a man who consid-ered himself a religious sage, but who had systematically destroyed the sanctity of the church he now inhabited.

The room was large, roughly twenty-by-thirty, stretching back underneath the sanctuary. Josie used her flashlight to poke around the perimeter of the room and could see where the SWAT team had searched through the boxes and tubs, seizing weapons and ammunition.

Josie sat down in one of the chairs and faced the lectern; what Gideon had surely thought of as his pulpit. She imagined the silver-tongued man quoting scripture to suit his needs, raising his fists and preaching against the government and the police state, and the hordes of people who were out to steal their free-doms. She wondered if the words he preached were so brilliant that she would have been moved in some way by their beauty. And then she stared at the place where she knew Cia's body had been found, clubbed over the head from behind with a metal pipe. Josie realized the only hope they had in getting Gideon's followers to tell the truth was to get them to turn against him.

When Josie arrived at the motel, Manny informed her that Otto had arranged the locations for the various interviews and had assigned Josie to Manny's office.

'And you're OK with me taking over your office for an hour or two?'

He lifted a hand dismissively. 'I've resigned myself to the fact that I've lost all control this week. It is what it is.'

Josie grinned and patted Manny on the arm. 'I'm sure your bonus check will be arriving in the mail any day. I'll text you when I'm finished.'

'That's fine. I'll be in my room next door if you need anything. And if I'm gone when you're through, just lock the door on your way out.'

Josie had selected Jackson and Thea Smithton for her two follow-up interviews. Jackson was the only other man in the group that Leon said wasn't issued a gun. Leon had intended to talk to Jackson to determine if he too questioned Gideon's culpability in Mandy's murder, but had been ousted before he got the chance. Thea made it clear that she 'hated' Leon. During her initial interview, she had told the police that she 'had no doubt' that Leon was guilty.

Outside Room 6 of the motel she heard boys fighting behind the door and a mother yelling for them to 'knock it off'. Josie had to knock twice to be heard, and then silence.

A woman in her thirties opened the door, looking as pissed off as she had sounded.

Black hair cut at a severe angle, several inches shorter on one side than the other, fit her bristly personality. She wore fuchsia-colored glasses and a bulky cable-knit sweater over a thin frame. Josie thought she could have passed for one of the Marfa artist elites.

Before Josie could introduce herself, the woman put both wrists out. 'Arrest me now. I cannot take this hotel room another minute.' Then she dropped her hands and turned to face her husband. 'Don't let them destroy the room.'

Her husband, who waved meekly at Josie, was slouching in a plaid chair tucked into the corner of the room. One of the boys remained standing in the middle of one of the beds while the other looked on from the floor where he was lying on his back.

The older boy on the bed yelled, 'Wait! Watch me do a guillotine leg drop on Billy!'

Without turning, Thea walked out the door and pulled it shut behind her.

Once they were seated at the small table next to Manny's kitchenette, Josie thanked the woman for coming and went through introductions and the formalities of recording the conversation.

'What information have you gotten about Cia and Mandy's murders?' Thea asked.

'Gaining information is why we're here today conducting interviews again.'

'It seriously can't be that hard. There's one person who makes sense. Track the *gun* back to him, and the *pipe* back to him, and you have your killer.'

'Who are you referring to?'

She rolled her eyes. 'As if you don't know. Leon Spinner. Would you like me to spell it too?'

'That won't be necessary. You suggest tracing the gun back to him. I was told that Leon and Jackson were the only two members who hadn't had guns issued to them. So how could Leon have used a gun to shoot Mandy?'

'First of all, it wasn't that Jackson wasn't *issued* a gun. He didn't *want* one. Just like Cia and Alaina *wanted* guns, but the rest of us *didn't*. Those of us who didn't want guns were conscientious objectors. We didn't see them as necessary. Leon was the only person who wasn't given a gun because he couldn't be trusted.'

'So how could Leon have gotten a gun to kill someone?'

Thea rolled her eyes. 'You've seized everything we have. You know how many guns were in there. He could have just taken one from the basement.'

'Were The Drummers all against guns when you started?' Josie asked.

'I have no idea. It wasn't something we talked about. It's not like guns were a part of how we identified.'

'I understand guns were a new acquisition. Why did Gideon decide to purchase them?'

'He didn't purchase them. They were given to us by a group who supported our mission.'

'But you said your mission didn't include guns.'

Thea tilted her head and pointed a finger at Josie. 'You're a sneaky one, trying to trip me up.'

Josie grinned at the characterization. 'I assure you, my goal isn't to trip you up. I want to find out what happened to Cia and Mandy. That is my only motivation. Once we find that out, everyone else goes home.'

'Fine. The guns didn't further our cause, they furthered theirs. I thought the whole thing sounded sketchy.'

'How so?'

She gave Josie a look as if she'd asked a dumb question. 'People don't give you something without wanting something else in return. Human nature. No way were those people giving us those guns without wanting something back.'

'Did you ever figure out what they wanted?' Josie asked.

Thea pursed her lips and stared at Josie, as if realizing she was offering too much information.

Josie willed the irritation she felt toward the woman to remain hidden and offered a kind smile. 'Thea, you say Leon killed both of those women. We have no physical evidence that links those guns to him. You've already said he wasn't even allowed to carry a gun. So help me understand the gun situation and the group that provided them. The more information we have to go on, the easier it's going to be to put a killer behind bars.'

Thea continued to stare at Josie without speaking.

'If we don't have the evidence to link to the crimes, then a murderer will walk away from here a free man.'

Thea leaned in slightly and lowered her voice. 'If I tell you this, will the others find out I said it?'

'Absolutely not. This is a confidential conversation.'

'You need to know that Jackson had nothing to do with it. He was the only man who had the guts to stand up to Gideon. He and I, and three of the other women, told the rest of the group we had no business getting involved with these people.'

'Did they have a name?'

'A guy named Robert Easterman came and talked to a few of us one night a week after we moved here. I found out later he'd already been talking to Gideon when we were in Idaho. It was Robert who found us the church for a dollar and convinced us to move out here.'

'For what purpose?'

'Gideon bought in because they hate technology. And the government. And the police. And you name it. It seemed to me that their main goal was to jam up everything they could get their hands on.'

'What was their actual purpose?'

'I don't know.' Thea rolled her eyes as if she was bored with the topic. 'They called themselves a militia. The EX-Sovereigns is their name. To me, they seemed like a bunch of grown men playing army for no reason other than they wanted to destroy things.'

'Were Leon and David a big part of this group?'

'Leon wasn't. That's the one thing I agreed with him on. He thought the group was dangerous and we shouldn't be involved.'

'Why would Gideon want to be involved with a group like that?'

'He talked about nationalism or some such crap. What does that even mean? He hates the government.' Thea smirked. 'The real reason is that Gideon knew the move to Idaho was a mistake and he was desperate to dig us out of the hole we were in. These idiots offered to pay him for helping them, and pretty soon we're all moving to Texas.'

'How much did they pay?'

'No idea. I didn't want any part of the details. Jackson didn't either.' She pointed her finger at Josie again. 'And don't you dare let on to Jackson that I told you any of this.'

'Understood. Let's go back to Leon. Do you know why he wasn't issued a gun?'

She laughed at the question. 'You need to ask that? He shot one of our members and killed his girlfriend. Gideon did not trust Leon, and rightly so.'

'If he wasn't issued a gun, how could he have killed Mandy?'

'Gideon's rifle was in the bedroom. Leon picked it up off the bed and shot her.'

Josie gave Thea a quizzical look. 'How do you know where the gun was located when you say Leon picked it up?'

Thea looked confused and started to speak, stopped, and started again. 'It's just a figure of speech. I mean, where else would the gun be in that room? It's not like there was furniture.'

Josie shrugged. 'There was a closet, the floor, a pile of clothes in the corner.'

'Are you serious?' She looked offended, shocked that Josie would make a big deal out of something she said. 'Fine then. He picked it up from somewhere. I don't know where he got it from.'

'But why? Why would he have shot her?'

'Some people say it was to make it look like the cops shot one of us. Like *you* shot Mandy. But I don't believe it.'

'Why?'

'Because that's not who Leon is. He's the least committed to the group, so why would he dream up something like that? But Cia? He was crazy about her. I think he shot Mandy to make it look like Gideon shot her. He hated Gideon because he thought he was having an affair with Cia. Or at least trying to. He was so jealous of Gideon and the sway he had over Cia. When all the shooting was going on, Leon knew people were hiding in their rooms, so he shot Mandy, then left Gideon to take the blame.'

'Do other people believe that as well?'

'I don't know. Some. You'll have to ask them.'

'Why would Gideon have allowed Leon to shoot her?'

'I have no idea. I wasn't there. I'm guessing Leon entered the room, grabbed the gun and did it before Gideon could even respond.'

Josie watched her for a moment but Thea's hard stare didn't flinch. 'From what I heard, even from other members, Leon cared for Mandy. A big brother relationship. You don't think it's odd that, basically on a whim, after the shooting started, Leon would run into Gideon's room, shoot Mandy, and leave? That doesn't seem odd to you?'

Thea's confident façade finally broke and she teared up. 'Everything about this seems odd to me. My family is devastated. I went from having the world figured out, to having it shattered overnight. I don't care who you put behind that gun, it's still going to seem' – she paused – 'odd, as you call it.'

Josie prodded Thea about Cia's murder but she hadn't heard the fight between Leon and Cia earlier in the evening. Thea and Jackson's bedroom was on the opposite side of the hallway, and at the other end. Thea said she and her husband spent most of their time with Annette and John, the other couple with kids, and didn't socialize very often with Leon and Cia because she thought he was 'an arrogant jerk'.

'What about Cia and Alaina? They shared a room together but it doesn't seem like they were good friends.'

Thea smirked. 'It was a contest to see who was Gideon's favorite. Who would be his right-hand girl. They both fell over each other trying to get his attention. I thought it was disgusting.'

'Do you think Alaina could have had something to do with Cia or Mandy's death?'

Thea frowned as if she'd never considered it. 'I already told you who I think killed those girls. I have nothing more to say.'

When she had finished, Josie stood from the table and thanked Thea for her time, following her down to the motel room.

Thea stopped at the door and gave Josie an irritated smile. 'Are you afraid Jackson and I might talk before you get the chance to grill him?'

Josie smiled. 'Interview tactics 101. Keep the spouses apart.'

With her hand still on the doorknob, Thea said, 'You know, we're good people. We were trying to do something important with our lives. And someone tore it all to pieces.' Her expression dissolved into tears as she pushed the door open.

Seconds later, Jackson walked out of the room looking worriedly after his wife, who motioned him toward the hallway without a word.

Josie introduced herself and shook his hand, but she could see his attention was focused on his wife's tears. Josie doubted she was a woman who broke down very often.

'I think Thea's fine. She's upset that things have turned out the way they have.'

He nodded once but didn't look convinced.

After the formalities, Josie started her questioning by asking him to describe his relationship with Leon.

He smiled slightly. 'I'm sure Thea gave you an earful when you asked her that. She can't stand him.'

'Why is that?'

'She won't admit this, but it had to do with our son, Jacob. He and Ringo were screwing around one day, roughhousing in the pews. Leon took out after them and Ringo got smart with him. Then Leon really laid into them, called them both a couple of smart-asses. Thea and I were in our room and heard the whole thing. Personally, I agreed with Leon. They were being a couple of smart-asses and deserved a dressing down.' He grinned and shook his head. 'But you don't talk to Thea's kids like that. She went tearing into the sanctuary and gave Leon forty kinds of hell for it. They had a couple of similar run-ins in Idaho, too. Nothing major. But Thea holds a grudge, that's for sure.'

'How about you?' Josie asked.

'Nah, no grudges for me. What's the point? Life's too short to waste it being angry all the time.'

'What do you think of Leon?'

'The main thing is, he's a soldier, and in my book that means something. He served our country so he deserves some respect.'

Josie nodded. 'It doesn't sound like you see Leon as a murderer.'

Jackson gave her a pained look. 'That's just it. I don't believe any of us would kill those two girls. I've lived with these people for years. We're good people! We care about each other.'

'Good people do bad things all the time. Jealousy, greed,

hate. Wanting money or power. Those are all pretty big motivators.'

'So you're saying we're all capable of murder? That's a pretty grim view.'

'Two young women are dead. Obviously someone in your group is capable.'

Resting his arms on the table, he put his head in his hands and was quiet. Josie allowed the silence to stretch out until he finally looked up at her with red, watery eyes. 'I have no proof. I can't accuse anyone in my family of something so terrible with no proof. That's all I have to say.'

'Who do you think killed Mandy? Just give me something to work with.'

He said nothing.

'You said you don't believe Leon did it, so who?'

He continued staring at the table, but she could see his resolve breaking, his shoulders sagging.

'Gideon was the only person in the room with Mandy. Do you think he killed her? Maybe someone found out he was having an inappropriate relationship with her. Maybe she threatened to tell someone.'

'That's a horrible thing to say about a man,' he said, his voice barely above a whisper.

'Gideon had already been accused of child molestation in other towns. If he thought he might face charges, maybe this was his way to avoid jail. Maybe Leon had told Gideon he was going to the police. Killing Mandy was the only way Gideon could ensure the police couldn't prove anything. And, in the heat of the moment, he wrongly thought that he could blame her death on the police.'

Jackson's face was pale and his lips had lost color. He said nothing but nodded slowly.

'That scenario makes sense to you?' she asked.

Jackson cried silently and continued to nod his head in agreement for a long time.

SEVENTEEN

Mayor O'Kane lived north of the mudflats – a dried-up lake bed that only reached lake status during the brief monsoon season in the fall. His home snugged up into the base of the Chinati Mountain range, just a few miles north of his millionaire pal and Artemis founder's home, Macon Drench. Like Drench's home, O'Kane's was a series of glass and charcoal gray steel boxes that fit around and into the mountainside. The severe angles of the home were in line with the sharp edges of the rock, and managed to blend more than clash with the rugged landscape.

Josie pulled down the long driveway that wrapped around boulders she assumed were native to the mountain but that looked so perfect as to have been helicoptered in by a landscaper. Aside from the deep green of the pine trees, color was mostly absent from the front of the home, and the rocks and dried grasses took nothing away from the mountains beyond. Josie stood for a moment taking it in, thinking he'd achieved both simple and breathtaking in one space.

He slid open a glass door that appeared to be the length of Josie's home and yelled, 'Come in! I'm in the back about to burn dinner.'

Josie stepped into the home and laughed before turning and sliding the door shut behind her. The effect was shocking. Color and textiles covered every surface, from luxe teal velvet curtains that framed the soaring windows to a purple tweed sectional that looked large enough to seat twenty. Pillows in every color and style were scattered about the room, some in large black leather baskets, others thrown about the sectional and several sling-back chairs. Vibrant oversized still-life artworks leaned against the walls and appeared to be waiting to find a permanent home.

'Josie! I'm in the kitchen. Come on back.'

She turned toward the voice and noticed the rich, sweet smell of roasting meats and vegetables. Down a short hallway she entered a kitchen that matched the color intensity of the living room, but sparkled with shelves of glass containers of every shape and size imaginable filled with dried goods and spices and liquids. And at the end of the room, a massive open-hearth fire roared.

In the midst of it, O'Kane stood above a sauce pot with his sleeves rolled up and his wild mane of gray hair looking more unruly than ever. He peered at Josie over glasses perched on the end of his nose and grinned. He reminded her of a grownup nineties rocker.

'I love to cook. I'm actually a damn good cook. But I'm also a mess. I could use a bit of training to be honest, but in the meantime, I'll wing it.' He pointed to a massive slab of wood that served as a kitchen island. 'Help yourself. Red or white. Pour me red.'

'It smells fantastic,' she said, finding the red among a mix of bottled vinegars and oils. She filled his glass and poured the same for herself. 'I appreciate the invitation, Mayor.'

'Oh, please. Not tonight. Simon will do, won't it? Come tomorrow we're back to Chief and Mayor, but tonight I could use a break. Yes?'

She smiled, glad to oblige. 'That would be nice.'

She watched him pinch spices and herbs from a variety of tiny glass bowls and snap them into the pot, stirring and tasting. 'Honestly, I'm thrilled to be mayor. I needed a challenge. But people lose their brains. I'm the same ass I was six months ago, so what's with the stuttering and deferring? We're a town of twenty-five hundred people. I'm not mayor of Houston.'

'You don't see it as a sign of respect?'

'For what? For getting a few more votes than the next guy? A pat on the back and a thank you sir is fine. But for god's sake at least speak your mind.'

'I'm free to speak my mind about department priorities and the bullshit of making decisions based on the politics of making someone happy instead of doing what's right?'

'That's fine! Please do.' He tipped his head back toward the cabinets behind him. 'Plates are in there, if you don't mind.'

Josie believed his sincerity, but doubted his follow-through.

She set the table as he pulled the tented foil off a standing rib roast surrounded by carrots and potatoes in a broth of red wine, rosemary and garlic.

'It's had just enough time to rest. A cut from the primal rib,' he said, carving her a slice and laying it on the plate with a ladle of jus and vegetables. 'Any cut of meat with the name primal attached to it is worth trying at least once.'

Josie refilled their glasses and they sat at a small kitchen table pushed against a floor-to-ceiling window that faced the mountains.

Simon pulled a crusty end from a loaf of French bread and held the loaf for Josie to do the same.

'What a great place to watch the wildlife,' she said.

'I sit at this window every morning and most evenings. Plenty of birds and such, but not the big prize. I've yet to see bobcat or mountain lion. Macon claims he's seen a mountain lion, but he's always seen one more or one bigger than everyone else.' He rolled his eyes and grinned. 'I suspect the old bastard saw a coyote and called it a mountain lion.'

They talked about the animals along the mountain, and then veered into local politics and the governor's race, until Simon became quiet and pushed his chair away from the table.

'This is a social visit, but one with an ulterior motive. I'm worried about you.'

Josie grew still. It felt like a very loaded statement and she had no idea how to respond. Worried about her ability to do the job, worried about her guilt or innocence? She opted for silence.

He sipped at his wine, taking his time. 'As your supervisor, I need to be careful. With every word recorded and lawsuits around every corner, I don't want to misspeak, which as a businessman, I rarely worried about. I have been informed by friends and family that I need to watch my tongue. Think before speaking and such. Don't tweet your temper tantrums was one astute piece of advice.'

Josie smiled but remained quiet.

'So here's where I step into it. I'm worried about your mental health.'

She choked out a laugh. 'Not what I expected to hear.'

'I'm serious. You are under a lot of stress from all sides. I looked into it, and I don't think we have any kind of mental health coverage as part of our health insurance plan. But it doesn't mean that it isn't important.'

She tilted her head. 'I guess I've not given it any thought.'

'That doesn't surprise me – thus the invitation to dinner. My father was a clinical psychologist in Belfast. I grew up in a family of mental health advocates and it frustrates me that there's still such a stigma.' He took a card out of his shirt pocket and slid it across the table. 'This is a therapist in Marfa with an excellent reputation. I would gladly cover expenses. I need a healthy chief.'

'A mentally stable chief?'

'Precisely. Do you have a support group here? Friends or family you can talk to when you get in a jam? A significant other?'

'My significant other works in Mexico, although he's not so significant anymore. We don't see each other often.'

He raised an eyebrow as if waiting for more, but she couldn't think of anything else to say about her relationship with Nick at this point.

'Dell keeps me grounded,' she said.

'The rancher, out on Schenck Road?'

'That's him. He says friends are a pain in the ass, but he's made an exception for me.' She grinned at the thought of him. 'And I have Otto and Marta. I'm fine. Really.'

Simon walked to the warming oven and retrieved an apple crisp, setting it on the counter alongside ice cream, bowls and spoons, dishing up the dessert in no hurry.

'Do you mind my asking why . . .' He paused, and sat back down with the bowls in front of them, raising a finger in the air. 'My friends think I pay no attention to what they tell me, but I do. Just this moment I came terribly close to asking how an attractive, intelligent woman would end up a chief of police in such a remote border town. But I caught myself and thought to rephrase. So, tell me, what made you choose law enforcement in Far West Texas?'

She laughed at his workaround. 'I imagine you have gotten yourself into quite a few jams.'

'I blame it on the soap my mother used to wash my mouth out with as a wee boy.'

Josie grinned at the image of the little Irish boy with the smart mouth. 'My dad was a police officer in Indiana, where I was born. He died in a line of duty accident when I was eight. My mom fell apart, or at least lost her ability to mother. I guess I went into law enforcement in part because I saw so much chaos growing up that I just wanted to stop it, or at least control it.'

'And do you think you've done that?'

She laughed. 'Not even a little. I've learned that law enforcement does very little to stop crime. We pick up the pieces after it happens. Families and communities and churches, and maybe even politicians have to make the changes.'

'Ah, so it's not the fault of the cops, it's the fault of the politicians?'

'Then let's blame the parents.'

'Makes more sense than blaming me.'

'And what about you? How does a millionaire tech guru end up in a town with the worst cell phone service in all of Texas, tackling border issues most of the population can't even fathom?'

'I'm from Northern Ireland. We know a thing or two about border issues. Are you too young to remember the IRA and the reunification of Ireland?'

'"Sunday, Bloody Sunday?" Bono taught my generation about the IRA.'

'Ah, U2. I was born in seventy-two, so I grew up in the midst of the Troubles. We lived in Belfast, but when I turned fifteen my father moved us to the coast, looking for sanity. My parents became innkeepers in Coleraine.'

'Sounds quaint. An innkeeper with a degree in psychology.'

He tipped his head. 'Quaint isn't how I'd categorize my childhood, but it wasn't bad. More chaotic than quaint, but they made a decent living. My mother was schedule obsessed and yet my brother and I were still left on the curb multiple times because she was off on some errand.'

'What made you come to the US?'

'College. And then a job. And then a girl. And then twenty

years went by and Ireland is now my childhood, and the US is my home.' He shrugged. 'No grand plan. It just happened.'

Josie stood and they cleaned the kitchen together, talking amiably, and she realized how much she longed for a partner, a man she could go home to at night, someone to talk to and plan with, making dinner and waking up together each morning to face the day. She was tired of text messages and five-minute phone calls. She'd spent more time talking to Simon that night than she'd talked to Nick in a month. And when they were finally together there were apologies and guilt and regret instead of happiness. She was done.

On the drive home, Josie replayed Simon's comment about seeing a counselor and tried to accept it as he had hopefully intended it. She wouldn't think twice about giving Martinez hell about going to see his heart doctor, but the mayor found it necessary to make dinner and offer a speech before even suggesting she might want to see a counselor for stress or depression. Her face flushed at the thought of it. Had he thought she acted depressed? Was she depressed? She had no experience with mental health issues – had never seen a counselor, had never talked to anyone about the experience of talking to a counselor, couldn't imagine how talking to a stranger would help her feel less stressed.

She took a last-minute detour and drove back into town to visit her mom. Talking about her mother with Simon had made her feel disloyal. She still felt a fair amount of unhappiness when she thought about her childhood, but she also acknowledged that her mother had done the best she could as a widow with a child.

She parked along the street a few houses down from her mom's and was glad she had at least finally hung curtains in the living room and actually closed them. The porch light was on, and the front door allowed her to see the living room was lit up. She hoped to find the front door locked. After being married to a cop, and losing him to criminals, Josie had always been appalled at her mother's lack of personal safety.

She knocked and looked through the glass in the front door,

and saw a Colt 45 sitting on the little table where her mom kept her keys. Her mother had never so much as touched a gun; she had made Josie's dad lock his in the safe as soon as he entered the house. Adrenalin flooded her system. She tried the doorknob and pushed the door open to find her mother tripping over the coffee table, laughing as she steadied herself, shocked to see Josie walking into her home.

'Well, shit fire. Look what the cat dragged in!'

Josie scanned the room for the owner of the gun, and stopped cold, her eyes settling on Gideon sitting in the middle of her mother's couch, his arms stretched across the back cushions as if he owned the whole damned place.

'What are you doing here?' she asked, not stepping into the room for fear that the anger she felt may come unleashed.

He grinned, self-satisfied, giving Josie a leisurely once-over before responding. 'I'm visiting this pretty lady. The question is, what are you doing here?'

She gestured toward the table. 'Whose gun is this?'

'Whose daughter are you? Lighten up, honey.' Bev laughed and knocked Josie on the arm. 'A man carries a pistol in his jeans, he has to set it down somewhere.'

Gideon leaned his head back and laughed. He finally looked from mother to daughter, wiping away fake tears. 'I see it now. The resemblance. Two beautiful women.'

Josie's mom screamed and laughed, slapping her thighs at the comment, which held no humor.

'What are you doing here?' Josie repeated. She noticed his Jerry Garcia hair had been washed and styled since she'd seen him last, and he wore a pink Oxford cloth shirt, unbuttoned far enough to see gray chest hairs curling around a gold chain, circa 1980s. She fought back a gag reflex.

'I stopped by to give your mother a quote on some house repairs, and she was kind enough to invite me over for cocktails. So I'm taking up your advice. I'm getting friendly with the locals.' He winked at Josie and tipped his glass at her.

She took a step toward him, her right hand settling on the butt of her holstered gun. 'Get the hell out of this house, you son of a bitch.'

'Hey, now. Wait a minute.' Bev looked from Gideon to Josie with the glassy, wide-eyed look of a drunk confronting conflict. 'Let's everybody calm down.'

Josie stepped in front of Gideon, grabbing his glass and sloshing alcohol down the front of his shirt. 'Get out. And if you come near my mother again, I'll have you in lockup before the day is out.' She set the glass down on the table and leaned in toward him before he could stand. 'Or I'll just meet you in the street and pistol-whip the worthless life out of you, while everyone in Artemis turns their heads and walks away.'

Gideon stood slowly from the couch and kept his eyes on Bev. 'I'm so sorry this lovely evening had to come to an end like this. Your company was divine, sweet lady.'

Once he had gone, Josie stood with her hands on her hips, looking at the floor, trying to get her temper in check before she faced her drunk mother. She had played out this scene too many times to count: as a kid being told she needed to spend the night at her neighbor's house because her mom had 'man plans'; graduating high school and leaving for the police academy only to get a call from a bartender needing a driver for Ms Beverly; then leaving Indiana in search of a quiet place in the world, finally free from the drama of family, only to receive the call from her mother to say she thought they should reconnect. When Josie had found Artemis, her refuge, however screwed up it might appear to the outside world, it had quickly become home to her. And now her mother was here, dragging her through the same shit memories she'd escaped. And here she was looking down the barrel of a rum bottle into her mom's crazy life. Welcome home, she thought.

'Why do you have to be so rude to people?' Bev said, swaying as she poured the rest of the bottle of flavored rum into her empty glass. 'Do you know what a bitch you look like to the rest of the world? That man wasn't hurting anything. He offered to fix that gutter hanging on the side of my house for free. You probably screwed that up for good.'

'Why would you invite him here?' Josie was so angry she had to stop to steady her voice. 'Two women were murdered in that church, under his watch. And you invite him over to get drunk in your living room? What the hell is wrong with you?'

'You didn't arrest him! He's obviously not the one who killed them or he'd be in jail!'

'You think guilty people don't walk the streets?'

'Well, if you'd actually talk to me every once in a while, maybe I'd know that.'

'I have a job to do. I'm trying to solve the murders of two girls while my own mother entertains one of the prime suspects in her home.'

Her mom crossed her arms over her chest and looked like a petulant child. 'Then you should have told me.'

'The man you invited into your home accused me of shooting that girl at the church. You sent me the Facebook post where he called your own daughter a murderer.' Josie lowered her voice to barely above a whisper. 'How could you invite him into your home knowing he spread those lies about me?'

Bev's expression faltered. 'I asked him about that first thing. He said he felt terrible about it when he realized that one of his own members had done it. He thought it was a stray bullet at first and it had to have been from the police. But then when he realized what had happened, they turned that man in. He feels terrible about it.'

Josie closed her eyes for a moment, trying to remain calm. 'Gideon was in the room with that girl. If Leon shot her, like Gideon now says, he would have seen it and never suspected me. Gideon never thought that a stray bullet hit her. One of those members shot that girl, stood four feet from her and pulled the trigger. I believe Gideon is a murderer, and I'm doing everything in my power to prove it. And you invite him into your home to make him cocktails.'

Her mother looked shattered. Josie turned, unable to carry on a conversation with her. 'Lock the door behind me. And do not let him in ever again.'

EIGHTEEN

Josie got home and washed up the few dishes in the sink, ran a dust cloth around her living room and started a load of laundry. Too wired to read a book, she stood in the living room struggling to come up with something to settle her thoughts. It was nine o'clock, and Dell typically went to bed at ten. She looked out her kitchen window and saw lights.

She called. 'You headed for bed?'

'Reading a book. Come on up.'

Josie hung up and tried to remember a time when she'd called Dell and he had not made himself available for whatever she needed.

She roused Chester off his sleeping mat in the bedroom. He pulled himself up one leg at a time to a sitting position so he could stretch his neck, pointing his nose all the way to the ceiling before slowly lowering his head. He could still get up in a hurry for a strip of bacon but he had aged over the past year, and the cold weather over the last two weeks had done him no good.

He plodded behind her to the kitchen, his nails clicking slowly on the wooden floor, clearly irritated to have been pulled from his nightly slumber. At the back door, Josie slipped her boots on and Chester turned his soulful Bloodhound brown eyes to her, questioning the late-night trip outside. When she put her coat on he began the dance, one foot up at a time, whimpering like a pup, sensing a trip down the lane to Dell's. The dog knew the difference between slippers and boots, and the latter always made for a better adventure.

The sky was clear, the temperature in the thirties. She thought about the areas of the country where cities had adopted policies to lessen light pollution. Looking in all directions, the only light beyond the stars came from Dell's little cabin up the lane. She breathed in the sweet smell of his wood smoke that mixed with the clear air, chilling the breath in her lungs. Josie loved the desert, but the cold winter air always reminded her of her dad back in Indiana. He'd loved winter, loved working the roads late at night after a deep snow had buried the city. He would come into the house off his shift red-nosed and smiling, trying to put his cold hands under her mother's sweater for warmth. She'd holler and smack his hands away, which only made him laugh and try harder. Josie could picture her little girl self, watching the commotion, laughing at their rough-housing, oblivious to the pain they would soon endure when he left them. She had so many questions to ask him, so many times she'd wanted his advice through the years. She knew that part of the emptiness that never left her came from his absence in her life.

Chester leaped up onto the porch and Dell, who must have been watching for them, opened the door and ushered them inside, grinning at the dog and following him into the kitchen for a treat.

Dell was in his seventies, though Josie had no idea what his actual age was. She'd never asked and he'd never offered. His hair was snow white and always neatly trimmed. He had the bearing of a former military man, disciplined and respectful, although he'd spent his life as a Texas rancher, taking over his parents' ranch when they died young, both in their fifties, of similar heart conditions.

She left Dell in the kitchen with the dog so she could stand with her hands over the woodstove. There was nothing more delicious than the radiant warmth of a fire on cold hands and body.

'The tea kettle's hot. How about a mug of chamomile?'

'That sounds perfect.'

Once she'd warmed up, she wandered into the kitchen to drizzle honey into their tea cups after he pulled the bags out of the steeped tea. He opened a tin of shortbread cookies from the counter and she took two, more grateful for Dell's friendship than she could ever explain to him.

She sat on the couch and watched him pet Chester with his slippered foot as he described some obscure book by Dostoyevsky that he'd been reading.

'But I don't guess you came up the lane to hear about my books. What's got you dragging this poor dog out of bed so late?'

She took a deep breath and exhaled slowly. 'I spent the day working two unsolved murders, then had dinner with my boss who suggested I might want to see a therapist. I ended my day at my mother's house. She was drunk, entertaining my prime murder suspect on her couch while his gun lay on her entryway table.'

He nodded slowly. 'I'm guessing you exchanged words with your mother.'

'I lit into her,' she said. 'I dislike myself and my mother in equal measure right now.'

'You two seem about as opposite as two people can be. Sounds like you both need some ground rules if you're going to survive living in the same town together.'

'How do you write ground rules for crazy? It's like writing rules for a cat.'

Dell grinned. 'That's why I stick with cows.'

Josie felt her face burn in frustration. 'I'm serious! She doesn't get boundaries. It isn't that she's selfish. She'd do anything for anybody. It doesn't matter if you're a criminal or the president, she'd help both in equal measure. But she expects the same from everyone else in the world, and most people don't operate like that. So then she gets her feelings hurt.'

Dell took a moment to respond. 'My dad was a drinker. It was before the days of using the word alcoholic, but he fit the bill. I watched my mother yell, negotiate, cry. He was never mean, but he put the bottle before us. He felt terrible guilt over it, but he never could change it.'

'So what are you telling me I should do?'

'Oh, I'm not telling you anything. Just saying there's no easy fix. You won't change her, so maybe let her know what you can accept and what you can't. That's what I mean by ground rules.'

'Like quit harassing your neighbor at nine o'clock at night?'

'Time doesn't matter to an old man like me. You come up the lane day or night. I can't say that I'd extend the same offer to your mother though. That woman wore me out.'

'She's quite a talker,' Josie said, laughing as he grinned and sipped his tea. For a self-described hard-ass who claimed friends were a pain, he was one of the kindest men she'd ever known.

'What's the latest on your Drummer case? Any closer to figuring out who killed those two girls?'

'You'd think with a limited number of suspects that narrowing it down would be easier, but it seems like all we do is talk. And then we've got this group called the EX-Sovereigns messed up in it.'

Dell nodded. 'Ned Bates got mixed up with them for a while. Said they were a bunch of lunatics and cut ties.'

Josie grinned and shook her head. She should have come to Dell from the beginning. For a man who kept to himself, he always had his finger on the pulse of the town.

'You're saying Ned was a member of the EX-Sovereigns?' she said.

'I don't think he got that far. He and some other ranchers went to a meeting or two with them. Maybe a year or so back.'

'Were you invited?'

'I was. Wasn't interested. Not my kind of thing.'

'What did they want with ranchers from West Texas?' she asked.

Dell waved her question off. 'Some nonsense about the government screwing the ranchers over. Taking their land from them. Ned's always pissed off about something so he bought right into it. I think the talk got crazier though. Those people wanted us to take up arms and file lawsuits against the government. I think I got a flyer on my door about it but I just pitched it. I don't know. Talk to Ned. He's never shy about offering an opinion.'

At ten o'clock the next morning, Josie borrowed the mayor's Escalade to pick up Mark and his team at the landing strip outside of town. She had started the day with her own team, reporting on the interviews conducted the previous day. The outcome had been disappointing but not surprising. The most positive development had been members airing petty grievances about one another, allowing the officers to draw up a list of alliances and divisions among the members, a list Josie intended to exploit.

The helicopter set down on the landing strip, which was little more than a paved patch of desert with an airplane hangar at one end. Mark and two additional officers followed her to the waiting SUV. Mark introduced his team members as Shanita Carter, a cybersecurity expert with Homeland Security, and Allan Holland, a domestic terrorism expert with the FBI.

On the drive into town, Josie brought the officers up to speed on the investigation, and then said she'd learned that the EX-Sovereigns had also communicated with a group of local ranchers.

Mark asked Josie to arrange a meeting with Ned Bates, and as many of the ranchers as she could round up. He also arranged for Otto to accompany Allan to serve the federal search warrant for The Drummers' mail, and then to meet at the church to organize and retrieve the paperwork in the offices with a focus on anything that might tie them to the EX-Sovereigns organization.

At 11:00 a.m. Mark held a briefing for Josie's team in the upstairs office of the police department. Downey and Townsend were there, as well as Martinez and Philips from the sheriff's department. Josie introduced the federal team and explained they were in Artemis to share the information they had gleaned on the EX-Sovereigns, and what they hoped to achieve by speaking with The Drummers. Mark wasted no time.

'The sovereign citizens movement is centered around the belief that even though the members physically reside in this country, they are separate or "sovereign" from the United States. Because of that, they believe they don't have to answer to government authority, which includes the police, payment of taxes, the court system. Typically, the sovereigntist groups have been about harassing public officials, filing fake documents, threatening and impersonating law enforcement. But the EX-Sovereigns group has organized its members more like a militia. We have drone video of members training with weapons in ground combat techniques in a small community in Wyoming.'

'When did they organize?' Josie asked.

'They were founded in 2009 by a man named Hayes Oolitic, right after the financial crisis hit the country. His main argument was that the government bailed out the banks but they let homeowners lose their homes. Save the banks, screw the people.'

Otto nodded. 'Well, they've got a point there. It still irks me.

GM and Chrysler got a handout while my next-door neighbor lost his ranch over a bad loan.'

'It irked a lot of people. Hayes took advantage of the anger and started spinning tales about how the government was scamming US citizens to fund big business. It didn't take much to convince a group of disgruntled citizens that what he was saying was the truth. He also provided his members with instructions on how to get back the money the government was stealing from them. He showed them how to reclaim funds using Form 1099-OID.'

'Did it work?' Otto asked.

'For some it did. The IRS was so undermanned at that point that only a fraction of the people who were attempting the scams were getting processed. We have records showing that Hayes received over half a million in refunds over a two-year period. His wife received a similar payout. This attracted a billionaire oilman from Wyoming who claimed Hayes was brilliant.'

'And is he?' Josie asked.

'He's a smart conman, but brilliant is pushing it. I'd say more opportunistic. When the IRS finally caught up to his schemes he was prosecuted and spent two years in a minimum-security prison while his wife ran with the conspiracy theories and spread their word to smaller groups across the west. While her husband was in jail, Melanie Oolitic fell in with a militia organizer named Bobby Lee Green. He's anti-everything except guns. The FBI estimates that he has the largest private gun collection in the nation. He could outfit an army and send them off to war.'

'Where does his money come from?' Josie asked.

'Family. His mother was part of the Getty family and his father owned part of a publishing empire out of Canada. Bobby Lee has never done an honest day's work in his life. But he's rich and angry, with a rough charisma that apparently appealed to Melanie. When Hayes was set free, the three of them bought a ten-million-dollar estate in Wyoming and set about dismantling the United States as we know it.'

'How do you go from tax fraud to taking down the electric grid across the country?' she said.

'Hayes came out of jail with new contacts, convinced that the government had screwed him over,' Mark said. 'Here's my theory. Hayes is a pudgy, pale numbers man who garnered respect and attention through his intellect. When he got out of jail he was smart enough to know that Melanie wasn't going to leave the charismatic Bobby Lee.'

'Better to join forces than lose everything,' she said.

'So what do three wealthy forty-somethings do in a mansion in Wyoming, with more guns than they know what to do with? They come up with a mission to use them. Their basic tenet is: we are going to free the people from the shackles the government has put around us. And the electric grid is the visual representation of that. The grid stretches across the country, connecting every household and business, making us completely beholden to its power. Without the grid, we fall apart.'

'Their goal is to destroy the country because they think our government is corrupt?' Josie asked.

'Not destroy it. Tear it down and then build it back up with these splinter groups it's funding across the country. Groups like your Drummers will help tear down the grid, and then step in with their weapons and dogma to restore order.'

The officers in the room sat quiet, taking in the magnitude of the undertaking.

'That's a massive plan. How close are they to moving forward with it?' Downey asked.

'That's why we're here, hoping to get information from The Drummers. The EX-Sovereigns' approach has been brilliant, at least in terms of avoiding detection. These splinter groups barely get noticed. They move into town and typically stir up trouble before people get tired of the fight and dismiss them. They're harmless kooks. So when the substations get blown up, nobody thinks too much about it. They just want their lights turned back on. Sound about right?'

The officers looked around the room at one another with the unsettling knowledge that their own community had done just as predicted.

'What you described is exactly right,' Josie said. 'If the murders hadn't taken place, The Drummers could have easily set up a community in the desert, funded by the EX-Sovereigns, and we'd have gladly allowed it. People would have been so relieved to see them out of the church that they'd have helped them move.'

Mark ended the briefing by explaining that they planned to pressure several members, letting them know that the federal government was looking into domestic terrorism charges against some of The Drummers for their role in the two murders.

He held a hand up in response to the skeptical looks from around the table. 'Remember, we expect ballistics will tie bullets from a gun registered to a member of The Drummers to three substations in West Texas. That's a serious felony. And I've heard from several different sources that Bobby Lee has met with at least one member of The Drummers on two separate occasions. Linking our investigation to your two murders is a priority.'

'We appreciate hearing that,' Josie said. 'I was concerned that our investigation might get lost in the rest of the drama.'

'I assure you, we won't let that happen,' Mark said.

'We have everything we need for a conviction on both murders: the bodies, the location of the crimes, the murder weapons, timelines and a finite list of suspects. We just can't match the weapon to the murderer,' she said.

'What are your next steps?' he asked.

'My plan is to find the member most willing to turn on Gideon. Someone knows more than they're telling us, but no one is willing to speak out against him.'

'You believe Gideon murdered both girls?' Mark asked.

'I do,' Josie said.

He looked at Otto. 'You don't look so convinced.'

'I'm not. I think there are a number of people who could have committed those murders, including Leon, Alaina and even Cia, but until the evidence proves it, we're screwed. And I can't help thinking that if Gideon was the murderer, wouldn't he have fled as soon as he was able? Why stick around at this point to continue with questioning unless he knows he's not guilty?'

'For that matter, why stick around at all?' Mark asked. 'He knows he's a top priority, so why keep himself under the spotlight?'

'Because he loves the spotlight! This is what he lives for.'

Josie took a deep breath. She'd not planned on sharing her personal information, but they needed to know. 'I stopped by my mom's place last night to check on her at around eight thirty. I walked up to her front door and noticed a Colt 45 sitting on the entryway table. She hates guns so I entered the front door unannounced and found Gideon sitting on my mother's couch with a drink in his hand. I won't go into my mother's personal business other than to say she'd had too much to drink. My point in telling you this is to let you know that Gideon is playing games with us. Or with me in particular.'

Otto was shaking his head. 'That arrogant bastard. You should have called me.'

'He left when I ordered him out, but he clearly loved the interaction.'

'All the more reason to get him behind bars,' Mark said. 'What's the story with Leon? Is he still in custody?'

'We cut him loose yesterday, although he didn't seem too excited to be back out on the streets. He has no money, no family to call, he's lost his girlfriend to murder. He doesn't seem to trust any of The Drummers,' Josie said.

'They are trying to frame him for two murders he claims he didn't commit,' Otto said.

'Is he still in the area?'

'He's at the same motel as the other members. Manny had another guest vacate, so we moved Leon in.'

Mark raised an eyebrow. 'He's staying at the same motel where his accusers are staying? How's that going?'

'I've not talked to him since the move, but he's on my list. I'm hoping this all might shake something lose.'

'You don't think he'll take off?' Mark asked.

'I think he would have if he were guilty. But I don't think you realize how isolated these people are. When they left to join Gideon, they gave up their families and jobs and homes,' Josie said. 'Not only does he have no money, but he has no credit cards and no credit to get one. When Hernández told Leon he was free to go yesterday, his response was, "Free to go where?"'

NINETEEN

The most disturbing piece of information that the team gleaned from the Drummer interviews was that fifteen-year-old Mandy Seneck had been in Gideon Masters' bedroom at six o'clock in the morning when the police arrived to serve the parole violation warrant, and no one had a good explanation for why she was there, including her own mother, or Gloria, Gideon's wife.

Gloria claimed to be an early riser. She said she was in the kitchen most days by four in the morning to begin mixing up biscuits and bread for the day. Three other females in the group substantiated the fact that Gloria was up early most mornings working on breakfast. While no one could place her in the kitchen on the morning of the murder, it was no surprise given the chaos in the church that day. Gideon claimed that Mandy had come into their room 'seeking refuge' because she'd heard something that frightened her.

More troubling was Charlene's response to her daughter's absence from her bed that morning. Marta had conducted the follow-up interview with Charlene and said the woman started the interview in tears, responding as you would expect any parent to after the loss of their child. However, when Marta abruptly asked the question, 'Why was your daughter in Gideon's bedroom at six o'clock in the morning?', she looked shocked. Marta said she blinked several times, as if she'd never stopped to consider the question. When Charlene didn't respond, Marta asked if Mandy ever slept in Gideon's room. Charlene looked offended and said it was a terrible thing for Marta to have said. Marta tried to play it off as an innocent question, as if Mandy might have wanted to sleep in Gideon and Gloria's room because she felt safe with them. Charlene said yes, maybe that was why Mandy had been in there. She'd gone looking for help, or had needed something that morning and couldn't wake her mother.

To Josie's frustration, Marta had not pushed the questioning with the mother. In hindsight, Josie wished she had conducted Charlene's interview. As a mother, Marta tended to sympathize with parents, especially those with young kids or a troubled youth. Josie would have pressed the issue, asking the mother to elaborate on a possible inappropriate relationship with Gideon.

Josie moved all of her paperwork to the conference table in the center of the office. She stacked her notes in one pile, the police report and follow-up summaries in another, Marta's drawing of the church and Leon's sketch of where each member slept alongside. She looked again at the diagram she had drawn that outlined each of the members' major alliances, along with those they didn't like or didn't support.

The two married couples with kids, Jackson and Thea and John and Annette, seemed to have conflicted feelings about Gideon and Leon, although all four of them openly admitted that they had no evidence to support their feelings. John had told Downey during his interview that the two couples were trying to secure a place to stay at The Farm, a commune in Tennessee that was founded in the early seventies and was still active. John said their biggest hurdle was finding transportation for the eight of them. Josie looked at her notes and tried to imagine how four able-bodied, intelligent adults had gotten to a place in their lives where they had no home and no financial means to transport their family to a different state.

She flipped her notes back to Charlene and tried to imagine her current mental state. Josie didn't have kids, but it wasn't a leap to imagine the anguish and anger the woman must have felt over losing her only child. The shooting had taken place three days ago. The woman was staying at a motel with her daughter's killer, and no one was offering any information to help the police solve the murders. People walked around in this oblivious state of wonder, acting as if they weren't even sure how they'd landed on the streets of Artemis. How was it that Charlene wasn't losing her mind with anger?

Josie stared down at the sketch of the church, and at the names she had written in the boxes representing the members' bedrooms. She looked at Gideon and Gloria's room in the center on the west side of the hallway, and then at Charlene and Mandy's room located on the east side at the end of the hall. Directly across the hallway from Charlene and Mandy's room was where Leon and Cia stayed with David and Alaina. Josie drew a line to represent a door out into the hallway from each of the rooms and then went back to her notes.

After the gun shots Charlene would have been frantic about where her fifteen-year-old daughter had gone, and listening intently to everything that was happening. If David and Leon were in their bedroom opposite arguing, Charlene would have heard.

Josie didn't have a degree in psychology, and she acknowledged that she was lousy at cultivating healthy relationships with the people she claimed to love in her own life, but she did have a good feel for what made others tick. She felt certain that the police grilling Charlene would get her nowhere, but a little carefully placed peer pressure might help.

Leon stood in the shadows of his motel room watching people walk the sunny streets surrounding the courthouse wearing jeans and sweaters, no coats or scarfs, no more shivering from the freezing weather, and yet here he was, a week from Christmas, completely alone in the world. With his hands shoved deep into his jeans pockets, he imagined Cia moving up behind him, smiling as she slipped her hands along his sides and around his stomach, lying her face against his back. He imagined the soft heat from her body pressing into him, dissolving the anger and fear like she used to do.

When he'd first returned to Portland from Iraq and found his family gone, he and David had quickly fallen in with Gideon, spending long hours at the pub, talking about war and philosophy and the possibility for change in the world. It had been the first time in his life that someone had been interested in what he had to say. Leon began to understand his own feelings about the world, and realized he had a core set of values that he'd never put much thought to, and certainly never verbalized. Gideon helped him understand that the world was more than just cause and effect; to live meant understanding politics and people and religion, and all of the nuances that come with the issues of the day. Leon smiled at the memory, at how excited he'd been back then.

He and Cia had lost track of each other during his last two years in the service. But when he'd started the conversations with Gideon, he knew Cia would love him. He'd stopped at the apartment she was sharing with a girl she worked with at a beauty salon. Cia did pedicures and manicures for rich women. She was good at her job, fawning over the ladies, telling them how perfectly shaped their hands were, how soft their skin felt, how strong their nails were. And she meant it – she loved caring for those rich ladies, making them feel good. That was her purpose. Until she met Gideon.

The night Leon showed up at her apartment, she opened her door and burst into tears when she saw him, then wrapped him in a fierce hug and for the longest time it felt like she would never let go, like she would be with him, holding tight, for the rest of their lives. He knew without a doubt that there would never be another girl like Cia, that he would never know love like they'd had that first year when they'd joined Gideon and Gloria and followed them across the country to figure out life, and, more importantly to Cia, to make a difference in the world.

When they'd set out from Portland to Idaho, Leon had imagined it was how the hippy culture had felt in the seventies: screw authority and the bullshit rules; we're here to treat people right and enjoy the earth. Gideon had made it all seem so simple in the beginning.

'Life isn't hard when you boil it down to what matters. When you don't care about a bank account full of money, or a house filled with knickknacks. It all becomes clear. You get out and see the world, you meet people. You figure out that love of life and people are what matters. Not rules and useless shit.'

And that had become their mantra. Alaina had made bumper stickers which they'd started passing out to people that read, *No rules – No shit*. But what had started out as a mantra focused on avoiding asinine rules and collecting material things, had turned into avoiding government interference at all cost and taking no shit from anyone – whether it made sense or not.

About a year into their stay in Idaho, Leon had brought up the shift in philosophy to Cia and she'd laughed it off, telling him he worried too much about words and not enough about living. They'd had their own bedroom in a government-subsidized three-bedroom apartment at the time. The irony of them accepting public assistance while slamming the government was not lost on Leon, but the rest of the group had figured they deserved it. They used Leon and David's service in the military as a reason that the entire group should benefit, and that thinking had already started to irritate Leon.

Cia had understood his frustration and had borrowed a car and a tent from a woman she'd met at the library where she worked, and she'd driven them to the Salmon River for a two-night getaway. They'd hiked in the rugged Sawtooth Mountains and fished in the river for their dinner. Leon had fileted the fish and they'd fried it in an old cast-iron pan they'd bought at a secondhand store on the way to the mountains. It had been one of the best weekends of his life, and images of Cia in the sunshine, hiking up the mountain pass, had pushed him through many rough days, knowing they would eventually find that happiness once again.

Leon noticed the glint of metal in the sunshine and realized Chief Gray was walking across the street toward the motel. He had a fleeting thought that she was coming to offer him the job at the police station. He tried to imagine that that had happened. That he'd been able to escape the church and start a job, to clear his head. Would things have turned out different? Would Cia still be alive?

He was shocked to watch Josie walk straight up to his room and knock on the door. He glanced around, feeling the unreasonable stab of guilt that any interaction with a police officer produced in him.

He opened the door and she asked to come inside.

She sat in the one side chair at a small table next to the TV, and Leon sat on the edge of the bed. She asked how he was coping with the investigation, and what his plans were now that he was free to leave.

'None of us has any money. It's all tied up in The Drummers, in some account to help us buy property. I have one hundred dollars to my name. And that's because I held it back for an emergency. I honestly think I'm headed for a city with a homeless shelter so I can work fast food to save a down payment for an apartment. I'm so angry that I'm here. That I let my life turn into this. That Cia's gone.' Leon leaned forward on the bed and put his head in his hands for a moment before looking up at her again. 'I used to see homeless people in Portland. And I'd think, what's their story? How does a man with a clear head end up on the street? And here I am.'

'I'd like to see you stick around a few more days. I think it would do you good to see this resolved before you leave.'

He nodded.

'There are ranchers around town who are always looking for good help. You may be able to stay in a bunkhouse for six months and save up enough money to get a start somewhere.'

'That would be great. I'm a hard worker. I just need a start.'

'Hang around then. Use me as a reference. I'll check with some locals and let you know if I hear of anything.'

'I appreciate it.'

'I also stopped by to talk about the investigation. I know this is hard, but I'd like to talk this through again.'

'I just want this done. I want whoever did this to Cia and Mandy to pay. I want them to rot in prison. So if I can help, I'll do it.'

Josie paused a moment, still thinking through how she wanted the questioning to proceed. 'Let me ask you something. What do you think of Charlene? As a person, and as a mother?'

He considered the question for a moment. 'I'm not sure how to respond without sounding like a judgmental ass.'

'You don't need to try for tact here. I'm just looking for an honest answer.'

'She's not someone I spent much time with. She gets caught up in all the little shit and misses the big stuff. Like she'd be pissed off that someone didn't screw the peanut butter lid back on correctly, while her daughter is sneaking out of her room at night to screw Gideon. She was freaking fifteen years old! And you can't tell me that Charlene didn't know about it. But she has this way of acting oblivious to anything she doesn't want to deal with.'

'Did you ever talk to her about what you believed was happening with Mandy?'

'You can't! That's just it. I've never seen her have a conversation about anything important. It's all avoidance. And yes, once I did try and talk to her and she shut me down. I was like, hey, I think something might be going on between Gideon and Mandy that she doesn't feel comfortable with. We were in the kitchen at the time, and she laughed and said something about Mandy having a schoolgirl crush. Then she went to her room, saying something stupid about a timer going off.' Leon felt nauseous at the memory. 'This is all so messed up.'

'I'd like to use your room this morning, to question Charlene about the morning of the murder.'

'You want me to leave so you can use my room?'

'No, I want you to stay. Charlene basically sold you out, like everyone else, and I believe it was to protect Gideon. I think Charlene is devastated and confused. I believe that when I confront her about that morning, with you sitting here next to her, she won't be able to lie about it to your face. I'm hoping to catch her off-guard, and hopefully get at the truth. I basically just want you to sit with us during the questioning. Are you good with that?'

Leon shrugged. 'Sure.'

'Do the other members know you're here yet?'

Leon choked out a laugh. 'I'm hiding out in here like some caged rabbit, too scared to go outside. I walked down to the diner last night just before they closed so no one would see me. I can't take much more of this.'

TWENTY

J osie borrowed two chairs from Manny's office and squeezed them into Leon's small motel room. She wanted the three of them sitting at the table, uncomfortably close.

Charlene answered her door wearing a pair of faded jeans and a hooded sweatshirt with Smokey the Bear pointing a warning finger about forest fires. Her frizzy red hair was pulled up off her neck in a banana clip that looked to be straight from the eighties. She smiled when she saw Josie, then glanced behind her nervously.

'I'd have picked up better if I'd known you were coming by.'

'No need. I just have a few questions. Would you mind clearing up some details? I have a room set up for us.'

Her eyes grew wide and she looked around absently as if she were forgetting something. 'No, that's fine. You mean now?'

'Yes, just for a few minutes. You shouldn't need anything. Just your room key.'

Charlene disappeared into the dark room, leaving Josie standing outside. She finally returned with her jacket and purse, stuffing her key into her front pocket, mumbling something about losing it.

As they headed toward Leon's door, Josie noticed Thea standing in the window of her room, watching them pass. Once they were inside, Josie motioned for Charlene to sit in the chair with its back against the wall. Josie sat to Charlene's left. As she was sitting down, Leon stepped out of the bathroom and took a seat to Charlene's right, effectively hemming her in.

Charlene's expression turned from scattered to panicked at the sight of Leon.

'Hi, Charlene,' he said.

'Hello. I see you're back out then. That's good.' She attempted to scoot her chair back but it bumped into the wall.

'Charlene, I understand this is terrible for you to talk about, but I also know you want justice for Mandy. You want the person who killed your daughter to pay for what they did.'

Tears welled in her eyes and she nodded but didn't speak.

'I want to talk about the morning of the shooting. I need you to walk me through exactly what happened when you woke to noise that morning.'

Charlene looked at Josie as if she were setting her up. Josie remained quiet. Charlene glanced at Leon who said nothing, keeping his stare fixed on her.

'I don't understand. I thought you always questioned us separately.'

'Sometimes it's better this way. Tell me about that morning, everything you can remember.'

'Well, I don't know. It was all so stressful. I can't hardly remember any of it anymore.'

'Where were you when you first heard the banging on the church doors?' Josie asked.

'In bed. Sleeping.'

'Was Mandy in the room?'

'Well, I don't know. I don't think so, but it was dark so I couldn't see over to her mat.'

'Did you get out of bed when you heard the banging?'

'Not at first. I was scared. Gideon kept telling us the police were going to come for us. I just thought that it was coming true.'

'Did you turn a light on?'

'No, I was too afraid at first. I just sat there. I heard someone run down the hallway to the sanctuary where they were banging. I think it was David, and I heard Leon telling the girls to go to the basement.'

'By the girls, you mean Cia and Alaina?'

'Yes, Leon was telling them to go. I didn't know what to do so I just sat there, until I heard the gun shots and then I was terrified.'

'So, you heard gunfire, but you didn't get up to make sure Mandy was OK?'

Charlene's eyes widened, realizing she'd made an error. 'Well, yes! I did! I just meant at first I was so shocked and I couldn't see anything. Then after I got my bearings I was frantic. I called

Mandy's name. I crawled over to her bed and when she wasn't in it I just sat there, trying to understand what was happening.'

'Were there any lights at this point?' Josie asked.

'I don't remember. I guess there were flashlights. I could hear people talking. I called out Mandy's name but didn't hear anything.'

'Where were you at this point?'

'I was on the floor, sitting on Mandy's mat. I could hear Jackson yelling. And then I remember hearing David and Leon coming down the hallway and telling the women to get the kids and go to the basement. I heard Alaina and Cia go to Annette's room to get the kids, and I thought about going with them, but I didn't know where Mandy was. I was too scared to move. I called her name several times but people were running around by then. It was crazy and I called for Mandy but everyone ignored me. So I just sat there.' Charlene looked at Josie with tortured eyes. 'I just didn't know what to do.'

'While the women were getting the kids to go to the basement, what were the men doing?'

'They were in the rooms, with their guns. David was giving orders.'

'And David and Leon were across the hall from you? Did you hear them fighting?'

Charlene glanced at Leon, her eyes filled with the terrible memories of that morning.

'You need to tell her everything you saw and heard,' Leon said. 'Just tell her the truth. That's the only way we're all going to get out of this mess.'

'I heard you and David fighting about Cia and Alaina. About putting them in the basement with the guns, and how the women and kids shouldn't be down there guarding all the guns. I hollered across the hall to you, asking if Mandy was with you, but no one answered. Then I heard more gun shots.' Charlene broke down sobbing, lying her head in her arms on the table.

Leon brought a cold washcloth from the bathroom and a handful of tissues. Once she regained her composure, Josie continued quietly.

'When the men took the guns into the rooms to guard the windows, were the doors to all the rooms open?'

Charlene took a moment to respond, still wiping her face with the cool cloth. 'Yes, they were all yelling at each other, talking about what they were seeing outside.'

'So you could see Leon and David in their bedroom across the hall from you?'

She nodded.

'And could you see into Gideon's room?'

She closed her eyes, tears falling again. 'Not from inside my room. But Mandy was in there the whole time. I thought she was in there, but I didn't know for sure. I just kept calling her name.'

Josie waited several minutes until Charlene was done crying. She wanted her full attention.

'You originally said it was Leon who shot Mandy. But you saw that Leon was in his room when the shots were fired. Why would you blame Mandy's shooting on Leon, when Gideon was the one who was with her?'

Charlene sat in silence, shaking her head.

Josie grew frustrated with the woman's avoidance. 'Charlene, I need you to help me understand. Your daughter was murdered, and you'd see Leon sent to jail for her murder when you know someone else shot her. Don't you want to see her killer pay for what he did?'

She faced Josie, her expression angry through her tears. 'I don't know who killed her! People were telling me what happened. I was in my bedroom, terrified, with guns going off. People were yelling and screaming. And after it happened Gideon told me what happened. I believed him.'

'You didn't stop to question what he said? You didn't stop to think it couldn't have happened the way he said it did?' Josie said.

Charlene stopped crying and her body slumped back into the chair, her cheeks sagging, her eyes drained of emotion. 'He loved her. He said he had a special plan for Mandy. Those other girls were jealous of her, but I knew Gideon had a plan.'

'Who was jealous of Mandy?'

'Alaina and Cia.'

Leon choked out a laugh but said nothing.

'It was mostly Alaina. She bullied Mandy, would say mean

things to her about being a whore. It was terrible the things she said.'

'Why would she do that?' Josie asked.

'Because Mandy was his favorite, and Alaina knew it.'

'Mandy was fifteen!' Leon said.

Charlene looked at him with an expression that pleaded for understanding. 'You know what it's like to finally be chosen for something special? To have your baby chosen? I was so proud of her. And I thought he was going to help her. And then when things started to go bad I didn't know what to do.'

Leon banged his fist on the table and Charlene jumped. 'I told you things were bad. I told you he was messing with Mandy and you ignored it.'

Charlene shouted back, 'If what you said was true, what kind of mother does that make me?' She leaned her head back against the wall and moaned. 'Everything is falling apart. Mandy was all I had aside from my family here. David and Alaina are leaving now. I don't know what to do or where to go. I have no one.'

Josie waited a moment and then leaned into the table, invading Charlene's personal space, almost close enough for their arms to touch. 'Do you believe that Gideon shot Mandy?'

Charlene grew still again, avoiding Josie's stare, but she nodded slightly.

'Are you willing to say that in court? To describe how you saw David and Leon fighting in their room just before the second set of gun shots? How David left the room in anger and Leon remained? That Leon was in his room when the shot that killed Mandy was fired?'

Again, a slight nod.

Josie glanced at Leon who was staring at Charlene with no pity, just anger.

'What happened to Cia?' Josie asked, her voice quiet and as kind as she could muster.

Charlene looked surprised at the question. 'I don't know. I swear it.'

'Your room is right across the hall from where Cia was sleeping. Did you hear her get up the night she was killed and walk to the basement?'

Charlene stared at Josie and pressed her back against her chair, moving as far away from Josie as possible.

'Yesterday afternoon, I walked down the hallway into the kitchen and down the basement steps when the church was quiet,' Josie said. 'Those old wooden floors creak and moan. Someone had to have heard Cia walking down the hallway toward the basement. Mandy had been murdered, the police were surrounding the building. People weren't lying in their beds sound asleep.'

Charlene's face clouded with memory. 'I didn't hear Cia get up. But I do remember Gideon's door open and close that night. Because I woke up and my first thought was Mandy, and looking over to make sure she was on her mat next to me. And I remembered she was gone all over again.'

'I need you to think back to that night, to that moment when you heard the door open and close. What do you remember hearing? Which way did the footsteps go?'

Charlene's face was red and swollen from crying. Josie watched her stare vacantly at the washcloth on the table, concentrating on the memory, dredging up horrific details from a night she wanted desperately to forget.

'I remember laying there,' she whispered, 'listening to those steps go down the hallway, toward the basement. I remember looking at my little alarm clock on the floor and seeing it was two in the morning. And thinking how will I get through the rest of my life like this? And thinking how my poor innocent daughter would never know another day. And that I will rot in hell for eternity for what happened to my baby.'

'Does Gideon know that you saw Leon in his own bedroom when Mandy was shot?'

'No. The only person I told was Cia.' Charlene covered her eyes as the tears began flowing again. 'And now she's dead too.'

After leaving Charlene, Josie walked across the street and called Mark. She explained what she had learned.

'Mark, this woman knew her own daughter was being sexually assaulted and was almost certainly murdered by Gideon. And after she told Cia of her suspicions, she was murdered too.' Josie took a moment, still overwhelmed at what she'd learned. 'She's a monster. How could any mother allow this to happen and not do something? We were parked across the street! All she had to do was come and tell us what was happening, and Cia would most likely be alive.'

'We can explore charges against her,' Mark said.

Josie could hear from the tone of his voice that Charlene wasn't his interest. 'On top of that, David and Alaina are leaving. They both knowingly falsely accused Leon of murdering Cia. We need to bring them in again before we lose the chance. Do you want in?'

Mark sighed and swore under his breath. 'I got word from Downey that ballistics came back with a positive match. The gun with Gideon's prints was used to murder Mandy Seneck. Ballistics also confirmed that the gun that was used on your substation outside Artemis was also used on the other two substations in West Texas. The gun was issued to David Jonas. Purchased in Mexico from a gun buyer in Wyoming.'

'Was the seller in Wyoming EX-Sovereigns?'

'I don't have confirmation yet. I just talked to the judge about a federal arrest warrant while we get our ducks in a row. He knows the rush.'

'So let's bring them in.'

'No, I want an arrest and Miranda rights on David. I want everything that's said today admissible in court. No technicalities. I'll head that way, but I'm thirty minutes out. Grab them now before it's too late,' he said.

'I'm on it.'

David and Alaina sat hand in hand on the motel bed as Josie read David his rights. Alaina cried quietly, but David stared intently at Josie.

He frowned deeply and cleared his throat as if preparing to make an announcement. Josie got the feeling that they had been waiting for this moment. 'I know what I did was wrong. Gideon was screwing around with Mandy. I told him that he had to stop, that she was too young. He wouldn't listen to me though. He claimed they loved each other.' David shook his head in disgust, wincing at the words.

'David, I just read you your rights. You've been advised to wait until an attorney is present.'

He teared up, shaking his head. 'I swear to you, I was trying to help. Leon was ready to go on the attack, but I was trying to save us. I didn't want Gideon's screwing around to tear apart everything we'd worked toward.'

'You didn't think you needed to protect Mandy? A scared young girl?'

'I just thought if I could get Gideon to see reason then we could get back on track again. Then he came to me, the night before you showed up with the search warrant. He told me that Mandy said she was going to tell her mom everything. He made her stay in his bedroom that night so he could keep an eye on her.'

'With Gloria in the room?'

David frowned. 'She slept in her office. She and Gideon had a fight over Mandy, and she slept on a cot.'

'So Gideon was in the bedroom alone with Mandy?'

'Yes. Then when he heard the police at the door in the morning, he lost it. Mandy was in his bedroom, she was angry and crying. In a panic, he used the shots fired. He thought it would look like she was caught in the crossfire.'

'You do realize that the police didn't fire first? Gideon fired the first shot out of his bedroom window,' she said.

David didn't respond. He held the miserable expression of a person who knows he's in the wrong, and that his excuses aren't helping.

'Gideon admitted to you that he shot her?' she asked.

David nodded. 'Later that day. I asked him point blank and he said he'd had no choice. He said that Mandy and her mother were going to the police and they would destroy us all. He convinced me to make it look like Leon had done it. He assured me Leon wouldn't be arrested, but it would cast doubt. If the police couldn't prove one person over another then no one would be prosecuted.' He glanced at Alaina who was staring down at her hands.

Josie said, 'You were willing to help a man who'd molested and murdered a young girl walk free while you allowed a man you served at war with to go to jail?'

David opened his mouth then closed it, shaking his head, apparently unable to speak.

Alaina looked up, her expression desperate. 'We could have left. I tried to get him to just leave. We could have gotten money from Gloria and taken off for California. I have an aunt in LA that would have taken us in. But David wouldn't do it. He said what he did was wrong, and he had to pay. So he's turning himself in. Surely that makes a difference.'

David stood from the bed and remained silent as Josie escorted him out of the room to the car.

TWENTY-ONE

Otto followed Gloria back into the motel room following Gideon's arrest. Otto had developed the best rapport with her, and had convinced her that he wanted to help the remaining members get a fresh start away from Artemis.

When Mark's team had interviewed her, Gloria had given up almost nothing in terms of the EX-Sovereigns. Mark said that she had supported her husband one hundred percent, but that her responses had felt rehearsed, as if she'd been saying the same lines for fifty years. However, when Otto talked with her after the arrest, she broke. He convinced her that she could help Gideon the most by offering information about the EX-Sovereigns.

'Give us names and addresses. Talk to us about your records. This may be Gideon's only hope of any leniency.'

Gloria sat in the motel room chair by the TV for a long time, not crying, just staring at the floor, apparently weighing her options. Otto called it wait time. There were many awkward moments sitting with suspects and witnesses in silence, allowing them the time for their overloaded brains to process information. He'd found that silence could be a great motivator.

She finally stood and pulled two worn ledgers from under her side of the mattress. She handed them to Otto. 'This has everything. What they sent to us, contacts, addresses and names. My notes about their expectations. You promise me this will help Gideon?'

'I can promise you that without this, he has nothing. With this information, at least the jury will see you're remorseful and willing to cooperate and make amends. That's all Gideon can do at this point.'

Otto left with the information, knowing that it would do little to convince a jury of Gideon's remorse. He was certain that if the case went to trial, Gideon would grandstand and the jury would hate him, especially women and parents.

* * *

Josie was in the intake unit at the jail finishing up with David
Jonas when her cell phone buzzed. A text from Mark read:

> *At the jail. Otto got ledgers from Gloria.*
> *Going to question Gideon again about EX-S.*
> *Thought you'd want in.*

She found Otto and Mark in the observation room connected
to the interrogation room where Gideon was sitting with an
attorney.

'That was fast,' she said.

'That's what we thought. The attorney's known for working
with militia groups. His name is Evan Carillo.'

'He can't be long out of law school,' Otto said.

'He's older than he looks.'

'I can relate. I *feel* older than I look,' Otto said.

Mark grinned but let it go. 'He's represented several of the
homesteaders refusing to move off federal land in Oregon and
Washington. There's no doubt the EX-Sovereigns are footing
the bill. The attorney told one of the officers that he's been
staying in Marfa for the past two days, basically waiting for
the arrest.'

'Is he a nut?' Otto asked.

'No. And he's got a hell of a track record. I don't know if
he actually supports their cause, but he's figured out there's
some deep-pocket private funding and he's taking advantage,'
Mark said.

'So what's the plan?' Josie asked.

'You seem to push Gideon's buttons. Every time you've been
mentioned in an interview he blusters.'

'Glad to hear it.'

'I'll take care of questioning, but I'd like you to go in with
me. Feel free to jump in if you think something needs clarifying.
We're honing in on the Sovereigns. The ledger shows that
Gideon met with Bobby Lee Green at least once. We want to
know about the initial meeting and expectations.'

The fluorescent lighting in the interview room gave Gideon's
skin an unhealthy bluish tint. His hair lay flat and oily against

his head and his eyes had the vacant look of a man facing ruin.
The only thing that seemed to revive him somewhat was seeing
Josie enter the room behind Mark. His flatline expression turned
into a smirk, apparently for her benefit.

Evan Carillo stood and shook everyone's hand, appearing
pleasant and kind.

After the technicalities, Mark said, 'I'm going to speak very
candidly. You will go to jail over the murder of Mandy Seneck.'

Carillo threw a hand up in the air. 'Seriously? That's how
we're starting this conversation? You are not clairvoyant. You
have no idea whether my client is going to jail.'

'The prosecutor has everything he needs: the body, the motive,
the murder weapon you used—'

'Since Gideon didn't kill anyone, it clearly isn't *his* murder
weapon.'

Mark continued, 'Your fingerprints, David's statement, eye
witnesses who have now provided their statements on record
that you were the only person in the room with Mandy when
she was shot.'

Gideon tried to speak but Mark raised a hand to stop him.

'None of that is up for discussion. There is no bargaining or
deal to cut. You will go to jail for the murder of Mandy Seneck.
Where you can earn some favor with the judge and jury is with
the murder of Cia Mulroney. You cooperate with us on information concerning the EX-Sovereigns and I can guarantee you a
more favorable consideration.'

Carillo started to object but Gideon cut him off. He had lost
the smirk and was staring intently at Mark, sensing a lifeline.
'I want into the witness protection program.'

Josie watched Mark's poker face for some reaction, but he
remained still. How could Gideon possibly think he warranted
protection after Mark told him he would do time for murder?
She also noticed Carillo's raised eyebrows as he looked down
at the table. Even he thought the request was absurd.

'Gloria and I will need new identities. You set us up a new
life and I have plenty of information I can give you about the
EX-Sovereigns.'

Josie couldn't hold her tongue. 'How do you think a new
identity will benefit you? Your Facebook video about me killing

Mandy is now all over the internet. Last I looked, you have over 500,000 views. Congratulations on your new-found fame.'

'Don't be a smart ass. You're the one wanting information from me. You're the one begging *me* for help.'

'Let's be clear,' Mark said. 'No one is begging you for anything. You raped and murdered a fifteen-year-old girl. Keep it up and we both walk out of here and tell the prosecutor to stick it to you as long and as hard as he can.'

Gideon turned in his chair toward Mark, facing his body as far from Josie's line of sight as he could manage. 'What can you give me in exchange for information?'

'The information you provide about the EX-Sovereigns shows the jury that you are cooperating. That you feel remorse for your actions. It goes a long way toward convincing the jury that you aren't a complete monster.'

Carillo placed his hand on Gideon's arm. 'I would tread lightly. Don't perjure yourself over information that you may not know or understand.'

Mark raised his eyebrows and leaned back to examine the attorney. 'Perhaps there is a conflict of interest here, Mr Carillo? I would think offering a client counsel that goes against his best interest, just so that you can protect another client, would be grounds for disbarment.'

Josie was shocked at the advice as well. Carillo was clearly trying to protect the EX-Sovereigns.

'I'm doing no such thing. This is—'

'This is bullshit is what it is,' Gideon said. 'I don't have any loyalties to them.'

Josie watched Carillo clench his teeth. The EX-Sovereigns were footing the bill for his legal aide.

'Tell me who contacted you first, and what they wanted,' Mark said.

Over the next hour, Gideon described how a member of the EX-Sovereigns first contacted him via email when they were living in Idaho. Bobby Lee was the person who convinced Gideon that the purchase of the church and the move to Artemis would be great for The Drummers. Bobby Lee had promised that if they set up a temporary settlement at the church, and proved they were serious about becoming a satellite group for the EX-Sovereigns, that they would in turn fund the purchase of land in Arroyo County and help the group develop a permanent settlement. They would also receive financial help with food and necessities until they were able to get their feet on the ground. In exchange, Gideon agreed to help further the EX-Sovereigns' mission. Because of David Jonas's military experience, he became the front man for the group, and was the person who communicated directly with Hayes Oolitic about the substation shootings.

At the end of the meeting Carillo stood and packed up his briefcase. Without looking at Gideon, he stated, 'I believe you are correct. There is a conflict of interest at play here. I am recusing myself from this case. Mr Masters, you are free to find other counsel.'

Carillo walked out of the room without another word, leaving Gideon dumbfounded. Josie followed Mark out of the room, with Gideon stammering after them, demanding a new attorney. Josie smiled for the first time that day.

'I'd call that a win,' Mark said.

'Score one for the good guys.'

'You want to head out for something to eat?'

'I'm worn out. I'm going home to pet my dog and drink a beer.'

Mark grinned. 'I'd say you're owed that.'

'And tomorrow is well past my weekend. I'd like the morning off. Head to Big Bend, beyond the cell phone towers, and get some sunshine. Otto and Marta can cover for me, and Martinez is on duty. You OK with that?'

'You bet. We're transporting Gideon tomorrow morning. My partner and I will drive him to Odessa. He'll fly from there to Fort Worth, to the federal prison.'

'That has a great sound to it.'

'Just check in when you get back in range. Enjoy your day off.'

Having hiked countless miles and kayaked through all five of the major canyons in Big Bend National Park and Big Bend Ranch State Park, Josie still took the same precautions as when she'd hiked the first time. She planned her route that night and made two copies: one to drop at the ranger station and the other to post on her windshield when she took off. As one of the most remote areas of the lower forty-eight, she knew the risks of solo camping and hiking, so Chester was always an appreciated companion. She no longer took him hiking in the summer months, when temperatures along the river could reach well over one hundred degrees, but he loved it in the winter.

For Josie, the Big Bend had never just been about escaping; since her first time hiking the park she had felt as if her body belonged among the mountains and hills, trekking mile after mile through the narrow cut-thrus, taking advantage of a hidden mountain water source, navigating the canyons and mesas and high-country prairies, finding grateful shelter in the late afternoon when the sun, even in winter, could still sap every bit of energy from your body and your spirit. Part of the allure had been learning how to survive in such an unforgiving environment; pushing herself to face unknown fears and then dealing with them, mentally first, then physically. She liked the simple way of life: cooking over a fire, camping under the stars, relaxing into an orange sunset that stretched across the horizon, then waking to a magnificent yellow sunrise, knowing that that same sun six hours later could take your life. A simple life, with a complex set of rules that had to be both understood and intuited.

Her last big trip had been a solo nineteen-mile hike on the Rancherias Loop Trail at Big Bend Ranch in the Bofecillos Mountains. The hike had taken three days, with two days spent camping along Panther Creek, taking in the red rock canyons. She'd hiked past a deserted homestead and fence line where cattle once made their way north from the Rio Grande. Hiking the area had pushed her limits; she couldn't imagine the grit it must have taken to call the place home.

Josie woke before dawn and arranged the dog's pack first, filling water on both sides of the unit that she would strap around his chest. Chester would carry a gallon of his own water and some of his food. The first time she'd tried the pack out with him, he'd taken it willingly, walking ten miles without ever trying to wrangle his way out. He seemed to understand the pack was for his own good and was fine to carry his own load.

After getting the dog's gear ready she filled her CamelBak water bag and an extra gallon they would drink from first, along with several jugs she would keep as extras in her Jeep. Her plan was always to take double the water she needed. Even in the winter, hydration was critical in the desert. She had participated in several park rescues and knew the dangers of hiking unprepared, from sun stroke during the day to hypothermia at night.

She packed her survival kit and strapped on an outside-the-waistband holster for her off-duty Glock 43. She typically only carried concealed, but hiking alone, she wanted it known that she was carrying if she came across someone unexpected.

With lunch and snacks packed, she carried the load out to her Jeep Wrangler, a 2010 white soft top that could handle anything she threw at it. When the PD received the new drive home patrol cars, Josie had sold her truck and bought a 4x4 that she could take into the desert without fear of ruining the suspension as she climbed over rocks and boulders in the arroyos. She counted the Jeep as one of her better purchases.

Driving south on River Road, they made it to Presidio where she fueled up the Jeep and she and the dog ate a McDonald's breakfast that would hold them through to lunch. It had warmed up enough to tie back the soft top and roll the windows down, allowing Chester to lift his head into the wind, his snout working overtime taking in all the new smells, his long ears flying out behind him like a little girl's pigtails.

The drive from Presidio to Lajitas hugged the Rio Grande along the bottom of the Big Bend Ranch State Park and was Josie's favorite – often driving it for miles on end without seeing any other cars. Once she left the paved road, the park map noted roads designated for high-clearance four-wheel-drive vehicles. It wasn't quite rock crawling, but it was close enough to generate a good adrenalin buzz.

She posted her travel plans at the ranger station located close to the center of the park, and she and Chester set out on the drive that required a spare tire, preferably two. After making her way up a rock-strewn slope, she slid down a sandy wash just outside the mouth of the Arroyo Mexicano. Josie parked her Jeep and geared up Chester, whose nose was to the ground even as she tried to buckle on his pack.

She trudged up into the soft sand of the arroyo and headed down the box canyon toward their destination, the Mexicano Falls. Cottonwood trees, looking lush in the desert setting, with leaves in various shades of yellow and green, grew up out of the arroyo where shallow pools of water and occasional streams began to appear. As she made her way up the canyon, she stopped to look at trees whose gnarled roots wrapped around rocks and boulders where rushing water had eroded away the soil.

After a two-hour hike up the canyon, allowing Chester plenty of time to stray and return, they finally made it to the falls where he headed straight to the shallow pool of water to drink. Josie placed her hand under the icy cold trickle of water coming off the canyon wall and cupped water into her mouth. Crystal clear and delicious. The waterfall wouldn't appear until the rainy season, but that meant flash flooding down the arroyo, and a hike she wouldn't attempt.

She walked around the area, admiring the colors along the canyon wall: green ferns and red and yellow vegetation she couldn't identify. Tired from the walk, she finally lay down on a flat rock and let the sun soak into her bones like a tonic. She could hear Chester sniffing out the rocks, in and out of the water, like a kid with a new playroom full of toys. She drifted off to sleep with one hand resting on the butt of her gun in her waistband, and didn't wake up until she felt movement on her foot. She jerked up to see Chester staring at her, ready for lunch.

After a sandwich and apple, and a bowl of dog food and another romp through the water for Chester, they loaded up and took the long trek back to the Jeep, stopping to look at the bright pink blooms on the tasajillo, or the Desert Christmas cactus. She counted it as a perfect day: sunny sixty-degree temperatures for hiking, no bumps or bruises, and a head cleared of the tragedy of the past few days.

It wasn't until she was back in her car and on the edge of the park that she heard her phone pinging with text messages, missed phone calls and voicemails, stacking up one after another.

Everyone she worked with knew she'd gone out of signal at Big Bend through the afternoon, so she was certain the messages would not bear good news. With the Jeep pulled off to the side of the road, she opened her phone and scanned through texts from Otto, Mark and the mayor, all asking her to call immediately, but none of them leaving details. She scanned several voicemails and selected the longest from Mark, hoping for specifics.

Josie, it's Mark. I don't even know how to tell you this. Gideon is gone. We took the route through Pinto Canyon up to Marfa, counting on it cutting off some time. A half hour into the drive we came across a massive cattle crossing. We were ambushed. Men came up from behind in ATVs and before we realized what was happening they had guns in our windows. They took Gideon. Handcuffed us to the fence with no communication. They were gone over an hour before dispatch realized there was a problem. Call me.

She listened to his message twice. She called and went through to his voicemail. She called Otto next and he picked up immediately. She didn't pull back onto the road for fear of dropping the connection.

'I just got out of the park. What the hell is going on?'

'Gideon is gone, escaped or kidnapped. We don't know yet. A trooper found Mark and his partner about two hours ago. So Gideon's been missing about three hours.'

'Was anyone hurt?'

'No. They were on Pinto Canyon. Mark said it appeared like a legitimate cattle crossing, so he stopped the car. There was no way around. Within a few minutes two ATVs came up on either side of them and four men jumped out with automatic weapons drawn. Mark and his partner each had the windows open, watching the cattle move, so within a few seconds the men had weapons pointed inside the vehicle.'

'Did Gideon seem to know what was happening?'

'Mark couldn't say. He and his partner were pulled out of the car, masks were pulled over their heads, and they were taken to a nearby fence where they were handcuffed.'

'This is unreal.'

'Are you headed back?'

'Yes. I'll swing by my house and drop the dog off, then I'll head to the jail.'

Almost two hours later, Josie joined Otto, Mark, Downey, Townsend and Sheriff Martinez at the Arroyo County Jail where the group had convened in the conference room. Case files were spread across the table amid maps and photos. Mark apologized as soon as Josie entered the room, obviously embarrassed by the turn of events. He filled her in on the basics, stating that an all-points bulletin had been issued, but they had no information as to the vehicle the apprehenders had used to take Gideon. They also still had no idea whether they were friend or foe to Gideon.

By seven o'clock, the team broke up, with no more information than they had collected hours before. After pouring through case notes and everything they could find on the EX-Sovereigns, there was little else to go on.

TWENTY-TWO

I t was after seven o'clock when Josie made it back to the police station. She took the stairs slowly, feeling twice her age, back and feet aching, eyes burning. The original team who had worked on the murders had sifted through every detail collected during the investigation, including pertinent information from the FBI concerning the EX-Sovereigns. Their best guess was that a local sympathizer had arranged the ambush; someone who knew the Pinto Canyon shortcut to Marfa, and the fact that the area was both remote and cattle country. The sheriff's department was trying to locate the retired CEO who owned the land, but he appeared to be out of the country. It had been one of the worst losses of Josie's career.

Inside the office she flipped the lights on and noticed a plastic evidence bag on her desk: her gun had been cleared and delivered. She carried a Beretta Px4 Storm Compact. The first time she'd held the handgun it had felt as if it had been made specifically for her, with a familiar heft to it. Since surrendering her duty gun she'd been carrying her backup but had felt uneasy without her Beretta.

She retrieved her gun-cleaning kit from the closet. She laid a white cloth out on the conference table and sat down with her gun and the kit, glad for the mindless task. The smell of gun oil and the feel of smooth metal gliding across metal was satisfying in a way she couldn't quite articulate.

With the barrel assembly taken apart she applied the cleaner to a patch and began rubbing down the inside with a metal pick that she'd watched her dad use at the kitchen table to clean his work pistol. She'd picked up his habit of laying out the pieces in order, always on a white cloth, meticulously wiping until the patches were free from the black carbon or lead or copper residue. He had taught her to check each piece for buildup, how to oil the spring and apply the gun grease. Josie's mom had never had any interest in firearms and would leave the kitchen when the two of them sat down to take his guns apart. Her father wasn't a big talker, but when he sat at the table, enjoying the rote mechanics in front of him, he would talk about random things, not just police work, but stories of his childhood in rural Kentucky, squirrel hunting with his grandpa or drag racing on a dirt track in high school. Decades after his death, she still mourned her life without him.

Josie heard the door open downstairs and someone talking to the night dispatcher. A few minutes later, she listened to the quick steps up the stairs and looked up from the pieces of her gun to see Mayor O'Kane knock twice and enter.

He raised a hand. 'Don't get up. You look hard at work.'

'Have a seat, Mayor. There's some burnt coffee in the back. Can I pour you a cup?'

'I'll pass. I won't stay long. I was in the office late and saw the light upstairs.' He gestured toward the gun. 'You put in a long day. Don't you think this could wait until morning? Maybe get a good night's sleep?'

'Some people do bonsai, some people tie fishing lures. I clean my gun for relaxation.'

He tipped his head. 'To each his own.' After saying that he wouldn't stay, he pulled out a chair across from her and sat down. 'I stopped by to check in. I listened to your voicemail earlier about Gideon but I wasn't able to respond. Any good news?'

Josie picked up a clean patch and ran it around the coiled spring. 'Not a damn thing.'

'No indication who took him?'

She shoved the magazine back into the gun and looked up. 'Not at this time. We're speculating a sympathizer, but,' she shrugged as she laid the gun on the table, 'we don't have much to go on.'

'What's the latest with the other murder? Cia?'

'We're still working it. Although I'm worried with David and Gideon's arrests that we're going to lose the remaining Drummers. Then the odds of finding Cia's killer plummet.'

She was surprised he didn't push her for more information. Instead, he watched her slip the tools back into the kit, saying nothing as she folded the cloth and returned it all to the cabinet.

When she sat down at the table he said, 'I'm guessing you've been around me long enough to know that I don't tread lightly. I don't beat about the bush very well.'

She laughed at his struggle. 'Actually, in America we usually say beat *around* the bush.'

He grinned. 'Damned Irish roots.'

'Although, I could argue that this is a perfect example of someone beating around the bush. What are you not wanting to tell me?'

'I enjoyed having you over for dinner. You are completely different than any woman I've ever spent time with, and I'd like to see you again. However, there is the mayor and chief issue that I'm not completely at ease with.'

All she could manage was to nod, not saying a word in response.

'I've noticed the police department isn't big on policy. In fact, there's no policy on dating fellow officers, or supervisors for that matter. But beyond the policy, if you feel at all uncomfortable with this, say the word and we'll never discuss it again.'

She said nothing for a moment, wondering if she was too tired to process a response, or if this was her brain's attempt at self-preservation.

'All right then. I'm going to take that wide-eyed look as a signal to end this conversation. I'm afraid I've never mastered the art of nuance. Better to let the bird out of the cage and either shoot it down or let it fly.'

She laughed at the description. 'I'm sorry. You just caught me off-guard. When you walked in, I assumed you were here about Gideon. This just surprised me.'

'Maybe another friendly dinner? I hear you like to hike. Maybe somewhere local?'

'Do you like to hike?' she asked, glad for the slight diversion.

'I do, but I rarely get out beyond the property.'

'I have the perfect place. How about when this mess with The Drummers is settled I'll show you one of my favorite local trails?'

He slapped his knee and stood. 'The bird will fly. I'll check back and we'll set a date for it.'

'Sounds good.'

She listened to his footsteps as he left the building and placed her hands on her flushed cheeks. 'What the hell have I just done?'

The following morning, Josie sat at her kitchen table eating a bowl of cereal, flipping through the news on her phone, when a text came in from Mitchell Cowan. She had called him the day before with an urgent request and had been waiting for a response.

- *Stop by my office on your way to work.*
- *Good news?*
- *Depends on your definition.*
- *Be there in 30 min.*

Josie found Cowan sitting in his office, frowning over his computer screen. He motioned toward the chair across from his desk and pitched his reading glasses onto a pile of papers.

'I owe you an apology. When you called yesterday and asked about the test, I knew instantly I'd made a grave error. In that situation, a check for hCG levels in the blood sampling should have been done. I was in such a hurry to get results and get my lab cleared that it didn't even cross my mind.'

'It didn't cross my mind until yesterday, so don't beat yourself up. What did you find out?' she asked.

'Mandy Seneck was pregnant. I'm estimating eighteen weeks. I can give you the specifics on how I determined the information, but I am certain. To answer your next question, it will hold up in court. I'm in the process of determining paternity, and have requested DNA from Gideon Masters. Because it was a homicide his DNA was collected upon arrest. I hope to have paternity established by the end of the week.'

'Is eighteen weeks far enough along so that others would have been able to tell?'

'Like her mother?' he asked.

'Exactly.'

'Most likely, yes. Typically a woman will start to show between twelve to sixteen weeks. That doesn't mean that she couldn't have hidden her pregnancy, but I believe her mother would most likely have suspected something.'

Josie sat still for a moment, taking in the information, remembering the photo of the girl wearing the white night-gown stained with blood. 'That poor girl. Her mother ought to be held accountable as well.'

Cowan pursed his lips. 'For a fifteen-year-old? Do we really want parents held legally responsible for every fifteen-year-old girl who ends up pregnant?'

'This girl wasn't sexually permissive though. She was being pursued by a man old enough to be her grandfather. And her mother knew it.'

'Did the girl ever report Gideon, even to someone within The Drummers?' Cowan asked.

'No. Although there were members who were troubled by what they thought might be happening.'

'So parents should be held accountable if the sex isn't agreeable to the fifteen-year-old, but they shouldn't be held accountable if the teenager is sexually active?'

'You just put words in my mouth. And I am far too tired for this kind of debate. Just get me the formalized results as soon as you can.'

Josie stood and walked toward the door.

'I don't typically follow investigations too closely. I prefer to stay removed,' he said. 'Easier that way.'

Josie turned to look at him. His face was drawn, tired, but his eyes were angry.

'This man was a monster, Josie. He raped and murdered this young girl.' He paused for a moment and had to clear his throat to continue. 'I just hope you get this sociopath behind bars.'

At 7:45 a.m. Josie left Cowan to meet with Ned Bates and a group of other ranchers he'd offered to gather. Ned was a prin-cipled man who complained to anyone who would listen if he thought his rights had been violated. Local politicians hated him because he argued every point. He was built like a bulldozer and had a deep, imposing voice that both men and women paid attention to, whether they liked it or not. But Ned was honest, and apolitical. He didn't care what side of the line you stood behind; if you screwed with him or his rights, you would catch his wrath.

As a third-generation West Texas rancher, Ned was also a vocal supporter of the industry. He raised several hundred head of Hereford cattle, still ranching on horseback. Of the six ranchers in the room, their operations ranged from 2,000 acres to over 50,000. The only one with significant money was Charlie Tanglewood. He was the largest landowner present but his money hadn't been earned from ranching. He'd gotten rich off oil in the Permian Basin, and then cashed it in on a ranch that he knew would only break even, if he was lucky. He openly admitted that he'd already experienced wealth; now he was pursuing a dream.

The group of five men and one woman sat with tables pushed together in the middle of the Hot Tamale, most of them already eating a breakfast plate piled high with scrambled eggs and sausage and biscuits, smothered with salsa and hot sauce that Lucy made herself from home-grown habanero chilis. Josie gave her order to the waitress at the counter, took her mug of coffee and sat down with the rowdy bunch. She enjoyed the talk, listening to the bullshit and bravado, the woes of cattle ranching that ranged from scraping by to working alongside millionaires. They talked about the 420,000-acre Brewster ranch that had gone on the market for 320 million dollars, and how the market was being affected by the oil boom.

Once the food was gone and the coffee mugs refilled, Josie got their attention.

'I'm sure Ned told you this meeting is about the EX-Sovereigns. I'll tell you everything I know in exchange for everything you know. Deal?'

'Fair enough,' Ned said. He looked around the table and the rest gave a nod.

Josie spent the next half-hour providing the background on The Drummers connection to the EX-Sovereigns, from their time in Idaho, all the way to their purchase of the church and promise of land once they had completed several tasks to demonstrate loyalty.

'Ballistics proved that David Jonas, one of the lead members of The Drummers and a former Marine, shot out all three substations in West Texas. This was directed by Bobby Lee Green.'

Josie watched the news ripple around the table. Several of them swore under their breath, glancing from one to another.

She went on to explain the master plan to destroy the electric grid, and how rural West Texas was just a cog in the machine. Their expressions turned from shock to anger as she shared Mark's description of what could happen to the country if they were allowed to succeed.

Ned leaned on the table and chopped at the air with his hand, his anger showing red on his face. 'I want you to know, when Bobby Lee Green met with us, both individually and as a group, he never once mentioned taking down any kind of electric grid. We'd have kicked his ass all the way to Mexico. Every single one of us.'

They nodded, echoing the violence that Bobby Lee would have encountered had he suggested any kind of vandalism to the town.

'So why do you think he approached you? What would have been the point in getting you on their side, knowing you would eventually find out their intentions?' she asked.

'I can tell you why they approached me,' Charlie said. 'They wanted monetary support. I could tell he was feeling out my political views, but I made it clear my politics is my personal business and I sure as hell wasn't sharing it with some outsider from Wyoming.'

'How did they explain their interest in West Texas? Did they get into their sovereigntist beliefs at all?'

'Oh yeah,' Ned said, nodding. 'They eventually opened up about that. It's what shut down the group meeting pretty quick. When they met individually with us, they just stopped by each of our ranches. Probably scoping out the land, the money.'

Stella Rosario spoke up. 'When he stopped by my place, it was more about them supporting ranchers, shoring up the ranching tradition in the west. I thought it sounded sketchy then, but I was curious what their angle was. When they asked if I'd meet with the other ranchers I agreed.' She grinned. 'Free steak dinner, why not hear them out?'

Ned frowned. 'If I'd known—'

Johnny Dades laughed. 'Hells bells, Ned. A guy says he wants to bring a truck full of steaks and cater a dinner on your property? You're gonna say yes.'

Josie grinned at Ned, who crossed his arms over his chest and frowned at the good-natured ribbing.

'They had Steak and Ale out of Odessa cater the dinner. They put on quite a spread,' Johnny said. 'It was worth a little bullshit.'

'Was Bobby Lee the only member to show up?' she asked.

'Another man named Robert was with him. I never caught his second name.' Johnny looked around the table for confirmation but got blank looks and shrugged shoulders. 'Bobby Lee started out pretty tame, but he laid into the beer pretty hard. By the end of the supper he'd started talking second amendment rights. Then he got into the government taking our land.'

'*Seizing* our land,' Stella said, rolling her eyes. 'He must have said the word seizing twenty times.'

'Honestly, it didn't take long and we were all looking around the table at each other like, this guy's a nut case,' Ned said. 'We finally shut the party down at about nine o'clock and told him we weren't interested.'

'Did he contact any of you again?' Josie noted the shaking heads. 'How did he make his initial contact?'

Ned lifted a hand. 'For me it was an online ranchers' forum. Bitching about hay prices. Nothing political. Someone commented back to something I posted, but I can't remember if it was Bobby Lee the first time. I don't remember the details, but somehow he got involved and said he was flying into Odessa. Said he'd like to talk to some locals about ranching issues. That's how that dinner got set up.'

After the meeting Josie forwarded Ned's social media information to Mark. The goal was to determine patterns in making contact with local groups so the feds could make a more targeted effort at monitoring their actions.

Mark called Josie before she'd made it out of the diner. He explained that he'd spent the day digging into Bobby Lee and Hayes Oolitic and found that both men had dropped Charlie Tanglewood's name in several social media posts as being a supporter of sovereigntist rights.

Josie laughed. 'Charlie won't be happy to hear that. And he's got enough money to fight the bastards.'

She could hear Mark rifling through papers. 'How old is Charlie?'

'I'd guess in his forties.'

'Married?'

'No. Nasty divorce. I overheard one of the ranchers harassing him about it.'

'We might be able to put his anger to good use. See if you can schedule a follow-up meeting with him this morning at his place. You name the time and I'll be there.'

TWENTY-THREE

J osie slowed her patrol car to a crawl as she wound her way down the driveway of Tanglewood Ranch. A mile down a dry arroyo she passed through an ocotillo forest with hundreds of the spiny shrubs pushing crooked green fingers toward the sky, reminding her of an underwater seaweed scape.

Located in the foothills of the Chinati Mountain range, the ranch boasted a ten-mile riverfront along the Rio Grande. Stretches of flat ground were dotted by the tail end of the mountain range, like the ragged tip of a dinosaur tail. And among the rocks were deep brown canyons where the dry earth had split, with boulders that looked as if they'd been tossed off the side of the cliff, created in one tumultuous shake of the earth, while in reality it had most likely taken centuries to create.

Given the grand landscape, the home was a low, unimposing ranch made of Texas stone and cedar. Several barns and outbuildings were located to the south of the house. Josie parked her car in front and wondered if the solitude suited Charlie. He'd struck her as personable, a fairly social person who might struggle with the extreme quiet. To Josie, the ability to trade people for the earth seemed the ultimate exchange. To live in an area so completely untouched by humanity, so devoid of technology and modern anything, was a life that not many people in the world could afford, or perhaps more telling, wouldn't want even if they could afford it. It was Josie's definition of heaven on earth.

She parked next to Mark's rental car, a nondescript black SUV, coated in a thick layer of desert dust. Mark and Charlie stood to the side of the house in the midst of a cactus garden peppered with clumps of dried native grasses.

Charlie walked them around to the back of the house where a pergola provided shade from the sun, now directly overhead. 'I thought we'd take advantage of this warm weather and sit outside, if that's OK with the two of you?'

Mark agreed amiably, saying he'd left six inches of snow in
Washington.

The native desert landscape stretched around to the rear of
the house where several chairs sat under a pergola. Only one
chair appeared used, with a brimming ashtray on a side table
next to it, and a trashcan beside it overflowing with empty
bottles of Shiner.

Charlie motioned for them to sit. 'You two need a beer? Or
a water? I'm a two-drink man out here. Keeps life simple.'

Josie and Mark declined while Charlie grabbed himself a beer
from inside and lit up a cigar. He popped the top and tipped his
cowboy hat at Josie. 'You won't mind if I keep this on? I'll burn
my head out here with that big ball of sun overhead.'

'Won't bother me at all,' she said.

Mark filled Charlie in on his position within the FBI, and
his current interest in the EX-Sovereigns. 'I understand Josie
has explained their agenda.'

Charlie nodded.

'Are you aware they're using your name as a person who
supports their cause?' Mark asked, watching Charlie's expression
carefully.

'*My* name?'

'I assume they think your wealth and status will bring
respectability to their organization,' Mark said.

Charlie laughed, loud and open-mouthed. He held his cigar
up in one hand and the Shiner in the other. 'If I'm their front
man for respectability, then they got a major PR problem. I
may be rich, but respectable I ain't.'

Mark glanced at Josie, grinning.

'You see why I choose West Texas over Washington?' she
asked.

'What do you think about working a sting with us?'

Josie looked at Mark, surprised at his use of words. He was
clearly buttering Charlie up for an adventure. Mark hadn't filled
her in on his plan, guessing correctly that she'd support it.

'Bring it on,' Charlie said.

'We're closing in on their organization fast. But I'd like to
get a candid conversation with Bobby Lee before our team
heads to Wyoming. I'd like you to call him and tell him you

want to make a major donation. Tell him you're furious with what's happened here in Artemis with The Drummers, and you'd like to be a vocal front man for the EX-Sovereigns. See if he'd be willing to come here to your ranch to meet. Find out exactly what they want from these small rural towns.'

'If you're about to take them down anyway, what's the point?' Charlie asked.

'There are groups like this all over America. The more we understand about their thinking, and their method for recruiting, the better we get at profiling.'

Charlie winced. 'Why'd you have to go and use a term like that? That's what makes sons of bitches like me dislike feds like you.'

'Profiling?' Mark asked.

'Exactly.'

Mark sat back in his seat, looking confused. 'We profile every day. How could we do any police work without understanding a person's or a group's psychology and behavior? We do that to predict their next move. I promise you that our nation would be overrun with terrorists if we weren't able to analyze their movements.'

Charlie waved an arm in the air. 'All right, enough. I get it. I just hate those terms.'

Mark looked relieved that he hadn't pressed the issue. 'Would you consider having Josie pose as your fiancée? I'd like to have a law enforcement officer in the room. She may clue in on questions to ask that may not occur to you.'

Charlie laughed again. 'I hope my ex gets wind of this. She'll lose her shit if she thinks I'm remarrying.'

'Do you think there's any chance Bobby Lee would recognize me? I've been in the news over Mandy's shooting,' Josie said.

Mark frowned. 'I've seen the stock image they're using. It's a grainy photo they took of you in uniform with your hair pulled up, back when you signed on with Indianapolis Metro PD.'

She grinned. 'Yeah, that was a few years ago.'

'Honestly, I think Bobby Lee will have a laser focus on Charlie's income. I doubt he'll pay much attention to the girlfriend serving the beer.'

Josie rolled her eyes. 'I bet you're enjoying this.'

*　　*　　*

The next afternoon, Josie arrived at Charlie's place dressed in jeans and cowboy boots with a tailored white shirt and sterling silver and turquoise earrings, her hair hanging in loose waves over her shoulders. As she made the long trip down the lane again she wondered what it would be like to have enough money to live anywhere you pleased, from big-city high-rise to remote desert ranch. And she wondered what differentiated the urban wealthy from the desert wealthy, whether the need for space was an inherited trait or one born out of experience. Until Josie left Indiana in her twenties, she'd had no idea of her need for endless sky and the blistering heat of the desert sun, but once she'd found it, she'd known there was no going back.

She rounded a bend in the driveway and noticed a car in front of the house that hadn't been there the day before. It looked like an older model sedan, so she doubted it was Bobby Lee arriving early. She hoped Charlie hadn't invited someone else over to share in his adventure.

Josie got out of her car as a woman about her age, dressed in jeans and a T-shirt, left the house carrying a laundry basket full of supplies. They exchanged hellos and Charlie motioned Josie inside with a sheepish grin.

'The house needed a clean-up before inviting people in. Tina's always good about coming over for a down and dirty scrub-up.'

'That was nice of you to go to the trouble.'

'Yeah, well, it was pride more than being nice. Come on in and I'll show you around.'

Josie followed him down a hallway to three bedrooms: two sparingly decorated that looked as if they'd never been used, and a large master suite with Texas-sized log-cabin style furniture and a soaking tub big enough for two.

'Did a decorator do this, or do you have a natural flair?'

'Hell, no. I don't have a flair for anything but business. It's why Barb left me. She thought with all my money we'd tour the world and drink champagne and I don't know what all other kind of happy crap she wanted to do, but it didn't interest me in the least.'

Back in the living room he turned to Josie. 'Can you imagine a woman confusing me for a man who wants to jet around the world drinking champagne?'

'I can't imagine anyone making that mistake.'

Josie figured he must have had a well-executed prenuptial agreement for him to have been able to purchase the ranch after the divorce.

They walked through a sprawling living room ripped straight from the pages of a Southwest decorator's magazine, with a cowhide rug, pool table and a five-foot-wide antler chandelier.

'Just so I can establish myself, is this your decorating job, or did I come in and take over?'

'I sure as hell didn't do it. When Tina started cleaning for me I was living out of boxes and using a card table to eat on. It drove her crazy. She convinced me to give her a budget and she did it all.'

'So if it comes up, just think of me as Tina. I do the cleaning, and I did the decorating.'

Charlie motioned for her to move on in to the kitchen, appointed with stainless steel appliances and a massive granite countertop. 'Is this Tina's as well?'

'Yep. You may as well do the cooking. Otherwise we'll be eating Spam and eggs and rice a couple of times a day.'

'So I'm the cook too?'

'Maybe we should get married. You appear to be the perfect woman.'

'And what exactly do you do around the house?'

He grinned. 'I knew it was too good to be true. I do plenty. I take care of the outside. You take care of the inside.'

Josie asked Charlie to explain the ranching operations as she opened kitchen cabinets and figured out where the coffee-maker was. They decided to sit outside on the back porch, which was Charlie's domain. After they got settled, Josie would go inside and make coffee, and bring the drinks out.

'Not to tell you how to do your job, but if I was you, I'd bring beer out for the men. Bobby Lee got popped at Ned's steak dinner party, and that's when his tongue set to wagging.'

Bobby Lee Green arrived in a massive pickup truck that Josie couldn't imagine any car rental place keeping in their fleet. She assumed it was part of his persona – the successful businessman who gets what he wants. She had expected a big blustering

type, but he was tall and thin, smooth-shaven and pale; a man
her mom would have referred to as a pretty boy.

He shook hands and congratulated Charlie on his engagement.
Charlie laid his arm over Josie's shoulder and pulled her into
a tight hug. She forced a smile and patted his chest.

'He's the best,' she said. 'Come on in and we'll head through
the kitchen. I thought we could sit outside since it's so nice.
Can I get you something to drink? Coffee or a beer?'

'Whatever Charlie's having will be fine. Thank you, ma'am.'

Josie looked over her shoulder as she walked inside the house.
'You already know what Charlie's drinking.'

Charlie hooted and led Bobby Lee out back, already telling
him some story about the cows getting rounded up for market.
Josie's unease about turning him loose with someone the FBI
considered key to a critical investigation was subsiding. Mark
had made a good call.

She made a pot of coffee and found a small cooler in Charlie's
pantry, which she filled with ice and a half-dozen Shiners from
Charlie's refrigerator. She delivered the cooler first, then took
her seat with a mug of coffee and a hunting magazine she'd
found on his coffee table. She crossed her legs and flipped idly
through the magazine as the two talked about ranching operations. Bobby Lee finally steered the conversation toward the
EX-Sovereigns and what they hoped to achieve in West Texas.
Two beers in, and Bobby Lee's soft drawl had become more
animated. Josie stood quietly and took the cooler back inside the
kitchen where she refilled it. Neither man seemed to notice as
they grabbed another.

'I have to admit, after the meeting at Ned's place, I didn't
think we'd get much traction out here,' Bobby Lee said.

'We're not a quick bunch to bite. But we talked and there
are pieces to what you say that we support. But I'm only talking
for me today. Nobody else. Before I throw my money behind
you, I need to know up front what you're about. No sales pitch
like last time. Tell me what my money is going to support.'

Bobby Lee nodded and looked to the floor as if having to
refocus his approach. Josie figured he'd come to the ranch with
a sales pitch and had just swung at his first strike.

'All right then. Let's start with our name,' he said. 'It throws a lot of people. Some people think we're sovereigntist. And some people think we're against them because of the EX in our name. When we formed, our idea was, let's take the basic sovereign idea and make it bigger. Our purpose isn't getting out of speeding tickets or screwing with local law enforcement. We want out of the US government. It's a mess beyond repair. We've taken our case to the courts, to designate our rights as self-governing, free-born sovereign citizens.' Bobby Lee leaned forward, his eyes burning hot with intensity. 'But no US court will ever provide a fair trial. In fact, we've had several cases thrown out and fined as frivolous. So if they won't do things the legal way, then we take over by force.'

Josie watched Charlie nodding slowly, appearing to enjoy his role.

'I agree with you that Washington is a mess, and it doesn't represent me or my values. But without a government funded by taxes, what keeps China or Russia from coming in here and taking over our country?' Charlie asked.

'We have militia groups who are more than willing and ready to protect our citizens. We don't need billions of dollars in a defense fund to go patrol other countries in the Middle East. We spend our money here, in our own country, taking care of our own business. We don't understand Iraq or Iran any better than they understand us. So why in God's name are we sending our children into those countries to fight? My nephew lost his life in the Iraq war. And for what?'

Bobby Lee twisted the top off his fourth beer and handed another to Charlie. His pale cheeks were flushed red and perspiration dotted his forehead, even with the temperature hovering around sixty degrees.

'The loss of freedoms in our country grows worse every year. Companies want our data – they take it. The government wants to listen in on phone calls – they do it.' He pointed a finger at Charlie, having forgotten all about Josie. 'Mark my words, the EX-Sovereigns are the only group with the backing, the money and the members to make significant change.'

'Bobby Lee,' Charlie said, his voice pleading, 'I get all this. You are preaching to the choir, brother. I've seen what the government is doing to our freedoms. Why do you think I called you? I want to know what you're going to *do* about it? So far, all I hear is talk. All I see are pathetic half-assed attempts by a handful of militia groups to shake up the status quo. And nothing changes! Money and backing don't mean anything without a plan. Ain't that right, honey?'

Josie looked up, her eyebrows raised at having been drawn into the conversation. 'Whatever you say.'

Bobby Lee leaned back in his seat, smiling wide. 'That is exactly what I hoped to hear you say. Too many people don't understand the magnitude of what we're facing, and the organization that it takes to make a change. And when I say a change, I mean overthrowing the United States government. For the first time in the history of this country, the people are poised to take back what's rightfully theirs.'

'All I still hear is talk, brother!'

'We're going to blow this damn country up! That's what we're going to do! We have EX cells in every state, with most states averaging two to three groups operating as a network. With the size of Texas, I'd like to have at least five cells. I thought we were developing a group here with The Drummers but they were a dysfunctional mess, a bad call on my part. We need someone who can be a leader in the area. Someone like you who can understand the mission and find the right people to back you up. Right now, we need leadership, and we need boots on the ground.'

'Boots on the ground for what?'

Josie was staring at the magazine, leisurely sipping her ice-cold coffee, but she could feel Bobby Lee's eyes on her.

Charlie said, 'Oh, she's fine. She's on our side, trust me.'

Josie glanced up, looking bored. 'I have heard this conversation too many times to count, Bobby Lee. If you want me to leave, say the word.'

'You'll do no such thing!' Charlie said. 'We're in this together.'

'Together forever,' she said, feigning boredom.

Charlie winked and looked back at Bobby Lee with a grin. 'OK, be honest with me. You and The Drummers, you took out the transformers, right?'

Bobby Lee gave a lopsided smile, clearly pleased that Charlie had made the connection.

Charlie leaned forward. 'Look, I got generators. I take care of my own out here, so no skin off my back. But why the hell would you target West Texas? If you have all this money, why not go after Houston or San Antonio?'

'We're taking a lesson from the US government's own training manual. When a recruit joins the military, what's the first thing they have to do?'

'Basic training.'

'Yep. And the whole goal of basic training is to tear them down to build them back up. The drill sergeants yell and scream and scare the shit out of their ragtag group of pansies, and ten weeks later those kids are marching in step with a "yes sir", ready to load and unload and shoot when ordered. If Uncle Sam can do that with a bunch of kids, imagine what we can do with committed adults wanting a better life for their families?'

'So you tear down the electric grid?'

'To build it back up. Absolutely.'

Charlie nodded, his eyes sparkling. Josie looked back down at her magazine to hide the disgust she felt, trying to keep her own desire to ask questions in check. Charlie was doing fine without her.

'So big picture,' Bobby Lee continued, 'we get groups across the US to cause small-scale outages, which then ripple into a tidal wave.'

'But how do you get it back up again?'

'Each one of our groups is being trained to get their region up and operating within ten days, without the grid. Once the pockets are up and successful, and the electrical grid is a smoked-out mess, people will rely on their own communities for help. They'll do it small scale at first, teaching people how to generate their own power. I won't lie, it'll be rough, but we've been preparing for this for a long time. We've already got zero energy communities set up with geothermal and solar.'

Josie looked up from her magazine, surprised at the nod toward green living.

'But electric is just one piece. We're talking about rebuilding the country. We take out water, electric, gas and technology. Then each region builds their own community back up without

Big Brother defining every move. We don't need a third of our paycheck to go to a government to take care of things we can do on our own.'

'What does Bobby Lee get out of this?' Charlie asked.

'The satisfaction of seeing our country restored to what our founding fathers had in mind when they left England.'

'Come on, brother. I'm not buying it. Satisfaction doesn't motivate men like us. What do you get out of this?'

Bobby Lee grinned. 'Real estate. We already have planned communities in Texas, California, Ohio and South Carolina. We rebuild the country, one community at a time. And EX-S is selling it all.'

Bobby Lee laid out a detailed plan that included key cells and their locations, dropping names of major players in many of the areas. Charlie played along, asking for clarification and details, while Bobby Lee handed over the names as if reciting his pedigree. He clearly liked the connection to wealth.

As the meeting was wrapping up, Bobby Lee asked Charlie, 'Hey, what do you know about that group in town, The Drummers?'

Josie looked at Charlie who appeared caught off-guard. Judging by the way Bobby Lee worded the question, Josie took a chance that he was fishing for dirt, and hopefully had some of his own.

'I think they're crazy as hell,' Josie said. 'Did you hear two girls from there are dead?'

Bobby Lee's eyes widened. 'Yes! We were helping those people! That's the problem with some of these splinter groups. You never know how stable they are.'

'They do you any good?'

'They did what we asked of them. Had a couple of ex-military guys who we hoped would be helpful. But then we heard about the murders and shut off contact. I don't want any part of them.'

'Have they asked for legal help?' Josie asked. 'They sure need it.'

'The leader did. I think Hayes hooked him up with an attorney, which I told him was a mistake. He felt some loyalty to him though. We got some weird texts from a female in the group right before the second murder.'

'What was she wanting from you?' Josie asked, looking mildly surprised, hoping she wasn't coming off as inappropriately curious.

'She said something about Gideon not being who he said he was, or some bullshit like that. I don't really remember. You'd be surprised at some of the crazies we get contacting us. I just ignored it.'

'You heard that crazy bastard got arrested and then escaped?' Charlie said, shaking his head like he couldn't believe it.

'No shit? I hadn't heard that.'

Josie walked back into the kitchen, confident that Bobby Lee not only knew Gideon was missing, but had quite possibly had something to do with his disappearance.

By the time Bobby Lee reached the airport in Odessa, Mark had a team of agents waiting on him with an arrest warrant for tampering with government property. With the amount of information Bobby Lee had given up during the meeting, Mark couldn't take the chance that he might get spooked and detour out of the country. He had implicated himself in the transformer vandalism, but Mark would have to hustle to pull together additional warrants if they hoped to take the organization down.

Mark explained the arrest warrants for computers, phones, guns and records that the FBI would file against the Wyoming compound, and Josie filled him in on her own updates.

'Who do you think the female was that texted Bobby Lee?' he asked.

'Cia or Alaina. I don't see any of the other females being that engaged with what was happening. And since Alaina was still supporting Gideon at that time, I'd say it had to be Cia.'

'She knew something, and it got her killed,' he said.

'I may know what the something is. Our county coroner called yesterday. Mandy Seneck was pregnant when she was shot.'

'Son of a bitch. Gideon's baby?'

'They're doing the paternity test now.'

'Pretty compelling motivation for murder.'

'That's what I thought,' she said, shuddering again at the thought of Gideon forcing himself on the young girl. 'I still can't get over Mandy's mother not intervening. But what about Gloria, Gideon's wife? Her husband was sleeping with a fifteen-year-old, most likely in Gloria's own bedroom, while she's supposedly sleeping on a cot in her office? That's messed up.'

'Do you know if the girl entered the room after Gloria left? Had Gideon kicked her out of the room so he could share it with Mandy?'

'I haven't been able to confirm that,' Josie said. 'Gloria is still on my list for a follow-up interview.'

'Would Mandy's mother know any of this, or be willing to share it?'

'She claimed she didn't know where Mandy was. She avoids conflict, pretends it doesn't exist. That's what Leon claims. I doubt she'd admit it if she thinks it paints her in a poor light.'

'What's your take on Gloria? Are you thinking she might be involved?'

'I don't know. It's just eating at me. I can't imagine being in her place and allowing her husband, whom she appears to genuinely love and revere, to impregnate a fifteen-year-old girl.'

'I have to run. They're ready to transport Bobby Lee. I've got half an army on this son of a bitch. This will not be a repeat.'

TWENTY-FOUR

J osie woke the next morning to marimba drums. She sat up in bed, disoriented, wondering where she was. She looked toward her alarm clock but couldn't find it, further clouding her thinking. She noticed the light from her cell phone across the room and realized it was her backup alarm clock. In case of a power failure, she set her cell phone each night before going to bed. She turned the alarm off and looked back at her clock. Nothing.

She flipped on the light switch. Dead.

'Damn these people!'

Chester stood up from his dog bed and whimpered, worried by the outburst.

She checked for messages on her phone and found nothing. She skipped a shower, put her hair in a ponytail, put her uniform on and grabbed her gun. Once in her car she radioed her location and called Jeff Douglas with Tex-Edison Electric.

'Sorry to bother you. My electric is out. Have you heard about any outages?'

'I got word ten minutes ago about the outage in your area. I'll be headed your way in a few. Hoping for a squirrel.'

'You and I both. I'll be at the substation in five. I'll let you know.'

Josie stopped her car, glad to see no fire or blue light, but as soon as she got out of her car the stench filled her nose, like burnt hair, but with an overpowering acidic, metallic smell. She slipped gloves on, held a hat to her nose to block the smell, and turned her flashlight toward the chain-link fence. The entrance gate stood wide open.

As Josie stepped inside the enclosure she saw a large black mass on the ground and an extension ladder lying beside it. Steam still emanated from parts of the clothing, with about fifty percent of the body severely burned. From the pieces of frazzled gray hair and the heft of his gut and baggy jeans,

Josie was certain she was staring at the corpse of Gideon Masters.

At first look, it appeared that the victim had used the ladder to try and climb to the top of a large metal transformer. Josie was fairly certain that he had been forced up there. When the ladder had been allowed to fall forward, flinging Gideon into the transformer, he had died of electrocution.

She struggled to control her gag reflex as she turned from the scene and walked back to her car. Jeff pulled up ten minutes later.

'You look terrible,' he said. 'It wasn't a squirrel, was it?'

When Mark and his team showed up, Josie experienced a rare feeling – relief at turning an investigation over to the feds. They were angry enough at having lost a prisoner, but to lose him again to murder doubled the insult. Once the forensic team had confirmed Gideon's identity through an engraved medical bracelet, Josie left the scene. She drove home to shower off the stench of Gideon Masters, thinking, not for the first time, that Karma is a bitch.

The Artemis Police Department's evidence room was located in what had once been an alley between the PD and Tiny's Gun Club. When the closet upstairs at the PD had filled to capacity, the alley had been bricked up, with metal shelves installed along the walls.

Lou fished the key out of her desk drawer and handed it to Josie while she filled her in on a dozen new calls she'd missed that day.

Finally breaking free from Lou's lurid questions about the substation murder, Josie flicked the fluorescent lights on and found the box for Cia Mulroney. She retrieved half a dozen objects that had been collected from the room she had shared with Leon at the church: the smiling photograph of Cia and Leon that had been sitting beside their bed, a high school class ring, a dog-eared spiral notebook half-filled with random observations and lines of poetry with words written, crossed out, and written again, all in a scrawling cursive. Josie flipped through each of the pages but found only what appeared to be fictional

lines about love and nature. She found a small photo album
with pictures of high school friends, and judging by the resemblance, photos of her parents and her sister. A stack of
Greenpeace and Amnesty International stickers slipped out the
back of the album.

Josie looked over the dead woman's items with respect. She'd
always felt a sense of reverence toward a deceased person's
effects, touching the objects that often boiled down to the
essence of who that person had been at the time of their death.
Looking at the items in Cia's box, Josie saw an idealistic young
woman, happy and in love.

At the bottom of the box Josie found a plastic bag with
Cia's iPhone. Still charged, the phone required a passcode, as
she knew. When they had retrieved the phone, they knew that
gaining access would be unlikely, if not impossible, and would
take months of legal wrangling and money the county didn't
have. However, Josie had realized she might have a better
option.

After grabbing two stale donuts for lunch, she drove her car
the short distance to Manny's and knocked on Leon's door.
With no answer, she put her hands up to the window and saw
the made bed, and his belongings gone.

Josie entered Manny's office and found him sitting in his
recliner reading a book. He eased out of his chair and approached
the counter, chatting aimlessly.

'Manny, I'm in a bit of a panic. I need to see Leon and it
looks like he checked out. Did he leave town?'

'He didn't tell me his plans, but he left you a note. He said
that as awful as the past couple of weeks had been, if he'd not
had you believing in him . . .' Manny shrugged. 'He didn't
finish the thought, but I think we both know what he meant.'

Josie walked outside to read the letter, handwritten on
spiral-bound notebook paper in neatly printed letters.

Dear Chief Gray,
I took your advice and called a few ranchers around the
county to see if someone would allow me to work for
room and board. I actually got a job at the Knight Ranch,
free place to stay and a weekly check. I wish I'd done this

the day I stepped foot in town. Maybe things would have turned out different for Cia.

They asked me to start work right away, so they are picking me up first thing in the morning. Since I don't have a phone I wanted you to have a way to get ahold of me if you need anything. You will probably never know how much your belief in me meant. If I can ever repay your kindness, I will.

Sincerely,

Leon

Josie plugged Cia's phone into a charging brick and drove to the Knight Ranch, a thirty-minute trip out of town, tracking Leon down to one of the corrals. She found him leading a horse around by the reins. When he recognized her, he waved and walked the horse over to where she stood at the fence.

'Congratulations on the new job,' she said. 'You move quick.'

'I owe it to you. I called and talked to the farm manager yesterday morning. I told him you suggested I apply, and that you said he could call you as a reference. He didn't even have me fill out an application. I came out yesterday after lunch to get a feel for the ranch operation. Then this morning he put me out with the horses. Said he'd pay me for a day and see how I did. At lunch today, he told me the job's mine.'

'That's great news. I'm glad for you.'

'Gideon had us all convinced that the whole town hated us. When you suggested I work here in the county I thought you were crazy.'

Josie grinned.

'And here I am a day later with a job I'm excited about.'

She watched the light in his eyes and the animated smile as he smoothed his hand down the horse's neck. 'You look like a natural. Not bad for a city slicker.'

'This is what I thought our move out here was going to be.' He shielded his eyes toward the Chinati Mountain range, drenched in the late afternoon sunlight. 'This is what Cia and I dreamed about. The blue skies and incredible sunsets and that endless horizon.'

'Cia is actually the reason I drove out to see you today. Can you take a few minutes?'

'Sure. I need to get her back in the barn anyway. Did you find something?'

'I hope so.'

As they walked to the barn, she wondered what the news of Gideon's death would do to Leon; whether it would be felt as one more tragedy to digest, or justice served. The FBI was keeping the news completely confidential, wanting to control the investigation before the media grabbed the sensational death of the commune leader and twisted it into more drama.

When they reached the shade of the barn, Josie handed him the phone. 'When we retrieved Cia's phone we weren't able to break her passcode. I brought it with me today hoping you might know it.'

He held up his index finger. 'Yeah, unless she changed it. She had a fingerprint reader and she had me set mine. Hers is on mine as well, if I ever get it back.'

'I'll make sure that happens this week,' she said.

He accepted the phone and pressed his finger on the pad. Josie watched as the phone lit up.

'I need you to open her text messages.'

'I'm in.' He clicked a few times and passed the phone back to her.

Josie looked at the list of names and phone numbers. She opened the phone message that matched Bobby Lee Green's number. The messages were dated the night of Cia's murder.

Josie was surprised to see two different colors of text message bubbles, meaning Bobby Lee had responded to the texts. He had told Charlie and Josie that he'd thought Cia was crazy and that he had ignored her.

> - *Gideon is crazy!! He killed a girl. He's blaming an innocent person. He's going to kill my boyfriend. Can you help us???* (Sent from Cia at 11:45 p.m.)
> - *Talk to Gloria. She'll know what to do.* (Reply from Bobby Lee at 12:07 a.m.)
> - *We need someone from outside to help! Please!!!* (Sent from Cia at 12:08 a.m.)

There was no additional communication between them.

Josie flipped back to Cia's texts and clicked on Gloria's name. She was the last person that Cia had communicated with that night.

- *We need to talk. Tonight!* (Sent from Cia at 12:19 a.m.)
- *Answer me or I'll come get you out of bed!* (Sent from Cia at 12:22 a.m.)
- *Meet me in the basement in ten.* (Reply from Gloria at 12:35 a.m.)

Josie returned her attention to Leon who looked at her expectantly. 'What did you find?'

She closed the messages and handed the phone back. 'Can you get into her settings and change the password to "police" so that I can get into her phone without using the fingerprint reader?'

He did so, and tried the new password before handing it back. 'Can you tell me who she talked to before she was killed?'

'I can't get into specifics, but I want you to know that Cia believed in you. Based on those text messages, it's clear she understood that you'd been telling her the truth.'

Leon grit his teeth and turned from Josie for a long while before regaining his composure. When he turned back around his eyes were red, his expression angry. 'She was so proud, so determined to do things on her own. If she'd just come to me that night, maybe the two of us could have gotten out together.'

Back in her car, Josie called Marta to give her an update on the case, and asked her to sit on the motel to keep an eye on Gloria until they had a plan in place. Next, she sent a screenshot of the text messages from Cia's phone to Mark and Otto as a security measure.

She arrived back at the PD at six with carryout burritos from the Hot Tamale. Otto was already upstairs standing over the conference table, digging through reams of internet research from Mark's team and sorting through pages of notes and photographs. Mark had explained to Otto that he was still trying to piece together the hierarchy of the EX-Sovereigns based on the information that Bobby Lee had shared with Charlie and Josie.

As they began pulling together the evidence they needed to present for a warrant, Josie received a phone call from Marta.

'Gloria is gone.'

'What do you mean?'

'I'm standing here with Manny. She checked out earlier today. She didn't say to where. Manny says to tell you how sorry he is, that he should have called you.'

'Marta, I need you to go to each remaining person at the motel and see if they'll share where Gloria's headed. Don't bother with Leon, he's already moved out. I'll contact him personally.'

'I'll work room to room.'

'Make it clear that she isn't in trouble. You need her because you have critical news about Gideon. Nothing has been released on his death yet and we want to keep it that way. Tell them something has happened to Gideon and they need her immediately. If they think we're going after her they won't tell you anything.'

Josie asked Otto to call West Texas Mobile, the only cell phone company providing service to Artemis, to track Gloria's phone. They wouldn't get a GPS location, but if her phone was on they could find out what cell tower she was pinging. The PD already had a blanket warrant for technology used by The Drummers, so Josie faxed it to the company's legal division in Marfa while Otto worked with the clerk.

While they waited for word from West Texas Mobile, Josie called the Knight Ranch and explained to the farm manager it was urgent she speak with Leon. The manager had Leon call from his office phone.

'You mentioned that you'd help any way you could, so I'm calling in that favor,' she said.

'Sure, anything.'

'You mentioned during one of your interviews that you were close with Gloria. Did you know that she left Artemis today?'

'No. I haven't talked to her since they forced me out of the church.'

'Leon, I'm putting a lot of faith in you right now. You can't repeat this information. You understand?'

'I won't say a word to anyone. I'll do whatever you need.'

'Based on the text messages we got from Cia's phone, Gloria was the last person who talked with Cia before she died. Gloria knows what happened in that basement. I am confident that she can help lead us to the killer, but it's been almost four hours since she left. We have to track her down before we lose her. Do you have any idea where she might be heading?'

He was quiet for a moment. 'I don't know. She was so focused on convincing us that Artemis was our new home. I don't think she had a backup plan. And they didn't have kids. I don't know of any family.'

'Do you have her number?'

'Yeah, I know it.'

'Could you call her and ask?'

'I could call and say I'm leaving town, that I'd like to clear the air between us. That I miss her.'

'That would be a plausible response from you?'

'She was like a mother to me. I always felt like she understood me. More so than anyone outside of Cia. So when Gideon told me they were forcing me out for Mandy's murder, I was just . . .' He paused for a long while. 'I just couldn't believe Gloria would allow it. She knew that I cared about Mandy. That I would never have done anything to hurt her.'

As Josie was talking to Leon, Otto stood from his desk and twirled his finger in the air, grabbing Josie's coat and handing it to her.

'Call me back if you talk with her, just so I know where we stand.'

'I'll call her now and let you know.'

'Gloria's cell phone last pinged the tower west of Marfa just twenty minutes ago,' Otto said, holding the door of the PD open for Josie. 'It's such a remote area, and Gloria doesn't know anyone. She has to be headed toward highway ninety.'

As he pulled the car away from the PD, Josie looked over at him. 'How could she leave? She and Gideon didn't have a car. All they had was that crappy minibus that was impounded days ago.'

'Then someone picked her up. Maybe the EX-Sovereigns are more connected to The Drummers than they let on. Maybe they tipped her off after the conversation between Charlie and Bobby Lee.'

Josie called Manny. 'Didn't you tell me you installed a security system this year?'

'Yes.'

'With video cameras in front of the motel?'

'Yes.'

'I need you to drop everything and see if you can pull up the video for the time period when you said Gloria checked out. I need you to get the make, model and color of the car she left in. And see if someone picked her up or if she had her own vehicle.'

'I can tell you that part now. It was Nicki from Enterprise Car Rental. Over in Odessa. She came in my office looking for Gloria. So I called Gloria's room and told her Nicki was waiting on her. I was surprised because it's an expensive option to have a car dropped off that far from Odessa. But people do it. This isn't the first time I've seen it.'

'Call Nicki right now. Track her down if she doesn't answer. Get the rental information – payment method, drop off, etc. We need it immediately. Tell her there is an arrest warrant for Gloria Masters. Have her call me if necessary.'

Josie hung up and returned a call to Leon.

'I called Gloria but she didn't answer,' he said. 'Her phone said she doesn't have voice messages set up. I'm sorry I couldn't do more.'

As much as she trusted him, Josie couldn't help worrying about Leon's loyalty. If he tipped Gloria off, their only chance at tracking her down would be lost for good, but she'd been right to trust him thus far. With him settling in Artemis for now, she had to believe he had severed ways with The Drummers.

'We just learned that she's west of Marfa,' Josie said. 'Do you know where that is?'

'Yeah, that's the area we were looking to buy property.'

'I would have guessed she'd have been well out of Arroyo County by this time. Do you think she would have stopped at the property for some reason before fleeing?'

'I don't know. I can't imagine why. She and Gideon visited

a couple of times while they were still hoping to purchase it. Maybe she stopped for some sentimental reason?'

Leon wasn't able to provide an address so Josie tracked down the location through Junior Daggy, the realtor that Gideon had worked with to purchase the church.

'Are you telling me those people are still planning on buying property and settling here in Artemis?' Junior asked. 'I'd think they'd be running like the plague after what all's happened.'

'I don't think they'll be buying property, Junior. Please don't get that rumor started.'

TWENTY-FIVE

Otto drove in silence along River Road, hugging the Rio Grande, headed north toward one of the few side roads between Marfa and Artemis. The landscape varied between flat, open stretches of desert mesquite, ocotillo and sage brush, to glimpses of the mountains, colored dark rust at twilight.

'Why so quiet?' Josie asked. Otto was a talker when he drove. She wasn't much for conversation, but she enjoyed his ramblings, usually about his small farm and his treasured goat herd.

'I'm too old to be naive. Maybe those months I was away, working at the mayor's office, I lost my edge.'

'What are you talking about?'

'I couldn't understand how those members, those grown men and women, could buy into Gideon's load of horseshit. And then I did exactly the same thing. Gloria played herself off as a motherly type, wanting to help, caring for others over herself. And I bought right into it.'

Manny called back sounding out of breath, clearly caught up in the police intrigue. 'I've done it. I reached Nicki and she gave me everything. Gloria rented a white Toyota SUV, a 2020 Highlander. And get this. She's returning it to Odessa, to the rental store, tomorrow. So she's not on the run after all!'

Josie thanked Manny and relayed the information to Otto.

'Why wouldn't she just use Uber or something local? I know we're a small town, but there had to be a cheaper way than having a rental agency drop a car off from that far away. Especially for someone who claims to be broke,' he said.

'She probably figured no one local would take her. Or maybe she isn't good with technology. She does supposedly hate it. It was easier to get the rental car to run her errands than try to figure out Uber.'

'Maybe it's just the opposite. Maybe she understands

technology quite well and didn't want anyone following her movements once she had the car,' he said.

Josie received a text from Marta as they were turning onto the dirt road that led to the land The Drummers had been considering.

> *- None of the members I talked to knew she was leaving. Jackson said he thinks she'd fly out of Houston. She has a cousin in Tennessee she'd go to meet.*

'You think it's odd that Jackson is sending us in the opposite direction to where Gloria currently is?' Josie asked.

'Maybe she told the rental company that she'd take the car back tomorrow to throw us off. She could be planning to steal the car and head to Mexico.' Otto pointed ahead about a half-mile into the desert, illuminated by his headlights. 'You see white?'

'I do. Gloria's about ready to wish she'd taken the flight out of Houston.'

Otto approached the car slowly, spotting someone who appeared to be sitting on a folding chair.

'She looks to be by herself,' Josie said.

The land was rocky desert dotted with clumps of mesquite on all sides, with the low-lying mountains miles away. Some of the mesquite were eight to ten feet high, making visibility limited in the dark, but Josie didn't see any evidence of other cars. Gloria was sitting in a red folding chair, facing away from Josie and Otto's approaching car, apparently not worried about who was coming out to visit her in the middle of nowhere.

Otto parked his car with his headlights pointing toward her left side so that they could see her face in the dark. They approached her on either side of the chair, announcing themselves and walking carefully. She had not moved or said a word since they had exited the car and they had no idea what her mental state might be.

They both noticed the pistol on her lap and glanced at each other. Josie nodded at Otto, indicating he should take the lead.

'Gloria, we've come out here to check on you,' he said.

She continued to stare into the distance with no response as they walked to the front of the chair so they could see her. They stood about five feet away, giving her some space. Josie wondered if she'd taken drugs.

'Can you tell me why you have the gun?' Otto asked. 'Are you afraid of something?'

'You didn't come to check on me,' she said, her voice hoarse and difficult to hear.

'Why do you think we came?'

Josie took a step toward her and Gloria raised the gun to her temple. 'Get away from me.' Her voice remained quiet and flat.

Josie moved back as Otto raised his hands. 'Gloria, stop! Let's talk about this. Please put the gun down.'

Josie was certain she could rush Gloria and shove her out of the chair before she was able to register what was happening and take a shot. But the risk was that the flailing gun could go off and strike one of them.

Gloria's hand drooped, as if the gun was too heavy to hold to her head. The deterioration in her appearance and demeanor was shocking, as if she had aged twenty years in the past few days. She had no fight left.

'Help us understand why you're here,' Otto said.

She looked at Otto, squinting as if the question made no sense. 'You need to ask that?'

'Tell us what happened. Help us understand how this all ended so bad.'

She dropped both hands in her lap, the gun landing heavily on her thigh, but she didn't speak.

Otto leaned down to be closer to her, and Josie could see the wince of pain from his bad knees as he did so. 'We have Cia's phone. We've read the text messages. We know you were in the basement with Cia when she was killed. Why would you do it? Everything had already fallen apart. Gideon was going to be charged with murder. Why kill Cia when he was already going to jail?'

She looked mildly surprised. 'You think I killed Cia?'

Otto nodded once. 'You were the last person with her. I think you found out that Mandy was pregnant and Cia was making waves about going to the police.'

Gloria closed her eyes and turned her face away from Otto.

'You were trying to protect Gideon from Cia. Mandy was no longer a threat, and if Cia hadn't confided what she knew to anyone else, then you could have saved Gideon.'

She turned back to Otto suddenly, her expression angry. 'There's no saving him. He's an animal, what he did to Mandy. Gideon is where he should be, locked behind bars.'

They turned toward where the cars were parked, surprised to hear an engine approaching. 'That's Manny's pickup truck,' Josie said.

Jackson opened the truck door before it had come to a complete stop. 'Gloria! What have you done?'

He rushed toward them and Josie pulled her weapon, aiming at Jackson. 'Slow down. Put your hands up where I can see them.'

He looked barely phased at having a gun pointed at him. He raised his hands and yelled at Gloria, 'What are you doing, Gloria? You need a lawyer. Just keep quiet.'

'You come another step closer and I'll place you under arrest,' Josie said.

He stopped just a few feet behind Gloria's chair.

'I'm done with this. I'm done lying. We've all done wrong, Jackson. It's time to pay for what we've done.'

'Shut up!'

'Tell them what happened. Tell them so we can be free of this burden. Punishment is the only way back.'

'Damn you, Gloria. Shut up!'

'We know about the basement,' Josie said, her gun trained on Jackson, realizing she only knew a part of what had happened. 'You're better off to confess now. I promise you, the judge will be much more lenient than if we drag this through a jury trial.'

He stared directly at Josie, appearing to consider what she was saying.

'Gloria is right. Tell us what happened so we can move on. You can't run from this, Jackson. Too many people know.'

His frantic expression melted, and his shoulders slumped. In her peripheral vision Josie saw Otto manage to stand and take the gun from Gloria as Jackson began talking through tears. He began to walk slowly toward Gloria and Josie allowed him to move to the front of the chair and kneel down beside her.

'Why are you doing this? Make Gideon pay for what he did,' Jackson said.

Gloria looked at him for a long while. 'He will pay, but he's not the only person at fault. We all need to pay for our sins.' Gloria reached her hand out and placed it on his cheek, her eyes kind. 'Tell them everything. Make your peace.'

Jackson moved away from her, shuffling his feet in the sand. He stared out into the dark night before finally turning to Josie. 'I heard Gloria get up the night Cia died. When she couldn't sleep she'd head to her office. I would get up and keep her company for a while. Sometimes she'd cry on my shoulder, sometimes I'd cry on hers. It was tough times. Thea was angry all the time, pissed at me or the boys. Hating our life. Gideon had gone off the deep end and was having a relationship with a girl young enough to be his granddaughter. If I hadn't had Gloria to rely on, I'd have lost my mind. So when I saw her get up that night, and she went toward the basement and not the office, I knew something was up.

'So I followed her. I stood at the door and listened to Cia. She was stomping around, practically hissing at Gloria, as if the whole mess was her fault! What could Gloria have done about Mandy? It was Gideon's mess! I pushed the door open to say something, to make Cia think about her words. Cia started waving her phone in Gloria's face, calling her a monster for allowing it all to happen. Gloria was crying.' Jackson pressed his palms against his temples as if trying to hold his thoughts together. 'I just lost it. I hated that girl for what she was doing to Gloria. She opened her phone and started to dial 911, and I grabbed a pipe that was leaning against the door frame and ran up behind her and hit her on the head to stop her.'

Josie watched his expression turn soft, as if he were watching in wonder as the scene unfolded in his mind. 'Gloria started yelling at me, crying hysterically. She left to go get Gideon for help. I bent down and I could feel a pulse in her neck, but her head was bleeding and I knew it was bad. I just needed to end it before she woke up and accused me of whatever, and accused Gideon of what he'd done, and pointed the blame at Gloria who'd done nothing. So I took a plastic grocery bag that was lying underneath the table and I wrapped it around her face until she stopped breathing. And that was it.'

'And what did Gideon tell you to do?' Josie asked.

'He came down and told Gloria and me to leave. He told us to shut up, to say nothing. He said he would take care of it. And that was it. We left the basement and went back to our rooms. Our lives shattered.'

Otto placed Jackson under arrest and used Manny's pickup truck to make the trip to the Arroyo County jail for booking. Josie drove Gloria to the police station for additional questioning. Her demeanor had changed significantly. She talked about Leon, and how she had failed him, what a nice young man he'd been, and how she hoped he would find peace. A burden had clearly lifted. Josie had seen it countless times: the admission of guilt and the subsequent relief. She didn't think of clearing the conscience as a moral behavior as much as a psychological need. Josie thought back to the plaque hanging on Gloria's door, the one that read, 'Enter. Peace Awaits You', but she doubted Gloria would ever find the peace she had obviously been searching for throughout her life.

TWENTY-SIX

Cia Mulroney's parents asked to meet Josie at the Arroyo County Airfield. They had worked with the local funeral home to prepare her body for a flight back to the family cemetery in Portland. While Josie waited for the Mulroneys to arrive, she stood at the window in the small office in the airplane hangar, listening to a news report from Marfa Public Radio. The FBI had finally released details of Gideon's arrest, kidnapping and murder, and the radio had requested an interview with Josie. She heard the detachment in her voice, and felt the accompanying numbness in her body now that her part in the investigation was over. As she listened to herself recounting the arrests, the self-doubt she'd worked so hard to bury pushed its way into her thoughts. She wondered if she had responded sooner, if she had forced entry into the church immediately after Gideon announced Mandy had been shot, whether Cia might have been saved. But the fear of Waco had kept law enforcement at bay. She wondered if it was a matter of learning from mistakes made and saving innocent lives, or fearing past mistakes and allowing the fear to cloud good judgment.

Josie watched a car pull to a stop outside the office door. The couple remained in the car for a long time, not talking, putting off the moment they would remember for the rest of their lives.

The woman finally exited from the passenger side and the man a moment later, both of them grim-faced and moving deliberately, as if each forced step was at great cost.

Josie met them on the sidewalk and introduced herself, offering condolences.

'I'm Ed Mulroney, and this is my wife, Catherine.'

Josie shook hands, saying again how sorry she was for their loss. 'We have an office inside, if you'd like to talk or ask questions about anything. Otherwise, we can walk back to the hangar where the plane is waiting.'

Catherine glanced at her husband. 'We'd like to talk first.'

'The airport manager made his office available to us.' Josie led the couple inside and offered them seats around a small table next to the sunny window.

Looking anxious and close to tears, Catherine reached her hand over to her husband who took it and laid it on his lap. 'We'd like to know about this group, The Drummers. I've read everything online I could get my hands on, but I'd like to hear from someone who actually knew them.'

'I'll be glad to tell you anything I can.'

Before Josie could begin, Catherine continued. 'Even as a little girl, Cia was bighearted, throwing herself behind one cause after another. Always searching for something more. As her mom, I never knew whether to encourage her or to try and show her that some people weren't always deserving of her help.' Tears welled up in her eyes as she glanced at Ed. He said nothing, staring down at his wife's hand. 'And when we did try and point out someone's faults, she'd defend them as if her own life . . .' She stopped suddenly and choked back a sob, realizing what she was about to say.

Josie stepped in to move the conversation in a different direction. 'I would say The Drummers fit Cia's desire to serve a cause. I've had many conversations with most of the members. I've spent quite a bit of time getting to know Leon.' She noted the wince from Catherine and that Ed looked away at the mention of his name. 'I would sum the group up by saying that they were interested in living a life away from government interference. They wanted to live in a remote place where they could take care of each other, share their money and resources, and eventually have a place that would sustain them.'

'They were a commune,' Ed said, more statement than question.

'The leader, Gideon, didn't like that characterization, but it's how I thought of them. He also claimed to hate technology, but I think some of the members kept their phones. In fact, it was text messages from Cia's phone that helped us solve the case.'

Josie paused, waiting to see if either of the parents wanted to hear details. Neither of them spoke. She suspected one of them would be calling in the months ahead, wanting every detail from the report, but she understood the need to wait. Some families never requested the police report, preferring not to darken their memories more than necessary.

'You said you got to know Leon,' Catherine said.

'I did. I recommended him as a ranch hand here locally. He's working there now. I'm sure he would be glad to talk with you, if you'd like.'

Ed raised a hand. 'That won't be necessary.'

'I know Cia loved him. We just felt like he wasn't a good influence. Cia had a good job, was happy, had her sister and a group of friends. Then when he got back from the service they went running off after this group. She just gave everything up.'

Josie considered telling the couple that Leon was the lone holdout, that he had tried to convince Cia that Gideon was a murderer, but she decided that no good would come from that information.

Ed cleared his throat. 'I'd like to see my daughter.'

'Of course.' Josie looked at Catherine, who hesitated but nodded agreement.

Josie waited outside the hangar while the couple met with the funeral home director. He had explained to Josie that he would open the casket to allow the couple time alone with their daughter. An hour later, Mr Mulroney boarded the plane with the casket while his wife sat in the rental car and cried. She'd tried to thank Josie but had been sobbing too hard to get the words out and had walked away to shut herself in the car to suffer her grief in private.

Josie drove back toward the PD, thinking about the reasons she had entered law enforcement, and how she had been drawn to the notion of control. She liked the idea of black and white, of rules to follow with hierarchy and structure. The academy had taught her how to control a situation, and how every decision is orchestrated around the safety of everyone involved. The problem is that no matter how carefully an officer may plan a situation, it almost never works that way – from the driver who overreacts to a speeding ticket and escalates a simple citation into guns drawn, to the situation with The Drummers, where an arrest warrant spiraled into two dead girls. The need for control is critical, but more often than not, situations turn unpredictable, leaving victims and cops and criminals dissecting every move.

Late one night at the office, Josie had listened to a podcast from *This American Life* while organizing her files. A man named Graeme Patterson had talked about playing at a construction site when he was a child. One day, playing by himself at the site, he'd decided to create a seesaw with a plank of wood balanced on a brick, and another brick balanced on the end of the board. He then climbed up sets of scaffolding high off the ground and dropped a large rock, wanting to see how far the brick would catapult up into space. Instead, the brick flew straight up, toward the boy's face, barely missing him as it flew by his head. He talked about seeing the brick coming at him in slow motion, understanding for the first time his own mortality.

But what Josie found most interesting in the story was his discussion of the aftermath. He wondered what would have happened if he'd died and the police had arrived to reconstruct the crime scene. He imagined the forensics team showing up and finding a dead child who'd been killed by a brick, hitting him with incredible force under his chin – how his body might have fallen onto the board, dismantling the seesaw, creating a scene that would have looked nothing like the reality of a little boy playing. Josie had turned the podcast off and imagined the scene in her own mind, coming across the dead child, imagining a monster brutally killing the boy with a hard blow from a brick, then cruelly tossing it to the ground. Teams of officers would dissect the scene, creating a profile of the monster, worrying that a child killer was on the loose.

The story had stayed with her, influencing the way she processed a crime scene, making her wonder if all the possibilities had been considered, or at least the right possibility. She wondered at her own insistence that Gideon had committed both murders, while Gloria and Jackson had remained off the radar. It had come to a satisfactory ending, but it did make her question her own ability to examine people objectively. She learned that having the evidence – the smoking gun or the brick that might have killed the little boy – may lead to a conviction but didn't always lead to the truth.

TWENTY-SEVEN

Josie pulled the casserole dish out of the oven, burning the top of her hand as she did so. Sweating and swearing, she ran her hand under cold water before sliding two large loaves of garlic bread into the oven. Spaghetti with Ragu sauce, paired with buttered toast and garlic salt, had been a weekly staple at her house growing up, and it was still one of Josie's favorite meals. She had considered serving spaghetti, but had decided to up her game and attempt lasagna for the first time in her life.

It was Christmas Eve, and Josie was entertaining a small group of friends, something she had only attempted a few times in her life, and most of those occasions had been with her former partner, Dillon. He'd been the consummate host, and she'd tried to learn his good manners and grace, but it didn't come naturally. She felt clumsy and worried about the hundred things that could go wrong with the food, drink and conversation – especially with the conversation. The most important lesson she'd learned from Dillon was that a dinner party should be arranged around talkers and listeners. He'd convinced her that combining people from different backgrounds was always a good thing, as long as there was a good mix: a room full of talkers left people feeling as if they had been ignored, and a room full of listeners left people bored, with little to say.

Josie had realized several days ago that she'd been so consumed with work and the Drummers investigation that Christmas was days away and she'd barely given it a thought. She'd not spoken to her mother in over a week, and had no idea what she would do in terms of a gift, since the last time they'd spoken was a disaster. She knew what her mother wanted most was to be a part of Josie's life without judgment. She also knew that she had to stifle her disapproving comments if they were ever going to connect.

Josie had sketched out the dinner table arrangement on a piece of paper, strategically arranging her guests, hoping that the mix of cops and politicians and ranchers and former military would make for interesting conversation.

Her only mismatch in terms of a talker paired with a talker was Charlie and her mother. She was fairly certain that her mother would find the newly divorced Charlie attractive, and she was also certain that Charlie could hold his own against her mother.

The weather was perfect: blue sky and sunshine with temperatures in the low seventies combined with the glorious rarity of moisture in the air. Dell had cut a cedar tree from behind his barn and propped it up in a bucket on Josie's front porch, then strung colorful twinkling lights around it. Christmas music played softly in the living room, and she had tied a red bow on Chester's collar. It had been years since Josie had felt excited about sharing Christmas with friends, and she hoped the feeling would last into the new year.

Josie had confided to Delores that she'd never served eight people at once, and Delores had emailed her a sample menu and a timeline for preparations, along with an offer to help with the set-up. Josie had readily accepted. Otto and Delores had arrived an hour before, and Delores took over table arrangements while Otto set up folding chairs and took orders from his wife.

Josie heard the first guests arriving as she cut the lasagna. Simon walked into the kitchen smelling spicy and smiling, carrying two bottles of wine. 'Merry Christmas!'

'And same to you!' she said, offering her cheek for a kiss.

'What can I help you with?'

'Just help Delores make Leon feel welcome when he arrives. He could use some happy in his life.'

Delores took care of the welcomes and showed the guests to their places at the table while Josie lit the candles and dimmed the lights. With dinner complete and not burned, Josie watched the evening come together with pride. After Otto poured the wine and punch, she thanked everyone for coming and proposed a toast.

'Here's to a year surrounded by friends and family, filled with new beginnings and great adventures.'

'And a toast to our hostess for a beautiful evening,' Simon offered.

234

Tricia Fields

After much clinking of glasses the group settled into their seats, chatting about the weather, local politics, the price of cattle and the need for rain. Josie watched Charlie laugh at her mother, seeming to enjoy her stream of stories. Otto and Dell were deep into a conversation about winter wheat, and Delores was giving Leon the lowdown on West Texas living. Josie passed Simon a bottle of wine and thanked him for coming.

'If you and your mother don't have plans for Christmas tomorrow, I thought we could drive to Big Bend. Maybe we can take that hike we discussed. Your mom is welcome to come too.'

Josie smiled and nodded, suddenly overcome with happiness. She had worried so much over the past weeks about the country falling apart, about charismatic people abusing their power, about militias destroying communities and rebuilding the country around hate. But sitting in her living room that night, surrounded by friends and family, she knew that there was far more good in the world than evil, and as long as that remained true, humanity would prosper.